JUVENALIA

JUVENALIA

A VALERIUS MYSTERY

JENNIFER BURKE

To my family, for all their support.

—A MAP OF ROME, AD 58 —

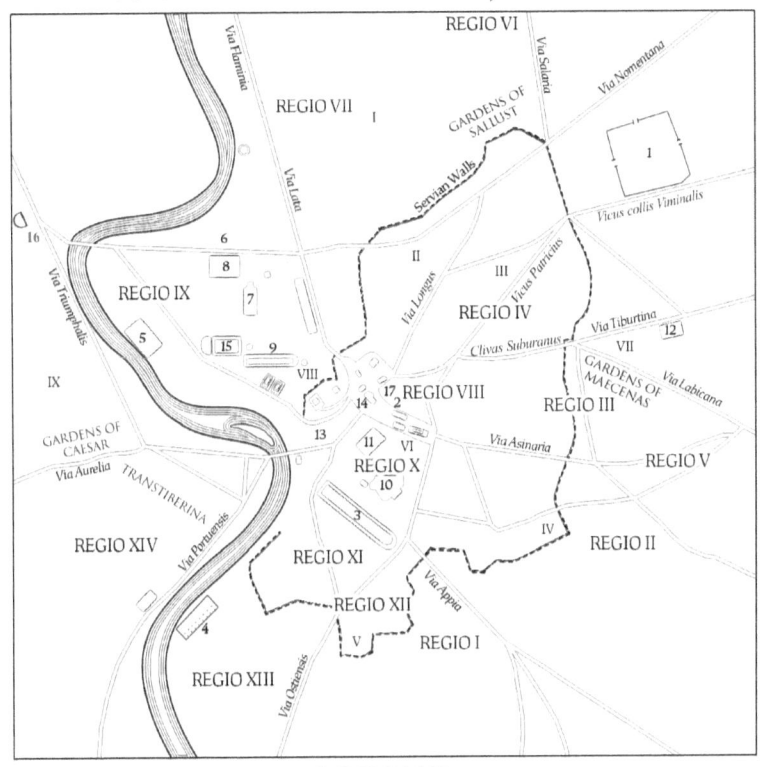

REGIO VI

REGIO VII

GARDENS OF SALLUST

Via Flaminia

Via Salaria

Via Nomentana

Vicus collis Viminalis

Via Lata

Servian Walls

16

6

8

REGIO IX

7

Via Triumphalis

5

15

9

VIII

IX

14

17 REGIO VIII

13

11 VI

REGIO X

10

Via Longus

Vicus Patricius

REGIO IV

Clivas Suburanus

Via Tiburtina

12

VII

GARDENS OF MAECENAS

REGIO III

Via Labicana

REGIO V

GARDENS OF CAESAR

Via Aurelia

TRANSTIBERINA

Via Asinaria

Via Portuensis

3

IV

REGIO XIV

REGIO XI

REGIO XII

Via Appia

REGIO II

4

V

REGIO I

REGIO XIII

Via Ostiensis

— LEGEND —

BUILDINGS

1. The Praetorian Guard Camp
2. Forum
3. Circus Maximus
4. Emporium
5. Navilia
6. Campus Martius
7. Baths of Agrippa
8. Baths of Nero
9. Circus Flaminius
10. Domus Augustus
11. Domus Tiberius
12. Praetorian Stables

13. Forum Boarium
14. Mamertine Prison
15. Theatre of Pompey
16. Theatre of Nero
17. Basilica Aemilia

HILLS

I. Pincian Hill
II. Quirinal Hill
III. Viminal Hill
IV. Caelian Hill
V. Aventine Hill
VI. Palatine Hill
VII. Esquiline Hill
VIII. Capitoline Hill
IX. Janiculan Hill

Dramatis Personae

The Family Aemilius

- Q. Aemilius Valerius: our hero
- Fulvia Drusa: his wife
- Octavia Junilla: his sister
- Julia Drusilla: his stepdaughter
- A. Caldus Ruso aka Mouse: his stepson
- G. Aemilius Lucullus Maro: a mad relation
- Marcia Laeta: a mad relation by marriage

Patricians, assorted

- Gn. Gavius Silanus: Fulvia's ex, Julia's papa
- Gn. Septus Severus: a neighbourhood magistrate
- G. Marcellus Naso: startlingly, a family friend
- G. Avitus Florian: a family friend about to become family

Slaves, assorted

- Juba: too smart to be a bodyguard, honestly
- Hursa: a punishment from the gods, probably
- Hermes: Lucan's slave, a scribe
- Idaeus: Otho's slave, a lackey
- Iris: Otho's slave, a triumph

Miscellaneous Items

- L. Junius Atreus: a vigile with a responsibility
- Lucilla: the responsibility
- Leander: a physician or mortician, whatever your need
- Gaius, Vibilus, Manius: vigiles, assorted
- Marcia Longia: a helpful neighbour
- T. Decimus Rufio: a Praetorian Guard
- Atius: a corpse
- Atia: his sister
- Erastus: a pretty gangster
- Mugo the Fish: not a fish

Historical figures (more or less)

- Nero: the Emperor of Rome
- Agrippina: his mummy dearest
- Seneca: retired, honestly!

Nero's In Crowd

- Petronius Arbiter: an author and playwright
- Lucan: a poet, and also Seneca's nephew
- M. Salvius Otho: an ambitious man
- Poppaea Sabina: his ambitious wife
- Litus: a poet and playwright, writing a play about Horatius
- Fabianus: a poet and playwright, *also* writing about Horatius.
- Entellus: a poet and playwright, not telling anyone what he's writing about
- Cilnius: a poet with a speech impediment
- Hosidius: a playwright with no confidence

The Theatre Crowd

- Marsus: an actor who is missing
- Ammenius: an actor who everyone wishes was missing
- Tertia: an actress
- Antigon: an administrator, not paid enough for this bullshit
- Fabia: a seamstress
- Nonus: a menace

Chapter One

Winter lay upon Rome like a shroud, but underneath the cold, grey threads of cloud, the city was very much alive, and in his house on the southern slope of the Viminal Hill, my new friend Petronius Arbiter was hosting a dinner party. Well, Petronius wasn't a friend, exactly, but he was certainly an important man to know, and so I had wrapped myself in my finest toga, had Hursa dig out a jar of the immortal Falernian, and here I was, spending an evening in the company of a man who counted the emperor as a close, personal friend—and who had obviously been encouraged to find out whether I ought to be elevated into Nero's immediate social circle, because I bet that not everyone got a personal tour of Petronius's library before dinner was served.

"Tell me about yourself, Valerius," Petronius said, and took a seat across from me.

A slave darted forward with wine and a dish of olives. Lamps brightened the room. Beside us, a brazier bled tendrils of warmth into the cool air.

Petronius was probably about thirty years old. He was an ordinary-looking man with close-cropped brown hair and unremarkable features, but with a cleverness in his expression that elevated his ordinariness to something that demanded attention. Petronius's gaze was sharp—probably as sharp as his pen. He was a writer, and he was just as vulgar—and twice as cutting—as the wags who wrote the scandalous graffiti on the sides of public buildings. They wished they had half his talent at skewering the rich and powerful with nothing but a stylus.

"There's not much to tell," I said. "And I'm certain there's nothing you

1

haven't already heard. I'm an open book, Petronius, and one nowhere near as entertaining as those you write."

"Flattery?" he asked, his eyes bright. "I'm almost disappointed, Valerius."

"It begins and ends there, actually." I swallowed a mouthful of wine. "I play social situations like I play latrunculi. I start off with a fairly standard move, then I diverge wildly away from the accepted conventions of the game. I let everyone assume it's to confuse my opponents, but really, it's because I don't have the patience to play properly. So I'm afraid from here on in, I'm completely out of flattery."

"How unexpected," Petronius said, arching a brow.

"As warned."

He snorted through a smile. "I can see why you're so popular these days, Valerius."

I laughed. "I don't think my charming personality is the reason for that."

In the months since the death of Marcellus Albanus, and my subsequent discovery of the legionary conspiracy and treason that had led to it, the magistrate Septus Severus and I had become quite the talk of the city—we were now firmly known as friends of the emperor, although those that knew *why* weren't saying, and so speculation was rife. Most of the social invitations I received were from men who hoped that wine would loosen my tongue. For once in my life, it hadn't, because being friends with Nero had made us enemies of his mother, Agrippina the Younger, and both Severus and I knew better than to let our mouths run. Agrippina had killed far more important men than us. So it had been quite easy to ignore those invitations that came from men just seeking gossip, provided they didn't outrank me by too much. But Petronius's invitation, I knew, had Nero's hand in it. And even I wasn't stupid enough to spurn an overture from the emperor, however indirect it was.

"It's definitely not," he said, raising his cup in my direction. "But just so you know, asking you to tell me about yourself wasn't a mere formality. I'm surrounded by poets and artists, most of whom have barely been outside the Servian Walls. And here you are, a hero of Corbulo's Parthian campaign. I'm certain nobody else coming tonight will even know what a Parthian looks like, let alone have ever killed one."

"If you wanted war stories, I can name a hundred men who tell them better," I said. "War isn't very much like how the poets tell it at all."

He hummed. "I suspected as much."

Petronius wasn't what I was expecting. So far, his conversation lacked the barbs of his written words. And for a man who was famous for humour that was as sharp as any gladius, and could draw blood just as easily, I'd seen no sign of it yet. Perhaps he was a famous writer just like I was a famous hero of the Parthian campaign; we were known for one thing that made up only the smallest fraction of who were really were.

"And now you're something of an imperial agent," he said.

Maybe that was the barb I'd been waiting for. I couldn't tell if it was supposed to sting or not. As a proud patrician I probably ought to have been offended at the implication I was *working*. We patricians didn't work. When we took official positions, it was as part of the complicated system of favours and honours that marked our progress up the flimsy ladder that was the cursus honorum. We didn't do it for anything as crass as money. We did it for power, which we told ourselves was a virtue.

"Hardly." I made an unhappy face as I turned the joke back on him, or at least launched myself onto its blade to show it didn't hurt. "Agents get *paid*."

Petronius laughed so loudly that the waiting slave almost spilled his wine. Maybe it hadn't been a barb after all.

Our conversation after that was a lot more comfortable. We talked about senators we were both acquainted with, and some of the rumours floating around about them. I was sure that Petronius knew whether some of the more scandalous rumours were true or not, but perhaps he was saving them as the chunks of meat in the rich stew that was his next volume of the adventures of Encolpius and Giton, because he didn't weigh in on their veracity. We ate the olives and drank wine until a slave came to announce that more of the dinner guests had arrived.

"Well then," Petronius said, rising to his feet. "Fire tests gold, as the saying goes."

I raised my eyebrows at him, wondering exactly how adversarial this dinner was going to be, and then followed him through to the formal triclinium.

I wasn't on the main couch with Petronius. I was settled to the couch on Petronius's left, between two men who appeared to be about the same age as me. They were both writers, or poets, or something. But the conversation flowed as liberally as the wine, and they were pleasant enough. Still, despite neither the wine nor the company offending my tastes, I would have preferred to be elsewhere. I hadn't been joking about the latrunculi thing—I was easily bored.

I only knew one other person at Petronius's party—the poet, Lucan, who had previously been a guest at one of *my* dinner parties. He was on the main couch with Petronius. He was a thin-faced young man who appeared dour until a smile lit up his features, and then was bright and lively. He looked as though he was barely old enough to have outgrown the purple stripe of his toga praetexta, but only a few moments in his company shattered that illusion. Lucan was clever and quick-witted; he had inherited the brainpower of his uncle, Seneca, but eschewed the dull Stoicism his uncle was famous for. He was good company, as was our host, Petronius, but my skin itched with the need to be elsewhere, and my face was starting to ache with the effort of keeping a smile plastered on it.

"Lucan!" Petronius said. "Give us a poem, my friend, since not everyone is here yet." His smile grew wicked. "If you can remember one without Hermes whispering it in your ear, of course!"

Lucan rolled his eyes, but the slave seated on the floor in front of the main couch—Hermes, presumably—looked offended on his master's behalf. Lucan dropped a hand to tousle the boy's curls as he answered. "Some of us, Petronius, are so filled to overflowing with inspiration that we cannot keep every golden word in our memory. Of course, you would not understand."

Petronius laughed, and as much as I didn't know this crowd, I certainly recognised the way they jabbed at one another with insults. Put swords in their hands and helmets on their heads, and I would have thought myself back in the military, throwing shit at my fellow junior tribunes and hoping to dodge it when it was returned with alacrity.

Lucan rose to his feet and recited a poem, which garnered much applause. I was aware of Petronius watching for my reaction. I clapped along with everyone else, and pretended I'd understood what in Tartarus the poem had been about. It was wordier and more flowery than the one he'd performed at my dinner party. It was possibly full of allusions that were too high for my wine-addled brain to grasp in the moment. Or even my sober brain, if I was honest with myself. I liked poems that told stories from the beginning to the end, not circled around the point like birds in the sky, never landing.

The tardy guests arrived just as the slaves were bringing in the first course. One of them was young and brash, his face flushed with good humour, and his hair whipped by the wind. He was combing it back into place with his beringed fingers as he strode into the triclinium. The other man, slim and unremarkable, scurried behind him, tugging at his tunic like an anxious schoolboy afraid of being given a rap across the knuckles for being late.

"Entellus, you missed Lucan's poem!" Petronius exclaimed as the first man settled himself in a space on one of the couches. "It was glorious! Beautiful! Heady enough to inspire the pricks of old men to get hard, and the legs of trembling virgins fall open!"

Entellus laughed loudly, but the man reclining with Lucan and Petronius on the main couch rolled his eyes. He was thin and narrow, and looked like an ascetic. Probably not though, in this company.

"We'll need to check your prick then, Petronius," the thin man said dryly, "since you're the oldest man we've got, and Jupiter knows there's not a single virgin in your house."

No, definitely not an ascetic.

The room erupted with laughter. Even the slave sitting on the floor, stylus and wax tablet in hand in order to catch Lucan's inspired words, giggled and ducked his head.

"Litus!" Petronius crowed with delight. "With a mouth like yours, and a wit to match, it's a mystery that you're not yet nipping at my heels."

Litus rolled his eyes again and didn't snap at the bait. I had the feeling that when it came to Petronius, there was no winning that game.

The second latecomer, the nervous looking one, took a place beside me.

5

He was around my age, with light brown hair the shade of muddy water, and a smile that seemed a little too shy for this crowd.

Petronius made the introductions as we dug into the first course, and I did my best to remember the names of my fellow guests and also follow the conversation, as it went in directions I was entirely unfamiliar with. Poetry and plays seemed to be the only topic of conversation in the triclinium, and I wasn't a particular fan of either. Still, at least the wine and food were excellent. The goat's cheese with wheat groats was *sublime*. I sipped my wine and stared at the fresco of nymphs on the wall, half wishing they'd step down onto the tiles and whisk me away from here. Petronius had hinted at a trial by fire, not boredom.

"Well, his plays are good," said the man next to me, "but are they good *enough?*"

I blinked at him, relieved to discover that he wasn't talking to me, but rather to the man on my other side.

"Y- yes," said the late arrival on my other side. Cilnius, Petronius had said. He'd been introduced to me as a poet. I hoped for the sake of his career that he wrote better than he spoke. He had an unfortunate stammer that made him sound like a nervous child every time he opened his mouth. He seemed pleasant enough, though not exactly outgoing—even a cup of wine hadn't drowned his initial shyness. I suppose I wouldn't be too eager to talk to strangers either, if I had to worry they might laugh at me before the introductions were even over.

"What do you think, Valerius?" asked the first man. I wanted to say Fabianus? It had been a while since we'd been introduced, and I'd been busy forming a close and loving relationship with the Falernian. He had dark hair, oiled curls, and light-coloured eyes that were some strange shade between blue and grey, and didn't match the rest of him at all.

"About what?" I asked.

"Hosidius," he said, and nodded at a plump man lounging on the couch opposite ours next to a man decked out in more gold than a dead Egyptian pharaoh, who had been introduced to me as Otho. "His plays are sound, but there's nothing exciting about them."

As someone who had yet to be excited by any play in existence, I was extremely unqualified to answer his question. "I'm afraid I don't know his work."

Entellus, the brash young man who had arrived late with Cilnius, snorted into his wine. "Well, you wouldn't be the only one!" And then he laughed.

I smiled and decided not to tell Entellus I'd never heard of him either. I didn't want him to stab me with his fish knife.

Jupiter, tonight was really going to drag.

Which was right when Juba, my bodyguard, slipped into Petronius's formal triclinium. His gaze sought me out, and found me, but he stopped and spoke first to one of Petronius's indoor slaves. Then he approached, keeping to the edges of the room and out of the way of the musicians who were currently performing, before closing the space between us. For a big man, Juba could move as quietly as a cat.

He leaned down beside me. "Message from Junius Atreus, sir."

Anticipation thrilled through me. "What is it?"

Juba raised his eyebrows. "He wants to know if you've ever seen a corpse with no blood before."

Junius Atreus certainly knew how to get a man's attention. There was no way I was staying for dessert.

I rose from the couch, and Juba helped arrange the fall of my toga. I approached the main couch and thanked Petronius for his hospitality, offered a promise to return it, and said my farewells.

"Oh, must you leave, Valerius?" Petronius asked. "I feel as though I hardly know you yet!"

There was no sharpness in his tone, but his gaze was as keen as the pointy end of a gladius. I had been tested here tonight, but I had no idea if I had earned Petronius's approval or not. I didn't know if he would take offence at my early departure, or if he didn't care at all.

"I'm afraid that duty calls," I said. It wasn't really duty as much as curiosity. Atreus had baited his trap well; of the two, I'd always been more susceptible to the latter. Also, I'd spent most of the afternoon complaining to Atreus about feeling more antisocial than usual, so it would have been churlish to ignore his rescue attempt.

"Until we meet again." Petronius smiled and saluted me with his wine cup, and I escaped the triclinium.

Juba and I strode through Petronius's atrium to the front door, where a polite and handsome young slave wished us a good night, and then we stepped outside. The street was dark and quiet, apart from the puddles of light cast by the torches at Petronius's portico. It was cold after the warmth of the triclinium. A slim little figure appeared in the darkness, and I recognised him as Manius, the world's littlest vigile. He must have been Atreus's messenger boy this evening.

"Salve, Valerius," he greeted me cheerfully.

"Salve, Manius. Where are we going?"

"The Aventine, sir."

I heard voices, gruff and impolite, and turned my head to look down the street.

Juba stepped in front of me, alert as always, and then stepped back again as my litter appeared out of the gloom.

"Trouble?" Juba asked.

Ledo, one of my litter bearers, said, "Just some drunk fools in our way."

Manius looked relieved not to have to deal with them.

I reached into the litter and hauled out my spare cloak. There was no way I was wearing my toga into the Aventine. Not only was it cumbersome and impractical, but the bleached white wool would also shine like a beacon in the night, attracting every cutpurse, and cutthroat, who haunted the shadows. There were some nicer parts of the Aventine—Atreus lived in a decent enough neighbourhood—but why tempt Fortuna?

I shrugged off my toga and bundled it into the litter, and then Juba and Manius and I set off on foot, leaving my litter bearers to take home a lighter load than they'd expected. We stayed silent as we reached the drunken fools Ledo had mentioned—I glanced into the darkness at the corner they were lurking on. Two men, maybe three. They didn't say anything to us as we passed.

We headed down the hill, Manius leading the way.

"How was your night, sir?" Juba asked as we walked.

"Interesting," I decided at last. "I have a feeling I've been noticed, and tonight was about winning Petronius's approval."

Juba hummed. "Impress Petronius Arbiter, and you may soon count the emperor as a friend. Did you impress him, sir?"

I snorted. "Juba, I was in a room full of playwrights and poets and philosophers. What do you think?"

Juba snorted too, the bastard.

"Exactly," I said. "*Exactly.*"

I didn't think I'd embarrassed myself—frankly, after some of my previous attempts to ingratiate myself with important men, this was a huge personal improvement—but neither did I think my name would be anywhere near the top of the list next time Petronius was helping Nero select his dinner guests. I had as much affinity for poetry and plays as cats did for water. It was fine, though. Being a friend to the emperor and being the emperor's friend were different things, and I was content to be the first. My ambition wasn't sharp enough to fret that I might never share Nero's couch, or his confidences.

"Manius," I said. "Did Atreus really say no blood?"

"Yes, sir!" he replied eagerly.

Juba and I exchanged a dubious look, but there was no fooling ourselves. Atreus's cryptic message had us hooked like fish on a line.

We followed the downward slope of the Viminal Hill, into the valley where the Vicus Patricius would direct us into the heart of the city. The streets grew more crowded the closer we got to the Forum. Light flickered as slaves with lanterns led the way for their masters' litters, and torches burned in colonnades and porticos, throwing shadows against the closed doors and shutters of shopfronts and workshops and houses. Rome was modest at night. Her public buildings shone in the day, but at night they were obscured in darkness and in flickering shadows.

From the Forum, it wasn't a long walk to the Aventine. Still, when we arrived at the Medusa Fountain and found the street crowded with spectators, it didn't stop Junius Atreus from elbowing his way through them and saying curtly, "What took you so long, sir?"

I rolled my eyes at his tone and set my own against it. Mine was the result of generations of illustrious patrician lineage and came with a sense of entitlement larger than the Colossus of Rhodes. It left Atreus's in the dust. "I left a very important dinner for this, Atreus. I do hope you're not wasting my time."

Manius looked anxious, but Atreus's answering glower hid a smile. "Come and take a look then, sir."

I might have hit him with my shoulder as I pushed my way through the curious onlookers. He might have hidden another smile at that.

The Medusa Fountain wasn't named for any snakish ornamentations, I'd learned on a previous visit to this neighbourhood, but for the girls who worked the loom in the nearby weaver's shop and who braided bits of wool through their hair, making the tight plaits stand up like snakes. The weaver's shop was closed tonight, but a few of the girls must have lived nearby, because I caught a glimpse of their serpentine locks in the small crowd. The fountain itself was plain—just a regular fountain with carved leaves on it, with the dedication to whichever consul or praetor had bankrolled it worn away by the years. The water spouted from a tap in a column into a square concrete trough that was usually occupied by bathing pigeons and sparrows. There were no birds bobbing tonight—instead, there was a corpse lying in the shallow waters of the fountain. The fountain was covered in grime and bird shit. The naked corpse, however, was pristine.

"Sweet Juno's tits," I said, because I'd never seen anything like it.

A few vigiles were keeping the curious onlookers at bay, and they let me and Atreus and Juba through. A thin, sallow man was kneeling at the edge of the fountain, inspecting the corpse in the light of a torch. Leander was the physician attached to the Fifth Cohort of Vigiles. The first time I met him he'd also been kneeling over a corpse, although that one hadn't been anything approaching bloodless.

"Good evening, Valerius," he said.

"Good evening, Leander."

In the light of the vigiles' torches, we stared down at the corpse.

The corpse was a man. He was naked, lying on his back with his limbs spread as though he'd fallen from a great height. He was a young man, a youth, really. He was lean, and lightly muscled. He looked less real than a marble statue awaiting the touch of an artist's paintbrush. In sculpture, the marble was carved to mimic the way that muscles and tendons were the shifting foundations upon which the flesh was layered. A statue might smile or scowl, according to the desires and talents of its sculptor; the corpse could do neither. He was lax and soft and devoid of any expression. He might have been handsome in life with his full lips, his high cheekbones, and his dark curls, but now he just appeared cold and empty.

He was white, whiter than even a corpse ought to be. There were two long cuts in his arms, from wrist to elbow, the skin split to reveal the pink flesh and muscle inside. Yet his arms were clean. There was a gaping wound in his chest, pale and pink instead of red and gory. It had turned a little dark at the edges—it was not a fresh wound.

Juba crouched down beside Leander to examine the body. "Look at those marks on his ankles." The skin was abraded around both the dead man's ankles, but again, the wounds were pinkish rather than red. "Looks like someone hung him upside down and bled him dry after stabbing him. It must have taken hours."

Juba was too smart to be a bodyguard.

"Exactly so," Leander said, giving Juba an approving look. "I've never seen anything like it."

I wrinkled my nose. "And why put him in the fountain?"

"Someone must have seen something," Juba said. He was right; even if there hadn't been a crowd before, this was the Aventine—the streets were never quiet, not even in the middle of the night. And the fountain was overlooked by a whole lot of insulae, each one bristling with balconies.

"I'm working on that," Atreus said. "A few neighbours thought it was workmen, coming to work on the fountain at night when it wasn't as busy. A pair of men. They had a handcart. Nobody paid too much attention, until a woman who went to get water raised the alarm. They were already gone by then. I'm hoping someone will be able to describe them, but…" He shrugged.

But it was dark, the cold had probably kept most residents inside and off their balconies, and what would they have seen from their vantage points anyway? Two men, from above and behind. Unless someone in the street had taken better notice, our murderous workmen might as well have been ghosts.

"Well, I'm sure word's getting around," I said. "You've got quite a crowd."

Atreus hummed. "Someone might know something."

I glanced behind us at the gawkers. The wine shop beside the weaver's had opened up to capitalise on the night's entertainment. What good was a show without a drink to go with it? The crowd seemed cheerful and curious. There was nothing like a gruesome murder to really bring the neighbourhood together on a chilly winter's night.

I pinched the edges of my cloak together and tried to regret leaving the warmth of Petronius's house for this. I couldn't, though, even despite the cold. I was no better than the modest crowd behind me; I was here to be entertained too. And a corpse drained of all its blood and then dumped in a fountain was always going to be more entertaining than a discussion about poetry.

Atreus gave me a moment to stare at the corpse and then asked, a brow raised. "How was dinner, sir?"

"The vine leaves stuffed with goat's cheese and wheat groats were a delight."

"And the company?"

"Less of a delight," I said. "But at least I had a better time of it than this fellow."

We both regarded the corpse again for a moment.

"Do you even know who he is?" I asked.

"No idea," Atreus said. "I'm hoping someone recognises him."

It took a while, but eventually Vibilus, one of Atreus's men, approached us with a woman in tow. She looked older than the republic, but still had a spring in her step as she wobbled towards us on her walking stick. Her hair was thin and grey, and her face was lined. She squinted at us.

"This is Marcia Longia," Vibilus said. "Says she recognises the dead man."

"I did *not* say that!" Marcia Longia corrected in a reedy voice, and poked

Vibilus with her stick. "I said I *might* recognise him."

Vibilus rubbed his side and glared.

"Marcia Longia," Atreus said, with more respect in his voice now than I'd ever heard him show in the nicer end of town. "My name is Junius Atreus. I'm acting centurion with the—"

"I know who you are, Atreus," Marcia Longia said. "You're the vigile who killed Bano."

Bano had been a standover man who'd controlled the Aventine despite the best efforts of the vigiles. And it had technically been Juba who'd killed him, by propelling him off a warehouse roof, because Atreus had been too busy stopping me from falling off the same roof at the time. But why split hairs? The important thing, for everyone involved and for the entire Aventine, was that Bano was dead and that I still got a warm glow whenever I thought about it.

"Do you think you recognise him?" Atreus asked.

The old woman tottered closer to the fountain. She raised her walking stick, and for a moment I thought she was going to jab the corpse, but she poked the edge of the fountain instead. "Well, my eyesight isn't what it was, but that looks like the boy who sometimes visits my neighbour. I haven't seen him in a while though."

"The boy or the neighbour?" Atreus asked.

Marcia Longia sucked her gums for a moment. "Both of them, come to think of it."

Atreus left Leander with the corpse, and his vigiles with the small crowd, and lent Marcia Longia his arm to assist her home. She lived in the insula that directly overlooked the Medusa fountain—four floors of apartments built around a central courtyard. Marcia lived on the second floor, and it took her an interminable amount of time to climb the stairs. Juba stepped on my heels more than once when I had to stop to wait for Marcia to take a breather.

"Who's your handsome friend?" Marcia asked once we were outside her door.

Atreus blinked at her. "Ah, this is Aemilius Valerius. He is here on behalf of the magistrate—"

"I meant the other one," Marcia said, and leered at Juba.

Juba preened.

"She said her eyesight wasn't very good," I pointed out when we'd finally seen the old woman inside and were heading down the dark corridor to her neighbour's door. "She's probably senile too, the poor thing."

"Yes, sir," Atreus said, but I could tell from his tone that he was hiding a smile as he knocked on the neighbour's door.

Juba, maddeningly, hummed a smug little tune.

Nobody answered the door, so Atreus knocked again.

Still nothing.

Atreus tried the door, and it opened with a creak. "Hello?" He peered into the darkness inside. "Juba, can you see if Marcia Longia has a lamp we can borrow?"

Juba padded away, and was back within moment, his face illuminated by the light of the small clay lamp he carried. He stepped into the apartment, holding the lamp aloft.

The apartment was three rooms. It was sparsely furnished with a couch and two wicker chairs in the main room. A jug and a few plates sat on a low end table by the couch. The cushions on the couch were flat and motheaten, and a thin layer of dust, probably courtesy of the open door to the balcony, lay over everything in the place.

Juba carried the lamp through to the other two rooms, shadows sweeping up the walls in his wake. He was back within moment, and he set the oil lamp on the table, illuminating the room with a flickering glow. "It's empty."

"Looks like it has been for weeks," I said. "If not longer."

I crossed to the balcony. Outside in the street, the crowd had parted to let a couple of vigiles trundle through with a handcart. I leaned on the railing and watched as they lifted the corpse onto the cart. Atreus came and stood beside me, watching the unfolding scene with his usual serious expression.

It gave me the chance to study his handsome profile, which was something I always enjoyed. I hadn't known him long, and I still liked to discover new things about him—a freckle hiding behind his tan, the way the lamplight caught on his eyelashes, the tiny patch of golden-brown stubble on his throat that he'd missed the last time he shaved.

"He wasn't killed here," I said. "The only creatures who've disturbed the dust in this place over the last few weeks have been the rats."

Atreus didn't answer, his gaze fixed on the fountain.

I'd met Atreus over a corpse, too. That night, I'd wondered if his protracted silences meant it was taking that long for my answers to sink in. It had been an uncharitable thought; if Atreus had been taciturn, it was only because he hadn't known he could trust me. And why would he? I'd been a drunken fool. I still was, in the right circumstances. But we weren't strangers anymore, and I liked the way our dry back-and-forth hid smiles behind it.

"Well," I said. "A man with no name, and no blood, murdered in an unknown place and brought here by unknown persons for an unknown reason. You have your work cut out for you, Atreus."

That made him smile. "It seems like it."

On the rare occasions that Atreus's work needed the attention of a magistrate, I acted as their go-between, because Septus Severus couldn't bear to deal with the vigiles. But apart from the strangeness of this murder—and I certainly appreciated Atreus using it as an excuse to allow me to escape dinner with Petronius Arbiter—there was nothing here to suggest Severus or I should take a particular interest in the dead man. At least nothing apart from my morbid curiosity, and it just happened that mine was an insatiable beast.

"Of course, I should like to be kept appraised. And I should probably supervise." I honestly had no idea who I thought I was fooling. Despite coming close to death on more than one occasion when we'd investigated the murder of Marcellus Albanus, I'd loved the thrill of chasing all over the city looking for killers. True, last time danger had come a little too close to home for comfort, but what were the chances that would happen again?

Please don't make a fool of me, Fortuna.

"If you insist, sir." This time, Atreus couldn't hide his smile. I even caught a glimpse of his teeth. Then he cleared his throat and set his face into a solemn expression as he regarded the corpse again.

I went back inside and wandered into the bedroom. It was too dark to see much apart from the bed, but I had no doubt that Juba had already checked it anyway. It seemed, to my cursory glance, as undisturbed as the rest of the apartment.

Atreus followed me inside, looking behind him. Juba was prowling around in the living room. Atreus let the back of his hand brush against mine, our knuckles bumping. "How was your dinner?"

He'd asked before, but this time he wasn't teasing me, and so I gave him an honest answer.

"I think it was a test to see if I get an invitation into Nero's close circle of friends," I said. "They were all there, apart from him. Petronius Arbiter, of course, because he's the gatekeeper, and Lucan. Otho and Fabianus. Cilnius. Hosidius. Litus and Entellus. Most of them I'd never heard of, but I think I was supposed to know their names. They were just a bunch of spoiled, rich young idiots. You'd think I'd fit in well, except they're all fucking poets, Atreus. *Poets.*"

"You like poetry."

"I like bread too, but that doesn't mean I want to listen to a bunch of bakers go on for hours about how they make it and then get into a pissing contest about whose tastes the best."

Atreus laughed softy.

"So thanks for rescuing me," I said. "It wasn't terrible, but I was glad to have an excuse to leave."

"Well, I'm glad I could do it."

Only in moments like these, in the middle of the night, could a patrician son of the illustrious Aemilii and a plebeian who actually worked for a living be equal friends. Scant moments, but I savoured them.

Of course, Atreus and I were also something more than friends, and my reputation would be ruined if anyone found out. Atreus's wouldn't make it out unscathed either, but the worst of the scandal would be reserved for me. Because Roman patricians weren't supposed to bend over for anyone, not even tall, lean men with hints of hazel in their eyes, strands of gold in their hair, and faint freckles across the bridge of their nose. If we were discovered, Atreus would probably lose his job, but I would absolutely lose my reputation—and destroy my entire family's for good measure.

I had a lot of trust resting on Atreus's friendship.

"Whose apartment is this, I wonder," I mused, peering into the gloom.

"I'll find out," Atreus said. "Marcia Longia might know. One of the other neighbours might, if she doesn't. If nobody does, I'll send someone to wake the owner of the building, but in a place like this he might not even know who's living here. As long as someone pays the rent when his man knocks on their door, why would he care?"

"You think the original tenants might have sublet the place?"

He shrugged. "Who knows? It looks as though nobody has been here for a while, and yet not only are there still lamps and cushions here, and there are tunics in the trunk as well. Somebody must still be paying the rent, or the landlord would have tossed it all out."

I could understand not lugging heavy furniture if you moved—it might even have belonged to the landlord—but your tunics? No, the apartment might have been dusty, but Atreus was right. Someone still lived here, even if they hadn't been here for a while.

"Still, all that to get the name of a man who clearly hasn't been here in weeks, just on the chance that he might know the murder victim because an old woman with bad eyesight said she thought she'd seen him here before. I wasn't joking when I said you had your work cut out for you."

He laughed under his breath, and his hand grazed mine again. "I know."

Atreus had a long night in front of him, whereas mine was almost at an end. Knocking on doors and asking questions—and sometimes knocking on heads and asking questions—was what Atreus did best. And he didn't need my help to do it in a neighbourhood like this one. The Aventine was his territory.

"Come to the house tomorrow for breakfast," I said. "Whenever you finish up for the night."

"I will. Thank you." It was too dark to see a smile in here, but I heard it in his voice.

Our knuckles bumped again.

I stepped out into the main room. "Let's go home, Juba."

* * *

It was after midnight when I arrived home at my house on the Caelian Hill, but I was sober enough that Hursa, the door porter, wouldn't be able to report my failings to my womenfolk. They'd have nothing to complain about over breakfast now, which was a shame for them. My wife and my sister loved nothing more than taking the moral high ground since they weren't allowed to wallow wine-soaked in the gutter with the men.

"Did you hear any good jokes at dinner, sir?" Hursa asked hopefully as he latched the door behind me.

"Not a single one."

His face fell, but then he brightened again. "Ledo says you went to see a dead body!"

There was nothing that happened under my roof, or even outside of it apparently, that my entire household didn't know about as soon as it occurred.

"Ledo should know better than to gossip." I tossed Hursa my cloak. "Tell Damos that Junius Atreus will be joining us for breakfast in the morning."

Hursa nodded and scuttled away.

Juba followed me through to the dimly lit atrium, and then treaded silently up the steps behind me. There was a lamp burning in my bedroom, spilling a soft glow of warm, golden light out the doorway.

"Goodnight, Juba," I said, letting him know there was nothing else I needed from him tonight.

"Goodnight, sir." He vanished into the darkness.

I washed my face and hands, stripped out of my tunic, fell into bed, and dreamed of absolutely nothing.

I woke with the morning and took a moment to listen to the sounds of the household. Sandals slapping on the tiles of the atrium; the brush of a broom across the floor; a distant clatter of dishes from the kitchen. I rose after a while, then splashed my face with water from the basin on the stand near the bed. Then I washed the bits of me that most needed washing and dug around in my trunk for a clean tunic. The events of the night before came back to me, but it wasn't Petronius's dinner party I thought of—it was the corpse in the Aventine, and the trunk full of clothes in the bedroom. Despite the dust, the place hadn't been abandoned. Someone had still been living there, whether it was the tenant, or the man whose corpse had been dumped there. Maybe the corpse was the tenant, or the corpse was a victim of the tenant. Or maybe the tenant had moved on, and the tunics there belonged to the corpse, who had moved in without anyone's knowledge. But someone had been living there. Maybe not spending much time there, since the neighbours had no idea, but the apartment hadn't been empty.

I thought of the corpse, his expression lax in death. Why would someone go to the trouble of draining him of his blood and then lugging him down the street to leave him in the Medusa Fountain? There were a hundred places to dump a body in the Aventine alone. A thousand, probably, if you had any imagination at all. So why the fountain? Atreus certainly had a challenge in front of him when it came to solving this murder. I mean, so did I, because there was no way I'd let him investigate this one on his own. A bloodless corpse? It was too fascinating to ignore.

I searched for a belt for my tunic, and then sat on my bed and laced on my sandals. When I was fully dressed, I headed downstairs to the informal triclinium for breakfast.

Fulvia and Octavia were already eating.

I crossed to Fulvia first and leaned down to press a kiss to her cheek. "Good morning."

"Good morning, Quintus. How's your stomach?"

"I'm not even hungover, I'll have you know."

My wife raised her eyebrows. "I meant after the corpse."

"There is not a single secret under this roof, is there?" I kissed Octavia's cheek too, and then took a seat.

Breakfast was puls with beans and onion and chunks of cured pork. It was warm and hearty, and perfect for a winter's morning.

"How was your dinner?" Octavia asked, and then laughed at me when I

19

raised my eyebrows in disbelief at the banal question. "No, you're right; I'd rather know about the corpse drained of blood and dumped in a fountain, too. It's all Hursa can talk about, and he's very annoyed that Juba won't tell him anything."

"Of course he is." I made a mental note to slip Juba a dupondius for his discretion, plus a bonus sestertius for annoying Hursa. "I invited Atreus for breakfast, so you can interrogate him to your heart's content whenever he arrives."

Octavia showed me a mischievous smile. "As though I needed your permission, Quintus."

Perhaps if I'd been more of a stern paterfamilias, I would have chided her. But I'd never been disciplined enough to be stern, not even with myself, and I was too happy to have this version of Octavia back—my smiling, teasing, sarcastic little sister—that she could have been gambling and drinking and fornicating in the Transtiberina every night and I wouldn't have stopped her. Fortunately, Octavia's idea of a good time was a lot more modest than that.

I told my womenfolk about last night's dinner, about my interview beforehand with Petronius, and about how out of my depth I'd felt surrounded by men who wrote poems and plays about the grand themes of love and war. We somehow moved into a discussion about gruesome deaths—those that we'd seen on stage, and how, my wife and sister speculated, the real thing wasn't usually as thrilling. It was an odd echo of the conversation I'd had with Petronius last night.

I'd been in the army, so I was no stranger to bloodshed, and while I didn't confirm the suspicions of my wife and my sister, I didn't deny them either. How could I? Once the hot rush of blood in battle had receded again and your suddenly sharp awareness had worn off like a fever dream you could barely remember upon waking, there was nothing exciting about inspecting the dead. Nothing stomach-churning about them either. Usually by the time you were staring at them, you were too tired to feel a damned thing. Perhaps a familiar face among them might send a faint jolt through you, but it was as far away as distant thunder on a fading summer's storm. It took a while after the battle was done for your mind to settle back into your body, at least in my experience.

I let the womenfolk steer the conversation, until they brought it full circle back to the Aventine.

"What I don't understand," Octavia said, her brow creased in thought, "is why the body was dumped in a fountain?"

"That's what puzzles me, too," I said. "A dead man weighs twice as much as a living one, but someone went to the trouble to move him, risking discovery on the way. And for what? To leave him in a public fountain, where he'd be discovered in moments, even in the middle of the night."

Octavia hummed around her spoon. "It's intriguing."

"I know," I said. "Which is why I told Atreus I'm supervising."

Fulvia laughed. "And how did he take that?"

"Oh, I think he knew it was going to happen when he sent for me."

Fulvia's gaze was knowing, and her smile was fond.

Our talk of murders was interrupted by Hursa, who was wearing a faintly confused expression and tugging at his wild hair. He shuffled into the triclinium. "Sir? There's someone here to see you."

"Oh, yes," I said. "Atreus. I told you last night that I invited him for breakfast."

"No, it's not Junius Atreus, sir," Hursa said, and blinked owlishly at me while the embers in his brain failed to catch into a flame.

I sighed. "Who is it, Hursa?"

"Oh!" He widened his eyes. "Sir, it's the philosopher Seneca."

Well, that was certainly unexpected.

Chapter Two

L ucius Annaeus Seneca was a man with his six decades of life experience written hard in every furrow of his brow. He was bald on top, but thin grey curls still clung to his skull as though he wore a laurel wreath balanced on his ears. He was overweight, but he wore it well, and combined with his stern face and his keen gaze it gave him an air of gravitas and authority. Even if I hadn't known who he was, his presence would have demanded my respect.

He rose as I entered the formal dining room.

"Aemilius Valerius," he said. "I've heard many things about you."

"Annaeus Seneca," I said, as we shook hands. "It's an honour to meet you."

"I know your uncle Lucullus Maro," he said. "He speaks highly of you."

He didn't know Uncle Maro very well, if that was the case. I adored Maro, and vice versa, but we also complained about each other as though we were persistent toothaches.

We sat, and Seneca picked at the knee of his tunic for a moment. "And, of course, both Anicetus and Tigellinus have nothing but praise for you."

Anicetus was Nero's spymaster, and Tigellinus was Prefect of the Vigiles. I'd unwittingly brought myself to their attention during the investigation into the murder of Marcellus Albanus—and the murders of a bunch of other important men. There had been days when it had felt like senators were dropping like flies. Not that I spared them any sympathy; traitors to Rome, all of them. I should have guessed that Seneca would know every little detail of that investigation. He had supposedly withdrawn from public life, but did men like Seneca ever truly retire? I doubted it very much.

Calliope brought wine and honey cakes. Seneca ignored them both, still fiddling with the fabric at his knee. There was something gnawing at the edges of his composure, disturbing the calm waters of his famous Stoicism.

"As does the general Corbulo," he added at last. "You are one to watch, Valerius."

To watch approvingly, I hoped, and not with suspicion. The problem with having the attention of powerful men—an emperor-maker, in Seneca's case— was that if you lost their support, you were given a swift and oftentimes mortal reminder of the scope of that power. Just because Seneca was a good man didn't mean he wasn't also a dangerous one. Sometimes, the most dangerous men of all were the good ones.

"You honour me," I said, because it was a more polite answer than *What the actual fuck are you doing in my house, Seneca?* Still, Seneca was one of the smartest men of the age. Of course, he heard the question, even if I didn't have the balls, or the blatant stupidity, to ask it aloud.

His plump jowls sagged as he turned the corners of his mouth downwards. "Last night, after Petronius Arbiter's dinner party, my nephew Lucan was attacked in the street."

My blood ran cold. "Is he all right?"

"He is safe and well." Seneca's expression was grave. "His slaves are a little battered and bruised, but no lives were lost."

The streets of Rome were notoriously dangerous after dark. The vigiles and Urban Cohorts couldn't be everywhere at once, and thieves and ruffians took advantage of the darkness to lay traps for unwary pedestrians. My womenfolk were not happy about my habit of nocturnally gallivanting throughout the city, but they'd never seen Juba in action. It would take a very brave man, or a total fool, to square up to my bodyguard. And, just in case such a man existed, I wasn't proud enough that I'd never turn tail and run.

"I was at that dinner," I said.

Seneca's expression said he knew. He straightened up, leaving his tunic alone at last. "Valerius, I believe Lucan was targeted by enemies jealous of his rising fame, and that his life is in danger."

"We're assuming, then, that it wasn't a random attack?"

Seneca fixed me with a gaze that left no room for argument. Not that I would have dared. "We are not assuming anything. We *know*."

Seneca, apart from being the foremost philosopher of his generation, had also famously tutored Nero when the emperor was a boy. A twinge of phantom pain stung my knuckles just thinking about it, but perhaps tutors weren't so quick to lash out with a cane when their charges would one day be wearing the imperial purple. And, make no mistake about it, Seneca had made sure that Nero, Claudius's adopted son, would be emperor. Claudius's natural son Britannicus, a possible future complication to Nero's claim, had died before his fourteenth birthday. Men in Seneca's position didn't get their hands dirty, but neither did they remain entirely clean. Perhaps the most dangerous man of all was the good man who weighed the death of a boy against the stability of an empire and felt no moral qualms at all about the result.

Britannicus's death had been purely political. It had even been necessary. Agrippina, Nero's mother, had been making noises about withdrawing her support for her son and giving it to Britannicus instead. She'd condemned Britannicus by her actions, whoever had actually slipped the poison into his drink, and on whoever's orders. Politics was a dirty game. If you were a Julio-Claudian, it was filthier than the mud of the Tiber.

"Do you believe the attack was against your nephew, or was it against you?" I asked.

Seneca might have been a Stoic, and above the common vices that tormented us undisciplined lower beings, but he was also one of the richest men in the empire. Providing the sort of philosophical and moral arguments that allowed the Senate to sleep at night after they all agreed to remember that Britannicus had been prone to sickness since childhood paid very, very well, but his wealth and his influence had made him enemies.

Seneca's grimace told me that he'd had the same thought. "An attack on Lucan is an attack on me. Whether that is the intention of the attackers, I could not say. Lucan's star is on the rise. I may have enemies, Valerius, but I am sure that Lucan has some of his own."

Of course he did. Didn't we all? I wasn't without enemies myself, and I couldn't even blame it on my ambition, since I barely had any. I had vague ideas of becoming a quaestor as soon as I was eligible, but anything else? Political influence? The governorship of some province? The ear of the emperor? None of that interested me. My ambitions were more modest than that. I had no desire to be remarkable, just respectable.

"We have an enemy in common, I believe," I said, and held his gaze.

Seneca surprised me by not talking around it. He snorted. "Agrippina? The woman is a viper, Valerius. She strikes directly."

He said it with a sort of admiration in his tone. They had been allies once. Agrippina and Seneca, along with Burrus, the Prefect of the Praetorian Guard, had all worked to secure Nero's future as emperor. But while Seneca and Burrus had stepped back from the throne as soon as the young emperor was able to stand on his own two feet, Agrippina had tried to tighten her grip rather than loosen it. Her son had outgrown any need for her, and she resented it. Hadn't she won him the purple? Where was Nero's *gratitude*?

Agrippina was a dangerous woman, and I didn't like to think about how she must know my name now after the business with the murders that had taken place over the summer. The murders and the suicides—more than one man had fallen on his sword after Atreus and I had discovered his treason, and his links to Agrippina.

"What happened to Lucan exactly?" I asked.

Seneca let out a slow breath. "He left dinner and was set upon in the street by a group of six men. He did not know them, he says, but he could also not describe them in the darkness. His men had lanterns, of course, but in the melee..."

I nodded.

He shook his head. "Lucan's bodyguard and litter bearers prevailed, and the men fled. That is all I know. They made no demands for money, which makes me think it was not a robbery."

I shrugged. "Maybe they thought they'd empty his purse when he was unconscious or dead."

It made sense that a man like Seneca would look for reasons to assume that this was political. He was a political creature. To him, every robber was an assassin in disguise. It didn't mean he was wrong, but it meant he had a blind spot. What was to say the men hadn't just been robbers? Except...

Unease stirred in my gut. "Where did it happen?"

"Only a block from Petronius's house."

I thought of the 'drunks' that had approached my litter bearers. They'd let us pass, even though to a robber I must have been as attractive a target as Lucan. Was it the same men? I hadn't seen six of them last night, but perhaps the others had been lurking out of sight. If so, Seneca's hunch was likely correct: the men had caused no trouble for me because they had been waiting specifically for Lucan.

My curiosity was piqued. "I'll look into it and see what I can find out."

Seneca let out a breath, as though he was relieved, and I was struck by the fact that even though there was no room for me to refuse to help him—I'd be a total idiot to refuse any request from a man of Seneca's rank and influence—a part of him must have still entertained the possibility of it. Or, even more curiously, perhaps his relief came from believing the matter was now as good as solved. I was unused to anyone having that amount of faith in me. Honestly, if he'd seen me bumbling around the city the last time I'd investigated anything, he would have looked more wary than relieved. Atreus and I had succeeded more because of good luck than good management. Fortuna, for all that she could be a capricious bitch, had always had a soft spot for me.

"Thank you, Valerius." Seneca rose, having not touched his honey cakes at all, and swept out of the room, off to spend the rest of the day mentally wrestling with ethics and duty, or whatever it was philosophers did to pass the hours.

I reached over and snaffled a honey cake. I was brushing crumbs off my tunic when Atreus slipped into the room as silently as a cat and took a seat uninvited. Also like a cat.

"You're late," I said, sending more crumbs into my lap.

"Hursa wouldn't let me in because Seneca was here. Even he knows I'm not important enough to meet Seneca." He flashed me a grin.

"True." I nodded at the plate. "Have a honey cake. They're still warm." Atreus dug in.

"Any news on your murder victim?" I asked.

He arched a brow. "It's been five hours."

"I liked it when you at least pretended to show me respect," I lied, and his mouth quirked. "Did you at least get the name of the missing neighbour who was possibly friends with the dead man?"

Atreus shook his head. "Not yet, but he apparently hadn't lived there for long. Marcia Longia says she always kept her distance because he seemed like a shifty character with a lot of bad friends. One of them threw her shopping down the stairs once when she was taking too long to go up them."

"Charming. But she doesn't know his name?"

"She says she avoided him after that, and she hadn't seen him around for a while, so she just assumed he moved out. Maybe she'll be more talkative if I take Juba with me to talk to her."

I didn't take the bait. "Hmm. Aren't you going to ask me why Seneca was visiting me?"

He broke off a piece of honey cake and ate it. "I presume you're going to tell me now."

"I *am*." I leaned forward. "Seneca wants me to look into a matter for him. Last night, his nephew Lucan was attacked in the street."

Atreus furrowed his brow. "Last night."

"That's right."

"Didn't you say—" He answered the question himself before he'd even finished asking it. "Lucan was at Petronius Arbiter's dinner last night, with you."

"Right again."

"What did you see?" he asked me.

"At the dinner? Nothing much. But as I was leaving, there were men lurking in the street. They didn't give me any trouble, but they might have been the same men who attacked Lucan. Which means they were waiting for him."

The furrow in his brow deepened. "Not a random attack then."

"So it seems."

Atreus nodded. "We need to talk to Lucan and see what he can tell us."

"No," I said. "*I* need to talk to Lucan, and you need to go home and get some sleep before your neighbour brings Lucilla home." Lucilla was Atreus's niece. She was four. Between his night shifts and his responsibilities towards Lucilla, it was a wonder I ever saw Atreus in daylight hours at all. "I'll take Juba with me to talk to Lucan."

Atreus's expression told me he wasn't happy about it, but he knew better than to complain and give me the chance to remind him I outranked him.

"Go and see Damos before you leave," I said, to soften the blow. "He'll wrap some cakes up for you to take home."

* * *

Lucan lived in a house on the Viminal Hill. He wasn't there when Juba and I turned up on his doorstep, and his helpful door slave, for the price of only a quadrans, told us that we would find him on the Campus Martius. I exchanged a glance with Juba at that, because slender Lucan hadn't struck me as the athletic type.

He wasn't.

On the northern end of the Campus Martius, between the hills to the east and the Tiber to the west, near the Mausoleum of Augustus, we found Lucan orating to the trees. Well, to the trees, to a rather bored-looking retinue of slaves, and to one of the other guests I recalled from last night: Litus. Litus was a tall, thin fellow, even thinner than Lucan, but with a sinewy sort of strength that made me think of a praying mantis. His eyes bulged a little too, which aided to the comparison.

"Valerius!" he exclaimed when he saw me, his face breaking into a smile that made me feel immediately guilty for thinking of him as an insect. "Lucan is reciting his newest poem! Come and tell us what you think!"

A slave produced a stool for me, and I sat with Litus in the shade of a sweet-smelling stone pine.

This end of the Campus Martius wasn't crowded. A group of children

28

played nearby, but they weren't close enough to be a distraction. Their high-pitched shrieks, carried away on the sharp breeze, were as faint as birdsong. The day was bright, with no sign of last night's clouds, and while the brilliant blue of the sky promised a cold night ahead, the weather was as pleasant as anyone could hope for a winter's day. The day bathed Rome's buildings in light; the Temple of Jupiter gleamed from atop the Capitoline Hill, where it stood head and shoulders over the rest of the city.

In the colonnade of a nearby building, men and women sold food from makeshift little stalls. There was a steady trickle of people to buy from them; we were only a short distance from the busy Via Flaminia, and clearly I wasn't the only person in the city who'd make a detour for a really good stuffed vine leaf. In fact, the brisk trade they were doing over there convinced me that Juba and I would definitely be paying those stalls a visit once we were finished here with whatever it was Lucan and Litus were actually doing.

"Keep at it," Litus said, waving a hand at Lucan. "Remember, you must project your voice in the same manner an actor does, but without the aid of a mask. This is no dining room recital."

Lucan sighed, adjusted his stance, drew in a deep breath, and—

"No!" Litus said again. "Jupiter, Lucan. Look at your feet! You're standing pigeon-toed!" He threw me a look. "It's good he's a poet, because he'd make a terrible actor."

I glanced at Lucan, who looked fondly exasperated at Litus's assessment rather than genuinely annoyed. It took a true friend, I supposed, to call you talentless and pigeon-toed and not get punched in the face for it. Last night, I'd seen a lot of barbed looks hidden behind polite smiles as all of the emperor's favourites fought to find a higher position in whatever pecking order they had, but there was none of that here today between Lucan and Litus. Their friendship appeared honest. Brutally honest, in Litus's case.

There was a boy sitting at Lucan's feet, probably still aged in his teens. It was the same slave from last night. He wore an unadorned green tunic, sandals, and balanced a wax tablet on his knee. He was looking up at his master, squinting into the bright daylight. He held a stylus clamped between split and swollen lips, and one of his cheekbones was bruised.

Lucan adjusted his feet and looked down at the slave.

The slave plucked the stylus free. "The muddy waters of the Rubicon," he said, without glancing at the tablet, "glide through the valleys."

Lucan corrected his stance. "The muddy waters of the Rubicon glide through the valleys." He huffed. "No, not muddy. Cloudy? Brackish? *Are* they brackish? Reddish?" He nodded at the slave. "Reddish."

The slave made a note on the tablet.

I'd never been much of a poet. I'd suspected writing the stuff was a tedious job, and it certainly appeared that way as Lucan and the slave proceeded to make a bunch of tiny changes that, to my mind, changed nothing much at all. The part that followed about the rain-bearing moon with its moisture-laden horns was nice, though, and I started to get interested in the story when Caesar's army crossed the Rubicon.

"No, no, *no!*" Litus exclaimed. "Your *feet*, Lucan! Watch your feet!"

Lucan made a rude gesture in Litus's direction. "Let me get the words right before I bother about my feet!"

"He is always like this," Litus told me in a teasing undertone that Lucan was meant to hear. "Tetchy." To Lucan, he said, "Come and have some wine, my dear friend, and wash your foul temper away."

Lucan came and sat, and a girl brought cups of wine for the three of us.

"I suppose my uncle has sent you to see me," Lucan said wryly. His mood appeared much improved with his first sip of wine.

"He did."

"And you could not say no."

"I wouldn't have dared," I admitted, and raised my cup to him.

A smile split his narrow face. "Yes, that's Seneca, alright. Well, as you can see, I'm fine." He nodded at the slave. "Poor Hermes took the brunt of it."

"What happened?"

"I barely saw a thing," Lucan said. "I was in the litter, with the curtains closed. The first thing I knew of any trouble was getting dropped onto the road when the men rushed my litter bearers. Hermes?"

The slave tucked a curl of dark hair behind his ear, exposing more of his bruises to the daylight. He shuffled closer to us. "I was walking behind the litter, sir, and didn't see much," he said, and showed me an apologetic smile as though he thought I might blame him for that. "I heard men running, and then shouting, and then my master's litter bearers were fighting with the robbers. I tried to get to my master, but I was struck. It was a cudgel, I think, but I didn't see it coming."

"They could have killed him," Lucan muttered, a shadow crossing his face.

"I don't remember anything much after that, sir," Hermes said. "I'm sorry."

"That's fine," I said.

"My bodyguards and litter bearers saw them off, thank Jupiter," Lucan said. "Cowards, to strike a skinny slave who can't even defend himself."

"Hermes may be vicious with a pen," Litus contributed, "but he's not much of a street fighter, are you, boy?"

"No, sir," Hermes said with a smile.

"A pen?" I asked curiously.

"He's my scribe," Lucan said. "And a sponge, it seems. Litus was the target of one of his poems last Saturnalia—Hermes was our king—and I think he still feels the sting."

Lucan's mouth turned down at the corners, and he shot Hermes a cold glare. But Lucan laughed—poets were strange—and Hermes smiled hesitantly, so I was probably wrong about the intent. I often was. The problem with looking for truth in every gesture was that you looked twice as hard for deception, and you inevitably found it whether it was there or not.

Lucan took a sip of his wine. "And now Uncle Seneca thinks it's a conspiracy instead of some random street attack."

"What do you think?" I asked.

Lucan gave me an assessing stare. "I think the old man is paranoid. Then again," he added with a wry snort, "I also think he's a lot smarter than I am."

"He may be," I said. "I passed the same men when I left Petronius's house last night. They didn't trouble me."

"Fuck," Lucan muttered, and dragged a hand through his hair. "Seneca will be insufferable about this."

"Twice as insufferable," Litus said brightly. "As impossible as that seems."

"Litus." For the first time, there was a note of actual warning in Lucan's tone.

"I tease, my dear friend," Litus said. "You know I only tease. It's pure jealousy. I wish I had an uncle as rich and influential as yours."

Again, he laid that note of jest over words that might have hidden a sharp sliver of the truth.

Lucan huffed out a breath, seemingly half amused and half exasperated. "Is there anything else you need from me, Valerius? I really do need to get this poem finished and rehearsed before the Juvenalia."

"The what now?" I asked.

"The Juvenalia," Lucan said. "To celebrate the shaving of Nero's beard, and his passing from youth into manhood. It will be a festival of music and plays and poetry. It was Petronius's idea, I think. Nero's theatre is almost built. We're all writing something, and we'll be performing too."

"If you can ever figure out where to put your feet," Litus said, and Lucan rolled his eyes.

"Performing?" I asked. Patricians didn't *perform*.

Litus laughed. "The theatre is in Nero's private gardens, Valerius. It's not public."

In which case, I supposed it was no different than a poet reciting his works at a private dinner party for friends. Still, it was bound to ruffle some stuffy old patrician feathers. Probably the sort that could do with some ruffling.

"What's your play about?" I asked Litus.

He made the face of a man who'd taken a swig of what he thought was mulsum only to discover too late that it was vinegar. "About the glory of Rome, of course. Except I had an entire act written about Horatius defending the bridge and then last night Fabianus, that greasy little prick, announces that his play is *also* about Horatius."

I sucked in a breath through my teeth.

"And he knew too," Litus said with a scowl. "That *fuck*." He groaned, his breath leaving him in a pained sound. "So now I have to rewrite the entire thing in less than a month. Maybe I'll do Aeneus. Or Romulus and Remus. I don't fucking know. What do you think, Valerius?"

I thought I was very glad that I was neither a poet nor a playwright. Searching for Lucan's attackers seemed like a lot less work. Or at least if I failed, it wouldn't be on a torch-lit stage in front of an audience that included the emperor himself.

"Um," I said, because I was clever like that. "Honestly? A lot of old senators like to make jibes about the fact that Nero has never led an army, so if I could write poetry, which I can't, I'd steer clear of heroes like Aeneus. I wouldn't want to set up that comparison."

"That's smart," Litus said, his eyes suddenly bright. He looked at me as though he was seeing me properly for the first time, and was surprised at what he'd discovered. "That's *very* smart, Valerius."

"I have my moments," I said. "Scant as they may be."

"Apollo," Litus said. "Nero is more of an Apollo than an Aeneus." He flashed me a broad smile. "And who wouldn't rather be likened to a god than a mere hero?"

I was sure that, in my case, it wouldn't make a difference, since the comparison would be scathing either way. But then, I wasn't an emperor.

"At least you're doing better than Petronius," Lucan said to Litus. And then, in response to my questioning look, he said, "Petronius is putting on a play, of course. A scene from his *Satyricon* that nobody has read yet. He says it's to be even funnier than Trimalchio's feast, except the only actor he says can play Giton has run off, and Petronius is tearing his hair out because of it." He snorted. "*Actors.*"

I hated plays, as a rule, but I wouldn't have minded seeing the Satyricon on stage. "Petronius doesn't seem like the sort of man who tears his hair out over anything."

Lucan laughed. "Oh, actors would make anyone tear their hair out, wouldn't they, Litus? Just ask Entellus."

Litus snorted. "Entellus is a fool."

I reined the conversation back to the matter at hand. "Have you any known enemies, Lucan?"

Before he could answer, Litus snorted. "Have you been paying attention, Valerius? We'd trample over each other and leave our best friends' corpses

33

crushed in the street in order to win the favour of the emperor!"

Lucan rolled his eyes. "That isn't true. There is some—"

"Viciousness," Litus said.

"*Competition*," Lucan decided. He should have been a politician like his uncle. "But it is petty and childish, that's all. None of us would actually harm another over it. That's ridiculous."

I caught Litus's gaze and saw that he didn't believe Lucan. Jupiter, if Fabianus had been here a moment ago while Litus was still angry about the Horatius thing, Litus might have strangled him to death. But his anger had been short and sharp, the bright flare of a flame that had been quickly extinguished. Would Litus have enough venom in him to hire thugs in a premeditated attack on his friend, even if they were rivals? I doubted it. Which didn't mean nobody else in this circle of poets and playwrights was incapable of some forward planning, but I still felt a motive for an attack on Lucan probably had more to do with his uncle than his poetry. Seneca was a very powerful man with some very powerful enemies. And in order to discover who they were, I'd need to talk to the one man in Rome who not only knew all the gossip, but who I knew I could trust never to lie to me.

I bid farewell to Lucan and Litus, leaving them arguing good-naturedly over iambic and lyric forms, and exactly how to position your feet when delivering a recital. Juba and I got a stuffed vine leaf each and ate them as we headed along the Via Flaminia away from the Campus Martius.

My mad Uncle Maro lived on the Esquiline, in a house of ever-changing appearance thanks to Maro's madness, his wealth, and his willingness to be constantly beset by an army of tradesman. There was always someone painting a new fresco, or knocking a doorway into a wall, or redesigning the gardens. Juba and I sidestepped a couple of men trying to carry what appeared to be some sort of sculpture through the front door, while arguing with the door slave about whether or not it would fit. I left Juba to watch the entertainment while I set off to find Maro.

My mad relation was sitting in the garden with a scroll on one knee and a jar of oysters beside him. I picked up the jar of oysters and took their spot, resettling them on my lap where they were nice and handy to grab.

"Quintus," Maro said happily. "I was just on my way to visit *you.*"

"Were you?" I popped an oyster in my mouth. "What for?"

"Do you remember that general from Narbo Martius?" he asked. "Well, he sent around another few jars of rosemary honey yesterday, and I thought your household could use some."

I didn't remember the general particularly well, but the honey? I'd be dreaming of that until the day I died. It was delicious. "Thank you."

"But here you are instead," he said. He narrowed his eyes and tilted his head. "And it's before noon. What's going on?"

"Well," I said, "I had that dinner party at Petronius Arbiter's house last night, remember?"

Of course he remembered. I was finally making friends with important men. He also knew me well, which was why he jumped immediately to the worst possible conclusion. "Jupiter, Quintus! Don't tell me you've stumbled over another corpse?"

"As if you wouldn't already know if *that* had happened," I said, and he grinned. "No, but last night a bunch of thugs attacked Lucan as he was leaving the same party. He's fine, but Seneca turned up at my house after breakfast and asked me to look into it. He thinks it was a targeted attack."

"And was it?" Maro asked keenly, his hairy brows drawing together like pugnacious caterpillars.

"Well, the same group of thugs saw me leaving and didn't bother me."

Maro sucked a breath in through his teeth. "Juno's tits, my boy. You really do have the knack of putting yourself right in the middle of a pile of shit every time, don't you?"

I chewed an oyster before swallowing it. "Apparently so."

He rolled his scroll up. "Well, what do you need to know?"

One thing I appreciated about Maro was that he always got straight to the point with me. "I need to know what enemies Seneca has."

One of Maro's eyebrows crawled up his forehead. The other one scrunched up over his eye. "Seneca? You want to know how many enemies *Seneca* has? Quintus, you'd have more luck counting the grains of sand in the ocean!"

Maybe the oysters could help me with that. I sighed as I ate another one. "That's what I figured. But I thought you might have heard something new? Something fresh?"

"Seneca's about as fresh as last week's bread," Maro said. He snorted. "He's *retired*, don't you know? Of course, men like him never really retire until they're going up in smoke on their funeral pyres, but he's not the force he once was. I'm sure he's fully appraised of all the latest gossip from the Palatine thanks to all the friendships he made there over the years, but that's not the same as having a direct hand in ruling, is it? Seneca might have Nero's respect, but he no longer has his ear."

"Do you think that bothers him?"

Maro reached over for an oyster. "Honestly? No, I don't think it does. Do you think that Publius Suillius Rufus pulled those public attacks against Seneca out of his arse? No, no. If Nero hadn't wanted Seneca attacked, then Seneca would not have been attacked. That was a *warning*, and Seneca was smart enough to turn it around on Rufus instead with his successful counter-prosecution. So, while the retirement was forced on Seneca, I don't think he's pushed back against it at all. He's still an incredibly rich man, and, unlike Rufus, he's not banished to the Balearic Isles. Seneca's smart enough to know that a wealthy retirement is no real loss when you play his sort of political games. He got Nero the purple and, more importantly, he got him out of Agrippina's clutches. That's a win for both Seneca and for Rome."

"So he wins and loses at the same time?"

"That's politics," Maro said, digging around in the jar for another oyster. "But no, I don't think Seneca is vying to get back his position as Nero's advisor. I think he's rather enjoying not having to look over his shoulder all the time."

"Stoics don't enjoy anything."

Maro snorted. "Not that they'll admit to, at least."

I let out a slow breath and stared at the pots of thyme closest to our garden bench. "And does Rufus have any friends who might be angry at Seneca on his behalf?"

Maro showed me a sympathetic look. "Not that I'm aware, Quintus. Have you considered that if Seneca has any enemies brazen enough to attack Lucan just to get their revenge, then it just might be the same one you share with him?"

An oyster turned in my stomach. "Of course. Although Seneca says she'd attack him personally, not through Lucan."

"Well, Seneca is a smart man," Maro said. "But be careful he doesn't give her too much credit. When a wolf is caught in a trap, it'll snap and bite at anything it can reach."

He had a point, damn him. I helped myself to another oyster to see if it would kill the sour taste in my mouth. It didn't. "Do you think Agrippina is a wolf caught in a trap?"

Maro squinted into the sunlight. "I think if I were Agrippina, I would be enjoying my retirement like Seneca is." He popped another oyster in his mouth, and swallowed it down, and then belched. He lowered his voice. "Then again, who knows how her mind works? I might be mad, my dear boy, but I'm not *crazy*."

I snorted, affection for the old man warming me. "Well, that's the problem with following a path of logic like Seneca's, isn't it? The illogical people don't. So is Lucan's attacker logical or illogical?"

"This conversation has taken a philosophical turn," Maro said. He reached out and poked me in the ribs and then beamed. "I hardly recognise you nowadays, Quintus!"

I wished there wasn't a sting in the compliment, but I'd earned it. After my return to Rome from the army, and my father's death, I had not risen to the position expected of a young patrician and newly minted paterfamilias. In fact, thanks to an extended period of malaise and more than one drunken incident in public, I'd very quickly started to sink. I was only now beginning to turn my reputation around.

"I hardly recognise myself," I said. "Life was much easier when nobody expected anything of me, Maro."

Maro slapped me on the back. "*I* always expected better of you, you young fool."

That was us. I was a young fool, and Maro was an old one, and we understood one another perfectly. When the whole city had thought I was nothing more than a drunken idiot, Maro had known I was better than that. And when the whole city thought that he was a mad old man who didn't have any room in his head for thoughts of anything apart from home renovations, I knew that he was cleverer than a hundred Senecas.

Maro regarded me unhappily from underneath his hairy eyebrows. "I have no idea what you've got yourself into this time, Quintus, but make sure you watch your back."

"I will," I said.

"And don't forget to take some of that honey home with you. It really is delicious."

* * *

Junius Atreus lived on the fifth floor of a not-quite-as-decrepit-as-its-neighbours insula in the Aventine. I usually visited in the afternoons, when he was just waking up from sleep after working all night. Atreus's place was small, but he kept it tidy enough. It was a bedroom and a living area only, with an alcove for a stove that I'd never seen him use, and a balcony off the living area that, although it caught a pleasant breeze, wasn't as restful as it could have been—it also caught every bellowed obscenity from the downstairs neighbours, whose only occupation seemed to be fighting. Apart from the impromptu gladiatorial school on the floor below, I liked visiting here. I liked taking off my sandals inside the front door and padding barefoot through the small apartment, and then sharing a modest meal with Atreus on the balcony, and whiling away the hours in his quiet, undemanding presence. We saw each other most days, it was true, since I had somehow landed a position as go-between for the magistrate Septus Severus and Atreus, but here, in his modest home, we weren't patrician and plebeian. We were friends.

In truth, of course, we were more than friends.

Today, I was visiting earlier than usual; it wasn't even lunchtime. Atreus sat beside me on the balcony, his long legs extended, heels resting on the rail. He was close to dozing, a cup of wine in his hand that sooner or later—probably sooner—he was going to end up wearing. I swallowed down my guilt, because I knew Atreus hadn't slept yet. He and his men had been dealing with the corpse in the fountain all of last night, and this morning, he'd collected his niece Lucilla from the woman who watched her overnight when he worked. Still, he hadn't turned me away when I'd turned up on his doorstep like a stray dog, complete with puppy eyes. I'd hoped when I'd sent Juba out with Lucilla to get lunch—Juba was smart enough to know to take a while—that we'd have a reason to go inside and draw the curtain to his bedroom, but half a cup of wine in him and Atreus was no use to gods or men.

"It's not your strange bloodless murder," I said, "but it's *Agrippina*."

Atreus made a noise in the back of his throat. "It's not Agrippina."

"Well pardon me for thinking Maro knows her reputation better than you do, Atreus." I was beginning to regret telling him he could have one of the jars of honey Maro had loaded me up with before I'd left his place.

That earned me a sideways look. "You're right. I don't know her. I don't know a damn thing about her. But I know people. And I know that if you take the time to hire men to attack your enemy, you'd pick a better target than your enemy's nephew. Why would she do that when she could have sent them to kill Seneca, or Burrus, or Anicetus, or even *you*? You have to be higher on her list than Lucan. Besides, from what you've said, even Seneca doesn't think it was her."

"I notice you didn't add yourself to that list of people she hates."

He gave me a wry smile. "Sometimes it's nice to be beneath the notice of the great. It's not Agrippina, Valerius. Not if the men let you pass to get to Lucan."

He was probably right, but it didn't settle my gut at all.

"It's not just me," I said, struggling to find the words to explain. "It's Octavia too. If Agrippina wants revenge on those who helped uncover her treason, then it's Octavia too."

My younger sister, unbeknownst to Atreus and me as we'd been investigating, had known exactly what Agrippina and the ex-tribunes of the Third

Gallica had been up to, and had even gotten herself involved by hiding a witness—her ex-husband's slave. If Agrippina had a list of people she wanted to destroy, I had no doubt that Octavia's name was on it as well as mine.

Atreus set his cup of wine aside. "It's not Agrippina," he said again. "But I'll put a watch on your house, just in case."

"Don't be ridiculous. Who'll stop the Aventine from falling to the gangsters if you have your men camped out on the Caelian Hill?"

"Falling to the gangsters?" I liked his crooked smile.

I waved at the street below us. "It's like the Transtiberina out there, Atreus." It really wasn't, but it made him laugh.

"I don't need you to do anything, Atreus. My house is as secure as the Tullianum these days. I just have to worry aloud, that's all, until I've bled the poison out." I let out a long breath. "I know that you're probably right, that it probably has nothing to do with Agrippina at all, but just don't be so quick to *tell* me, please, because we both know you can't be sure."

Atreus was silent for a moment. He gave me a solemn nod. "I understand, and I'm sorry."

I picked up his cup and took a sip of cheap wine. "I also don't need your apology."

He reached out and threaded his fingers through mine, and squeezed, and said nothing. We both watched the sky and listened to the sounds of the street below, and gradually the tension bled out of me.

"So, what have you found out about this bloodless corpse of yours, or his mysterious missing friend, Marcia Longia's neighbour?"

"Not too much," he said. "The landlord, like I thought, had no idea of who should be living there. I spoke to the man who collects the rent for him—he wasn't happy about being woken in the middle of the night—and he said that last time he went by, a woman paid him. He didn't ask her name. He claims he can't remember the tenant's name, which I'm sure is bullshit, but I have no way to prove it."

"Why would he lie about it? Do you think he's involved?"

"No, I think that a few months ago, some of my men cracked his brother's skull in a street fight, so now he wouldn't cross the street to piss on me even if I was on fire." Atreus snorted. "He also declined to come and have a look at the body to see if he recognised him."

"Someone must be missing him," I said, and Atreus looked at me like I'd said something ridiculous.

"The tenant or the body?"

"Either," I said. "Both."

"There are a lot of people out there who are never missed," he said.

"You're a pessimist when you haven't slept."

"I'm a realist."

Well, maybe. Atreus and I were from very different worlds. I was the only son of a patrician senator. I could trace my family history back to the founding of the great Roman Republic. My ancestors' names were recorded on public monuments. Atreus was a plebeian vigile from the Aventine who didn't even own a toga. When he talked about people who wouldn't be missed, I wondered if he included himself in that number. Although probably not. Atreus wasn't prone to self-pity. That was my specialty, usually when I was drunk.

"I think someone would be missing the dead man," I said. "With a handsome face like his? I'll bet he broke hearts wherever he went."

"Broke hearts and inflamed jealous rages perhaps," Atreus said.

"Maybe."

Atreus hummed. "I left a sign chalked up by the fountain, asking for anyone who knows him to come to the excubitorium. A lot of people saw his face last night; it's odd that nobody knew it. Maybe he wasn't from the neighbourhood. What are the chances his friend the tenant, who clearly hasn't been to the apartment in a long while, will stop by, see the sign, and realise it's his friend it describes?"

"Slightly better than none," I said, "so writing the sign was a good idea." I wrinkled my nose as I thought of the corpse. "How do you even drain all the blood from a corpse?"

"*Why* do you?" Atreus countered, and yes, that was the better question.

"I have no idea," I said.

He shuddered. "Me neither."

We sank into silence as we watched the street and waited for Juba to return with lunch.

Chapter Three

Not everything in life was night-time attacks on famous poets or distracting bloodless corpses dumped in fountains. When I arrived home that afternoon, Fulvia divested me of my rosemary honey and informed me that we were having guests for dinner. And then she rubbed her thumb down my stubbled cheek and raised her eyebrows. She didn't say anything, but she didn't have to. I headed upstairs for a shave.

Since I didn't have time to send for my barber, I leaned back on a stool and trusted Juba not to slit my throat.

"And what do you make of this business with Lucan?" I asked him.

He hummed. "I don't know, sir. He has interesting friends."

"I thought so."

Juba scraped the blade along my jaw. "I wouldn't trust any of them as far as I could throw them."

"Me neither," I said. "Though you could throw them a lot further than I could."

He snorted. "Maybe not Otho."

"Ha!" I closed my eyes as the razor flitted at the edges of my field of vision. "No, that might strain even you."

I dressed for dinner as evening was closing in; the day had been bright but short. The night brought cold with it, creeping across the tiles and seeping into the walls. I wore a toga over my tunic, which Juba helped fold me into, and then went downstairs to sit in my tablinum until our guests arrived. Xanthus slid the doors to the tablinum open as the house grew darker, opening up the tablinum to the atrium on one side and the peristyle on the other. Then he went and lit the lamps in the peristyle while I spun a stylus on my desk, and pretended I was working.

A faint clattering from the kitchens told me things were busy down that end of the house.

Hursa wandered back and forth through the atrium, scratching his scalp and squinting suspiciously in the direction of the front door, as though he was afraid our invited guests might launch a surprise attack instead of knocking. And then, when they did knock, he almost tripped over his own feet in his haste to answer.

I gave him a moment to get the door unbolted, and then rose and went into the atrium. I found Hursa trying to relieve my guests of their sandals so that they might put on indoor shoes instead. Good manners, except he'd somehow managed to take only one off Avitus Florian before turning his attention to Marcellus Naso, leaving poor Florian standing there with one foot off the ground.

"Xanthus!" I called, and the boy hurried out of nowhere, saw the problem instantly, and got to work on Florian's second sandal.

Florian showed me a grateful smile.

Avitus Florian and I were both men with dangerous personal secrets. The only difference was that I knew his. Florian was a Christian, or at least he had been when I'd met him. I hoped for his sake, and for my stepdaughter Julia's, that he'd rethought which gods to worship over the past few months. Strange foreign gods were fine to dabble in when you joined the legions and went off to the edges of the empire for a few years, but once you came home, they ought to have been packed away and forgotten about like the rest of your military gear. And while usually I wouldn't have cared what gods Florian chose to worship, since his reputation was his own to sink however he wanted, he had recently become engaged to marry Julia, and therefore his reputation was linked, however tangentially, to mine.

Still, Florian was a good man. It was why I'd kept his secret hidden and hadn't told anyone, even Fulvia. He was a good man, and there were few enough of them to be found in Rome, and I *liked* him. I especially liked how Julia had transformed from a petulant tantrum-prone girl into a thoughtful young woman since meeting him. Not that I believed Florian was solely responsible for that metamorphosis; none of us had come out of the Albanus business unchanged. Julia had grown up, and it suited her. I suspected I had grown up a little too. I was certainly less hostile than I might have been to the prospect of a family dinner to discuss wedding plans.

Florian was accompanied by his adopted uncle, Marcellus Naso. Naso had hated me once, and the feeling had been very much mutual, but that was water long under the bridge.

"Valerius," he said, and clasped my arm. "It's good to see you again."

"You too, Naso."

Naso was looking better than the last time I'd seen him. Then, he had still been stricken with grief. Tonight, his smile was soft but genuine, and his eyes were bright in his wrinkled face. This was a happy occasion, after all, even though it must have been bittersweet. The last time he'd thought to arrange a marriage for his heir, the girl had been the same one, but the nephew had been different. I would never be crass enough to tell him that Florian was an improvement, but I suspect he knew it.

I embraced Florian once he got his feet under him again, and he patted my back. When I released him, he was smiling broadly.

"Thank you for hosting us, Valerius. It's been too long." His gaze drifted over my shoulder. "Is Julia here yet?"

So much for the pleasantries. But who could fault him for being eager to see his fiancée?

"Not yet," I said. "Go through and have a drink. I'm sure she'll be here soon."

And probably champing at the bit just as much as he was.

There was a time in my life, and not that long ago, when I would have found their young love cloying, but not anymore. Life had enough nasty surprises in store for all of us who ever drew a breath, so why shouldn't they revel in the sweeter parts of it when they were given the chance? Life ought to be enjoyed whenever possible, not just endured. Fuck the Stoics. What did they know?

Julia and her father, Silanus, arrived just as Florian and Naso were being

45

settled in the formal triclinium by my household slaves. Julia looked resplendent in green—it suited her almost as well as it suited her mother— and Silanus, as always, looked like a turd wrapped in a toga.

He grunted at me in greeting, and then pushed past me on his way to the triclinium.

Julia floated after him in a cloud of floral perfume, but not before she stopped and gave me a pretty smile and a kiss on the cheek.

Dinner was excellent. The food was fresh, plentiful, and full of flavour. I spared a brief thought for the cooks of men like Petronius and Otho and the rest of that crowd who were engaged in a constant battle of one-upmanship; their cooks could have put Julius Caesar to shame with their grasp of logistics and battle plans. Damos, my temperamental cook, would probably smash me over the head with a roasting pan if I ever tried to play those sorts of games. I might have been the master of the household, but I knew my place, and it was not underfoot in the kitchen.

I dipped a chunk of bread in oil and chewed while the extended family discussed wedding plans. Naso was mostly concerned with finding an auspicious date, Fulvia was concerned about which of Julia's paternal relatives would be invited to the ceremony, Julia and Florian would have run off and eloped tonight if their soulful gazes could be believed, and Silanus complained unhappily that Julia wanted the ceremony to begin at my house instead of his.

"It is customary for the bride to be wed at her father's house before proceeding to her new husband's," he said. "Not…" He waved a general hand in my direction. "Not *here*."

"But I shall be staying here before the wedding," Julia said.

Silanus scoffed. "Whatever for?"

Julia darted a look at Fulvia.

"Well, we can discuss it at a later time," Fulvia said smoothly.

Silanus was right to be annoyed. As Julia's father, it was him giving her away to her new husband, not Fulvia and I. To deviate from that tradition would be wrong. Worse than that, it would be remarked upon, and men like Silanus hated to be remarked upon. But Julia had grown up in her father's house without any grandmother or aunts to advise her, so it shouldn't have surprised Silanus that she wanted to spend some time with her mother before her marriage, if he'd thought it through. There were things that Fulvia would want to impart to Julia now: women's matters. But Silanus had never thought through anything in his life, and he wasn't likely to start now.

"Julia is welcome to stay here beforehand," I said. "But there's no reason the ceremony shouldn't begin at Silanus's house. We'll pack her off back home on whatever morning Naso's calendar suggests is most fortuitous, and the wedding can take place that evening."

Fulvia reached over and squeezed my hand. "Yes, that will work, I believe." Julia nodded and let out an audible breath.

I thought back to my own wedding night, and how Fulvia had announced that she intended to use wax to prevent conception, leaving me no room to argue, and I suspected Fulvia would be training Julia to deliver the same speech. The announcement had been unnecessary in my case, but the last thing Julia needed from her and Florian's awkward first-time fumblings would be a pregnancy. She deserved a chance to live her life a little before risking it for an infant's.

"Valerius," Naso said, thankfully changing the subject before anyone had to spell it out to Silanus. "I hear you're making friends in high places nowadays."

"Oh, with Petronius and Lucan and all their artist friends?" I snorted ruefully. "I think I've accidentally fallen upwards into their circle. I'm sure they'll get tired of me when they realise I couldn't write a poem if the muses held a knife to my throat."

"But, Quintus," Octavia said, her eyes shining with evil, "you wrote so many poems as a boy!"

"And I'm sure you recall they were all terrible."

She laughed.

Yes, I'd grown up in the last few months. I'd slipped more easily into my unwanted role as paterfamilias. And I was never going to be the same head of the family that my father had been—Octavia never would have made fun of him—but this worked too. In fact, this family right here, the one made up of in-laws and stepchildren and unmarried sisters and soon-to-be-step-son-in-law's-adopted-uncles, was one that fitted me as comfortably as an old slipper.

And then—because my mind was perverse—in the middle of contemplating my familial contentment, I thought of the corpse in the fountain, naked and drained of blood. Despite what Atreus had said, I believed that someone must have been missing him. Whoever his family was, and wherever in the city they were currently sitting down to eat, I bet their dinner conversation wasn't as pleasant as ours. Were they wondering where he was and clinging uselessly to hope, or had they already resigned themselves to the worst?

My heavy thoughts cast a pall on the end of the dinner, and when our guests left, I went and sat on a bench in the peristyle. Fulvia joined me, shivering in the cold. I stood and unwrapped my toga so that we could use it as a blanket.

"Are you well, Quintus?" she asked, leaning against me.

The breeze carried the faint scent of laurel.

"I am," I assured her.

"I thought you might be unhappy with Silanus's presence."

"Oh, I always am," I said, and put an arm around her. "But no, it's not Silanus I'm bothered about tonight. I was content, but then I thought of the body in the fountain, and of a family that must be missing him. It was my own thoughts that dragged me down, I'm afraid."

Fulvia clicked her tongue and caught my hand in hers.

"Sorry."

"Of all the things you might apologise for, it's having a sense of compassion?"

"*All* the things? Do you have a list?"

"I update it daily," she said, squeezing my hand. "And share it with my friends."

Her teasing pulled my dark thoughts from me as though she was draining poison from a wound. "Lies and slander. I should bring a prosecution against you. I am close friends with a magistrate now, didn't you know?"

"Lies?" She hummed. "So it was some other man who ate the last boiled egg at breakfast two days ago? And a stranger who broke in to take a nap in your tablinum last week, and snored so loudly that Marilla Junia and I could hardly hear our conversation? And I have no idea who it was who abducted Aulus and took him to the races when he should have been with his tutor."

Jupiter! She *was* keeping a list!

"Lies," I repeated firmly.

Her body shook against mine as she laughed silently. "As you say, dear."

"Exactly. Because it's the duty of every good wife to agree with her husband at all times."

"A man wrote that, I expect," Fulvia said.

"Very probably," I agreed. "And he ought to have included something about agreeing with your husband also meaning not laughing behind his back."

"I have never laughed at you behind your back, Quintus," Fulvia said. "I much prefer to laugh in your face so that I can see your immediate reaction."

"That's very sensible of you."

She squeezed my hand again. "Yes, I think so."

Just as I had not ended up with the sort of family I had expected, I had not ended up in the sort of marriage I had expected. And I could not have been more thankful for it. Fulvia and I were not the sort of starstruck lovers who, if they were in a play, would spend hours sighing on the stage. Neither were we cold strangers who had to share space. I loved my wife. We were an unlikely match. She was older than me by over a decade, smarter than me by about a million times, and our marriage had been built entirely on convenience; I had needed a wife with a good name, and she had needed to escape her deceased second husband's awful relatives. But together, we worked. I could not imagine any sort of life without Fulvia, and I liked to think I'd grown on her. In a pleasant way, I hoped, and not like a fungus.

Fulvia was smart, beautiful, practical, and she played a mean game of latrunculi.

She could also read my mind.

She straightened up and released my hand at last. "Shall I set up the board?"

See?

She was perfect.

* * *

It was late when Hursa found me in my tablinum. He'd clearly been asleep. He was blinking owlishly at the lamp he carried, and shuffling his bare feet over the tiles as though he didn't have the strength to lift them. His yawns could have swallowed the universe.

Fulvia, having thrashed me soundly at latrunculi, had already gone to bed, and I was finishing my wine before intending to do the same. In the meantime, I was pushing the latrunculi pieces around the board, pretending I was Caesar, dividing and conquering Gaul.

"Sir?" Hursa wrinkled his nose in my direction. "Petronius Arbiter is here, and he says something about you going with him?"

"Specific as always, Hursa," I said. "What do you mean, I'm going somewhere with him?"

The man himself swept into the tablinum. "Valerius. The night is young, and so are you, and I have someone who wishes to meet you. Grab your cloak. We're going to the Milvian Bridge."

I blinked like Hursa. "We're going to the *what?*"

"To the Milvian Bridge," Petronius said, as though that didn't raise a hundred more questions than it answered. "You there, fetch your master's cloak."

Hursa scuttled away.

"And why are we going to the Milvian Bridge?" I asked, more curious than annoyed despite the late hour. There was no use pretending, even to myself, that I'd ever subscribed to that idea about going to bed early so that I could wake at dawn to begin the day's work of correspondence and politicking. The wheels of the empire turned just fine without me putting my shoulder to them, that was for sure, and I'd never turned down a mysterious midnight invitation in my life.

"Surely you know the Milvian Bridge, Valerius?" Petronius asked me as Hursa returned with my cloak, and Juba loomed ominously out of the darkness.

"Of course I know it," I said. I took my cloak from Hursa and headed towards the front door. Juba fell into step behind me and Petronius. "My father used to drag me along to look at it when I was a boy." In response to Petronius's blank look, I said, "My ancestor Aemilius Scaurus tore down the wooden bridge and rebuilt it in stone. My father hoped that seeing the works of my illustrious ancestor might inspire a similar devotion to public service and politics in me."

"And did it?"

"Not in the slightest." A gust of cold wind met me as I stepped outside into the portico, and I tugged my cloak around me. "I just don't remember it as being particularly interesting, so I'm curious as to why we're going there in the middle of the night."

"Because things are always happening on the Milvian Bridge, Valerius," Petronius said with a wink, clapping me on the back and ushering me towards a pair of waiting litters. "Always!"

He wasn't wrong.

Saturnalia wasn't for another few weeks but, when we finally arrived at the Milvian Bridge, it was apparent that nobody had told the people gathered there. It was the middle of the night, but the bridge was crowded. It was a festival atmosphere, complete with dancers and tumblers, and one man with a blue-painted face who was juggling flaming sticks. His audience tossed coins at his feet, and the dancers nearby threw him dirty looks. However light on their feet they were, and however tantalisingly close to entirely naked, who could compete with that?

The bridge had certainly changed since my father had dragged me here as a child, although he'd never brought me here after dark. Perhaps it had always been wild once the sun went down.

Petronius caught me by the elbow and led me through the crowd, and I looked back to check that Juba was following. Not because I felt unsafe, but because later, when I was retelling the craziness of this excursion to the Milvian Bridge to any interested listeners—my womenfolk, Uncle Maro, or Atreus—I wanted someone who could verify it had actually happened. Juba, who always knew what I was thinking, raised his eyebrows in acknowledgement.

A group of youths with drums and cymbals cavorted along the bridge. An actor in a painted tragedy mask performed a speech from a play. The cold night air was alive with the sounds of shouting and laughter, and the river below us reflected the torchlight back.

Petronius drew me across the bridge, like a moth to some bright display. Compared to some of the cheerful tableaux taking place on the bridge, the group of men that Petronius headed for appeared at first to be very drab and unexciting. There were five or six men, wearing tunics and cloaks. Not a single one of them was near-naked or juggling fire. None of them looked particularly friendly either. There were no welcoming smiles waiting for us, and for a moment, I wondered if Petronius even knew these men. Then my gaze dropped to the hobnailed boots that every one of the men wore, and I realised exactly who they were: Praetorians. They weren't in uniform, but there was no disguising those military-issued boots. And if the Praetorian Guard was here, or at least a small group of them, then—

The soldiers stepped aside as we approached, revealing a youth who had been leaning on the side of the bridge.

"Petronius!" he exclaimed, delight evident in his tone. And for some reason it was still there when he greeted me, as well. "And Aemilius Valerius!"

It was Nero, the emperor of Rome. He was a young man of average height. He was a little plump—as anyone would be, with the epicurean delights of an empire at their fingertips at every meal—his nose was a fraction too large for his face, his brow was pronounced, and his hair and his beard were more red than brown. He was a few years younger than I was, barely on the cusp of his twenties, and he carried the weight of an empire on his shoulders. Yet his smile was warm and genuine, and bestowed real handsomeness on his otherwise heavy countenance.

He and Petronius embraced, slapping each other on the back, as hearty as only old friends could be. And then, barely before I could process it, Nero was pulling me in for an embrace as well. I had met him a few times before, and even dined at the palace several months back, but this was a level of familiarity I had not been expecting. I supposed I had passed Petronius's tests after all.

"Valerius!" Nero said and slapped me soundly on the back. "It is good to see you again."

"You too, sir." I was aware that the Praetorians were watching us very closely, and I was fairly sure that if I slapped him back too vigorously, I'd find myself stabbed in the gut and then pitched over the side of the bridge into the Tiber.

Nero snorted. "*Sir?* Are we not friends, Valerius?" He slung an arm around my shoulders and said to Petronius, "The man uncovers a conspiracy against me, provides me all the evidence I need to finally banish my mother dearest, is brought into my inner circle, and still thinks we are not *friends*, Petro!"

Petronius grinned at me, and at the very-probably gormless expression on my face.

Nero laughed in my ear and then released me. "Valerius, you are a better friend to me than half the men I've known since childhood!"

I wasn't sure that was exactly high praise, given the circles Nero moved in. Or rather, the circles that turned around a man born to power as Nero was. It was probably why he liked his artists so much. I was sure they were just as prone to intrigue and treachery as the politicians and courtiers who surrounded the emperor on the Palatine Hill, but what was the worst any of them could do? Write a nasty poem about him?

"You honour me," I said, because even in my surprise at Nero's warm welcome, I hadn't completely forgotten my manners.

"Rufio," Nero said to one of the Praetorians. "Some wine?"

A request, not a demand. It was a small detail to notice, but I thought that it spoke volumes about Nero and the man he was. He was popular with the people for a reason.

The wine that Rufio fetched was nothing special, but Nero looked delighted at his first taste of it. I realised we were drinking exactly the same as everyone else on the bridge was, and that was what pleased the emperor, and that was why he came here. To be normal. Well, as normal as anyone in this crowd of actors and acrobats and fire-jugglers and exhibitionists could be. But then, what was more normal than a twenty-year-old man, newly emancipated from an overbearing parent, throwing his money around on cheap wine and cheaper thrills? Nero hadn't come to the Milvian Bridge to be the emperor; he'd come to have some pointless, drunken fun.

And it turned out I was an expert in pointless, drunken fun.

It seemed as though the whole of Rome stopped by while we drank and talked and laughed. Although Nero hadn't gone out of his way to draw attention to himself, of course word spread fast. An emperor cut from a different shade of purple cloth might have been afraid of the attention he was drawing—the Praetorians, watchful and narrow-eyed, certainly weren't fans of the way people pressed close to him—but Nero received the cheers and good wishes of the public with obvious pleasure. He even bestowed a kiss on the lips of a woman both bold and lucky enough to slip through the wall of the Praetorians, while Rufio growled like an unfriendly dog. I didn't blame him. What if the woman had intended Nero harm? It was Rufio's job to expect attack from all sides, and Nero, with his gregarious nature, was probably responsible for every single one of the grey hairs at his temples. And I had a feeling that the man who'd let the woman slip past him would regret his lapse when the Praetorians got back to their barracks later. Rufio didn't look like a forgiving sort of commander. He gave Lucan and the slave Hermes a careful look as he gestured at his men to stand aside and give them room to join us.

"Lucan!" Nero exclaimed. "Petro promises me that your newest poem is almost done."

Lucan embraced him and rolled his eyes. "Petronius and I have different ideas on that, I think. But it will be ready for your Juvenalia."

Nero looked pleased. "Is it the one you've been working on, about the civil war?"

"It's a *surprise*, Nero," Lucan said. "I'll say no more on pain of death."

"He's the emperor, you know," Petronius drawled. "He could actually arrange that."

Both Lucan and Nero laughed.

Hermes stood at his master's elbow, his gaze darting towards the rest of the activity on the bridge as fast as a flashing minnow moving through shallow water—the dancers, the actors, the fire juggler—but it always returned to his master. He was never more than a step away from Lucan, and always had his stylus and his wax tablet in hand.

The rest of Nero's artist friends, the ones I'd met at Petronius's dinner, all stopped by, of course, and watching them was like watching eager children vying for the attention of a more popular boy, certain that his approval would elevate them too. And yet, it seemed as though Nero was also trying to gain *their* approval. He might have been the emperor, but what was that except a trick of birth? Or, in Nero's case, partly a trick of birth but mostly the result of his mother's machinations? To be an emperor was to be chosen by the gods, but to be a poet was to be beloved by the muses, and the way that Nero talked warmly with his friends and listened intently when they spoke, it was obvious that it was the muses he worshipped.

A burst of drumbeats and the clash of cymbals from somewhere beyond the Praetorians distracted my attention for a moment, and I looked back to our party in time to see stick-thin Litus arriving, flanked by two plumper figures: Otho and Hosidius. I was a little surprised to see Litus and Hosidius turn up together, given that this morning when I'd seen Litus on the Campus Martius he'd basically been plotting to string Hosidius up by his own entrails for stealing his idea about Horatius. But I was fast becoming aware that this lot didn't just save the drama for the stage. Or the cosmetics, either. Otho was wearing enough eyeliner to make Cleopatra jealous, but he certainly wore it well.

Entellus, Cilnius, and Fabianus rounded out the crew, and the cheap wine flowed freely. I elbowed my way through a conversation about Catullus's filthiest poems to get to Lucan.

"I'm not sure I'd be wandering the streets at midnight if someone had tried to attack me," I said to him in as much of an undertone as I could manage and still be heard above the noise.

Lucan leaned back against the wall of the bridge. "You do realise we're surrounded by Praetorians right now?"

"Very true," I said. "But unless they also escorted you from home, it's still a little risky, don't you think?"

The corner of his mouth lifted in wry acknowledgement. "You sound like my uncle. Besides, I came here in my litter, and my litter bearers already proved their loyalty last night by fighting off the men who attacked me." He shrugged. "It was probably a random attack anyway. It's a dangerous city, Valerius."

"It's even more dangerous for the relatives of important men." I tried not to shake my head at the way he'd already talked himself around to the idea of a random attack when this morning, when we'd spoken, we'd agreed he had been targeted. Sometimes, though, that was a handy trick the mind played. It was far easier to breathe after an encounter with an instance of bad luck than to accept the fact that someone wanted to kill you.

Lucan threw me a wry look. "Perhaps, but there's nothing I can do to change that."

"True," I said. "Just watch your back, please. I'd hate to make an enemy of your uncle if you went and got yourself killed when I'm supposed to be helping you."

That won a laugh out of him, like I'd thought it would. "I'll do my best not to inconvenience you by being murdered, Valerius."

I clapped him on the shoulder. "Thank you. That's all I ask."

I glanced at Nero. He was laughing at something Petronius was saying, and his face was bright with good humour and no doubt the effects of the wine.

Below us, in the darkness, the water of the Tiber appeared black. A boatman, his skiff illuminated by a single lantern hanging off the prow of his boat, used a pole to push his way under the bridge. The light from the lantern broke into a thousand pieces on the surface of the water as he passed silently beneath us. I wondered what he made of the raucous activity above him. And while I wasn't envious at all of his lonely night-time work, there was a part of me that suddenly craved silence and darkness. It had been a long day, and an even longer night, and I'd been ready for bed when Petronius had turned up uninvited to drag me along here. I wasn't sorry I'd come, but now my bed was calling me, and I didn't like the idea of facing tomorrow with a hangover. And so I bid the emperor and his poets and playwrights farewell, and, waving off Petronius's offer of a litter, Juba and I began the long trek towards the Caelian Hill, and home.

* * *

The next morning, Atreus and his niece Lucilla turned up for breakfast. I liked Lucilla and she was always welcome in my house, but her presence pointed to a failure of Atreus's childcare arrangements. He paid a neighbour to watch her while he worked overnight, and often so he could sleep during the day, but this morning he informed me with a grimace that the neighbour was unavailable.

"You're welcome to stay for breakfast," I said, and Lucilla climbed up onto my couch beside me and began to pick over my honey cakes. "And Lucilla is always welcome to stay here."

It was an offer I'd made before, but it was one that bruised Atreus's pride. He grimaced and took a seat on the couch across from mine. Months ago, when Atreus had been injured, he and Lucilla had stayed with me for a while. Mouse, my stepson, and Perella, the daughter of Fulvia's maid Thetis, had enjoyed having another child in the house to play with, even though Lucilla was a little too young to join in some of their games. Not that she hadn't tried; it had amused me no end to see her chasing after them on her much-shorter legs, refusing to admit she couldn't keep up. She was as stubborn and obstinate as her uncle.

My point was that there were enough people in my household, between family and slaves, that adding one little girl would hardly make a ripple. Atreus could drop her off here every day, and she could tag along to lessons with Mouse's tutor, or eat snacks in the kitchen all day, or play with Perella, and there would always be someone to keep an eye on her.

Atreus's point was that Lucilla was his responsibility, and not mine. And— it went unsaid, although we both heard it clear as day—he was not for sale.

"It's fine," he said now. "I just wanted to come and see you and update you on the corpse in the fountain."

"Oh, you've found something?" I waved at Calliope to fetch some breakfast for our guests, before Lucilla ate all of mine.

Atreus grimaced again. "No, sorry. There's no news. But I wanted to let you know that, in case you were wondering."

If I hadn't known him better, I might have teased him about finding any excuse to come and eat my cook's honey cakes. But since he'd only bristle if I did, and then refuse every invitation to dine with me for the rest of his life just to make a point, I didn't.

"Well, I have news for you," I said, and filled him in on my visit to the Milvian Bridge last night.

"And the emperor called you his friend?" He raised his eyebrows. "That's good for your career. Congratulations."

I preened a little. "Yes, I imagine that I'll have no problems being elected as a quaestor once I'm twenty-five now. It's just a matter of not ruining it before then."

"Why would you ruin it?"

"That's my doubt talking," I said. "But, and I don't know if you're aware of this, Atreus, I do have a habit of getting drunk and telling dirty jokes about well-respected senators."

Atreus huffed out a laugh. He was very much aware. "You'll just have to spend the next year and a bit sober then."

"Jupiter, don't wish that on me!"

This time, his laugh was warmer, and Lucilla smiled at him brightly.

Calliope returned with puls and more honey cakes, which gave me the chance to relish the pleased expression on Atreus's face as he dug into a hot breakfast. I sometimes wished he'd allow me to give him more than the occasional meal, but we were still feeling out the unspoken rules of our friendship, and Atreus could get prickly if he thought I was stepping on his pride. I admired him and was frustrated by him in equal measure.

"Junius Atreus!" a delighted voice exclaimed from the doorway, and Octavia strode into the room. "And Lucilla! What a lovely surprise. Are you here to tell us you've solved the murder of the poor unfortunate fellow in the fountain, or to listen to Quintus tell you all about his new best friend Nero?"

Atreus threw her a wry smile. "Not the first, unfortunately. And Valerius

58

has hardly mentioned the emperor at all."

"He has mentioned him then," Octavia said with an evil gleam in her eye. She sat down on one of the women's chairs beside the couches.

"Excuse you," I said. "I have to find out who is trying to attack Lucan. If that happens to elevate me to the social sphere of Nero, then who am I to refuse his overture of friendship?"

"Who, indeed?" Octavia snorted. "But I am pleased for you, Quintus. By some happy accident, you may actually end up with a career yet."

"Aristotle said that everything that happens does so for a reason and out of necessity," I told her smugly.

She raised her eyebrows. "In all fairness to Aristotle, he never met *you*."

"This is what happens," I said to Atreus. "I try to eat breakfast in peace, and yet I am mercilessly attacked, and for what?"

"For a reason and out of necessity, I imagine, sir," he said gravely, and Octavia let out a burst of delighted laughter.

"I am attacked from both directions now," I told Lucilla, who hummed and nodded as she shoved another honey cake in her mouth.

After Lucilla had dug her spoon around in her puls for a while and entirely polished off her honey cakes, Octavia took her on a walk to find Fulvia and say hello. Atreus took the chance to move to the chair Octavia had vacated. He was close enough to touch, had Calliope not still been flitting in and out of the triclinium.

"So, nothing on your fountain corpse at all?" I asked. Since he was sitting, I did the same, swinging my legs over the side of the couch and paddling my feet on the tiles.

He let out a breath. "No, although I didn't have time to look into it last night. We had a busy night."

"Any fires?" I asked.

"Nothing major," Atreus said. "Although Vibilus got into a fight with some fool who left a torch burning in his shop with nobody to watch it. He said it was to deter thieves and didn't take kindly to Vibilus's suggestion that of course it would, since there would be nothing worth stealing if the place was ashes and rubble come morning."

The vigiles were a plain-spoken bunch, Vibilus more than most.

"And how did that work out for the shop owner?" I asked curiously.

Atreus shrugged. "Well, he'd stopped bleeding by the time he came around, so there's that."

It was hard to feel too much sympathy for anyone who flouted the city's laws on unattended flames, when so much of Rome was so close-packed that it took no time at all for fire to take hold and destroy entire neighbourhoods. It wasn't just his own livelihood, or life, that the shop owner had put at risk.

Atreus let out a long breath and stretched his legs out. "I'd expected someone to come forward by now about the body in the fountain, though. The whole neighbourhood knows about him. Why can nobody identify him? Even if he only visited his friend in the insula that overlooks the fountain, why can nobody give me the friend's name? It doesn't feel right."

"Marcia Longia said the tenant was shifty," I said. "He probably wasn't on friendly terms with anyone in the building."

"I just hope someone comes forward soon," Atreus said. "He'll really start to stink in a day or two. At least it's not summer."

"What will you do if nobody claims him?"

"We have an arrangement," Atreus said. "We pay into a funeral fund with a libitinarius, and in return, he collects any corpses from us that have gone unclaimed."

Undertakers, like actors and prostitutes, were excluded from the legal protections afforded by citizenship. Unlike actors and prostitutes, though, they didn't even have the consolation of being popular at parties, and most people would cross the street to avoid them. Libitinarii were ill omens, surrounded as they were by death. But I supposed the vigiles, who were no strangers to death themselves, might consider an association with an undertaker a necessary evil.

"Yours is a dangerous job," I said. "A funeral fund makes sense. The legionaries ran them when I was in the military."

Atreus dipped his chin in a nod, his gaze wary.

I wanted to ask him if he'd made any provision for Lucilla should anything happen to him, but I'd poked at his pride enough already this morning. I hoped he knew me well enough to know that when I said she was always welcome in this house, it extended beyond breakfasts. Atreus didn't have any other family, and no close friends that he had mentioned either. His job was a lonely one; he mainly worked nights, and the men he worked with were his subordinates, not his friends. Leander may have been an exception to that; the physician still technically came under Atreus's command, but his duties were separate enough that I couldn't imagine Atreus ever pulling rank on him. They seemed friendly, but I didn't know if they were close outside of work. The things I didn't know about Atreus could fill the Library of Alexandria, but the things I did know about him made up for it. He was smart. He was a fine leader to his men and earned their fierce loyalty in return. He was serious most of the time, which made his occasional laconic quips even more hilarious. He was a good uncle to Lucilla and put her needs before his own. All the rest—his past, his ambitions, whatever secrets he kept to himself—I had yet to learn. I hoped that we would know each other for long enough that one day I would know them. Until that day, it was enough that he was a good man, and that he guarded my secrets as closely as he guarded his own.

I didn't push him.

"Well," I said instead, "let's hope that someone claims the corpse before it stinks badly enough it drives even the rats out of the excubitorium. Is your sign still chalked up by the Medusa Fountain?"

He nodded.

"What about informers?" I asked, thinking of the chalk signs I'd seen belonging to the informer Kaeso whenever I went to visit my barber in Fish Alley. "Would it be worth paying them to see what they can shake loose?"

Atreus raised his eyebrows. "You mean pay them to ask the questions I could ask myself for free?"

"I mean pay them because they might get different answers," I said. "Didn't you tell me that the rent collector refused to give you anything at all because he hates the vigiles? Maybe there are some other people in the neighbourhood who feel the same way but wouldn't mind opening their mouths for a sestertius or two."

I could tell by his sigh that he hated the idea, but not enough to dismiss it out of hand. "Possibly."

"Well, something to consider, at least." I stretched. "Meanwhile, I still need to figure out who attacked Lucan, and it may be more urgent that your corpse in the fountain."

Atreus cocked a brow.

"I'm not saying Lucan is more important," I said. "Although unless the corpse in the fountain also proves to be a nephew of Seneca's, he certainly is. I said *urgent*, because the corpse isn't getting any deader, is it? Whereas Lucan may still be in danger."

Atreus conceded the point with a nod. "What's your strategy?"

I groaned. "I don't think I have one. At least with that entire Albanus mess, we had a dead body in a house, and a list of guests. But Lucan was attacked on the street. We can't even be certain that he was the target, except Seneca believes it to be true. Now, I'm not as clever as Seneca, so I take him at his word. But what if Seneca isn't as clever as he thinks he is?"

"That's what you're pinning your hopes on?" Atreus asked. "That Seneca has got it wrong?"

I let out a weary sigh. "No, he's not wrong, is he? If those attackers had just been waiting for any rich man to cross their path, they would have chosen me. Jupiter, they could have headed to the Milvian Bridge and had their pick of drunk patricians, since apparently that's where everyone is hanging out these days. So Lucan was definitely the target, but *why*? Why not Seneca?"

Atreus shrugged. "You said it yourself. Perhaps it's not about Seneca at all. Perhaps Lucan has made his own enemies."

A tingle of awareness, too unformed to be called anything close to certainty, prickled my skin. It made as much sense as Seneca's theory. Seneca assumed that Lucan had been attacked because he was his nephew, but Seneca could only look at this matter through his eyes, and they were eyes that had been clouded by a decades-long political career. If Seneca saw enemies in every shadow, he knew they were there because he'd made them. But it didn't mean they were the only possibility. Lucan had an entire circle of friends and companions that Seneca had no special insight into. And while Lucan might have scoffed at the idea, their petty jealousies might lead as far as an attack on another. Litus hadn't scoffed, and I'd seen it last night at the bridge, the way they moved so intricately around each other as though the sands were shifting under their feet at all times. Lucan was a young man with powerful friends—and it was a rare thing to make powerful friends without making at least a few powerful enemies along the way.

I pushed my empty plate away from me. "Atreus, how do you feel about leaving Lucilla here while we pay a visit to Lucan?"

His smile was the only answer I needed.

Chapter Four

L ucan lived on the southern side of the Esquiline Hill, just above the shallow valley that separated the Esquiline from the Caelian Hill. We were almost neighbours. When we arrived at his house, the door porter admitted us without question and showed us into the atrium. The atrium was light and airy, with lit braziers softening the sharp edge of the winter's chill. Most of the doors off the atrium were pulled closed, presumably to preserve the warmth of the rooms behind them. The door porter knocked on one of the doors and then rolled it open, and light and laughter spilled out from the tablinum behind it. The door porter beckoned us through.

Lucan's tablinum was bigger than mine, though it was just as messy and lived-in. If his household was anything like mine, then this was his sanctuary, the one room he could hide in safely, pretending to be occupied by important work as the head of the household, while secretly taking naps. There was even a comfortable-looking reading couch with well-dented cushions against one wall. The couch was unoccupied now though, because Lucan was seated at the table, and Petronius was seated on the other side of it, and Hermes the slave was perched on the end with a wax tablet balanced on his knee. Hermes slid off the table when Atreus and I entered and flashed me a quick smile before ducking his head respectfully.

"Valerius," Lucan said. "Good morning. What brings you here?"

Petronius leaned back in his chair, the wicker creaking, and stretched his arms up towards the ceiling. He gave a satisfied groan, and I wondered how long the pair of them had been in here. The table was covered in tablets and scrolls. Pens and styluses fought for space between them. "Is it breakfast? I was promised breakfast, but none has appeared yet."

Lucan gave him an exasperated look. "Hermes, go to the kitchen and see what you can rummage up for our guests, especially Petro, who won't stop complaining until he's stuffed full."

Before he did, Hermes grabbed a couple of stools from the far wall and brought them over for Atreus and me.

"We've had breakfast," I said, "but I always save room for a snack." I sat and gestured for Atreus to do the same. "This is Junius Atreus. He's an acting centurion with the vigiles. Atreus, this is Lucan and Petronius."

Lucan's expression lit up. "We've met, I believe. At a dinner party at Valerius's house. It would be several months ago now, just after all that business with the murders."

"Yes, sir," Atreus said.

"Atreus assisted me with that whole matter," I said, wondering exactly how much Lucan knew. The results of that investigation had remained under wraps, but to a man with a close relationship with Seneca? There was probably no such thing as a mystery to him when it came to palace politics and intrigue. Also, he was close friends with Nero, and Nero had proved last night at the Milvian Bridge that he wasn't shy about mentioning either the legionary conspiracy or the connection to his mother when it came to the murders. "And so I thought he might also be helpful to me now."

Assisted was, of course, a euphemism for 'he solved the whole thing, really, while I just bumbled around in his general vicinity.' To be fair, it had been my first investigation. I hoped that I was improving, but the omens were not favourable so far.

Petronius leaned forward again, his expression sharpening. "So you think it's one of us, then?"

"What?"

Petronius waved a hand. "You think it's one of us, of course. You're here to dig around in Lucan's life because you don't believe it was a random attack. And if it's not random, then it must be because Lucan is one of Nero's favourites, yes?"

I exchanged a look with Atreus. "Possibly."

Petronius grinned. "No need to be coy, Valerius. You're probably right, given that Lucan is as squeaky clean as a Vestal Virgin. He barely drinks and gambles, can you imagine?"

Lucan gave a long-suffering sigh, and I imagined this was a contentious subject.

"So?" Petronius leaned back again and crossed his arms behind his head, the picture of relaxation. "Which one of those jealous little serpents do you think it is? Fabianus? The man's never held an original thought in his head. Cilnius? No, he's spineless. Hosidius? Litus? Otho?"

"Perhaps it's *you*, sir," Atreus suggested.

"Me?" Petronius looked delighted at the idea Atreus thought he was a suspect. "No, it couldn't be me."

"Why not?" I asked.

"Well, because out of all of us, I'm the only one who has no need to be jealous of Lucan," Petronius said. His grin widened. "Because I'm a better writer than he is."

Lucan rolled his eyes and snorted.

"See?" Petronius's eyes shone with delight. "He makes no attempt to deny it."

I hadn't known Petronius long, but I had the impression that arguing with him would be a lot like banging your head repeatedly against a marble plinth.

At that moment, Hermes returned with a tray of dishes. Olives, bread, eggs, cheese, and nuts. He crossed to the desk and made an unhappy humming sound. Before he had to readjust the tray or find some other place to put it down, both Lucan and Petronius shoved the scrolls and tablets and pens and styluses out of the way. Hermes set the tray down with a grateful smile.

"This isn't breakfast," Petronius complained, but helped himself to an egg.

"It's what you get when you were never invited in the first place," Lucan said, and took an olive.

I took an olive, too. "So you're working now? On your pieces for the Juvenalia?"

It was amusing to think that on one side of the same table, Lucan was recounting the glorious rise of Caesar and the birth of the empire out of the ashes of the republic, while Petronius was writing his hilarious stories about a lewd slave boy and his filthy-minded master getting into all sorts of sticky situations. Two very different sides of the same literary coin, or something.

"Some of us are working more than others," Lucan said wryly, and then he frowned. "You really think it might be one of my friends who arranged the attack on me?"

"It's possible," I said.

"It's something we need to look into," Atreus added.

I took another olive and stood up. I wandered over to the shelves that took up a full wall of the tablinum. Each little square shelf was stuffed full of scrolls of all different shapes and sizes, some with tags hanging out, and some with none. There must have been hundreds of them, possibly more. My fingers itched to touch, but since my fingers were also currently oily from the olives, I kept them to myself.

"You have an impressive collection."

Lucan hummed. "Tools of the trade, really. To write poetry and history, you must read as much as you can."

"Tell me about your friends, please, sir," Atreus said, taking out his wax tablet and stylus. "The others who are also producing works for the emperor's Juvenalia."

"Well," Lucan said. "Petro, of course."

"Petro is above suspicion," Petronius said, and winked at Hermes, who stifled a giggle behind his hands.

Lucan smiled fondly at the boy. "You must make your own mind up there, Atreus. And Litus, of course, who is probably my closest friend apart from Petro."

"Litus is writing a play about Horatius at the bridge," I told Atreus. "At least he was, until he found out that Fabianus is *also* writing a play about Horatius at the bridge."

"He was very angry about that," Lucan agreed.

"But you're not writing the same thing as him?" Atreus asked.

"No," Lucan said. "I'm writing about the civil war."

Atreus nodded, making notes on his tablet.

"And then there's Entellus," Lucan continued. "He won't tell anyone what he's writing about."

"Probably because he knows it'll be shit," Petronius said.

Lucan ignored that. "And Cilnius—"

"C-C-Cilnius," Petronius said, imitating the man's stammer. "Talented enough, but obviously can never perform his own recitals. And Hosidius, who is also talented, but folds like a wet piece of straw as soon as he is the centre of attention. Frankly, Cilnius and Hosidius could murder every other poet and playwright in the city and still fail to get noticed at all, because neither of them has any confidence."

Lucan hummed in agreement. "Oh, and Otho, of course, but he's not a writer."

"Why is he in your group, then?" Atreus asked keenly.

"Because he *likes* writers, and he is obscenely wealthy," Petronius answered for Lucan. "He enjoys the arts, no question, but what he really loves is being flattered by artists for throwing his money at us, and being in the same circle as Nero. To put it frankly, Lucan has wealthy relatives, and I'm successful enough that I've made my own wealth, but to everyone else in the group Otho is a shiny fat purse just begging to be opened."

Lucan gave him what might have been a censorious look.

"It's true, Lucan," Petronius said. "Listen, we talk a lot about art and truth and beauty, and I think that most of the time we even believe our own bullshit, but pretty words don't pay the rent and keep the wolf from the door. Art is a luxury that some of our fellow writers can barely afford, and the patronage of an Otho or a Nero is certainly worth attacking for."

"Not just patronage," I said. "But influence, too."

Petronius smiled. "Well, yes. That's very true. Lucan and I don't need Nero's money, but to be able to steer his influence? A little push and prod here and there? I don't suppose there is anyone in the empire who wouldn't want that."

It was no surprise it was Petronius who immediately saw what I was getting at. While Lucan was writing high-minded poems about events ordained by the gods, Petronius's characters were rolling around in the gutter with the rest of us mortals. They knew exactly how the world worked, and so did their creator.

"And certainly, Otho's wealth doesn't mean he's not also as jealous and ambitious as anyone else in the group," Petronius continued. "He's only a little fish, too, when compared to Nero. Oh, don't give me that look, Lucan. Just because you're as clean as a freshly laundered toga doesn't mean you haven't noticed the stench rising off the rest of us."

Lucan took the comment with a faint, rueful smile, while Hermes looked quietly outraged on his master's behalf.

"You'll want to talk to the rest of them, I imagine," Petronius said.

I took my seat again and reached for a couple of nuts. "Yes. Very much so."

"Otho's having a dinner party tonight," Petronius said. "You should come." And then, because he was a clever man who knew exactly how things worked, he added, "And you too, of course, Atreus."

✳ ✳ ✳

Atreus and I headed to the excubitorium of the first century of the Fifth Cohort of Vigiles for lunch. It was quiet at this time of day, or as quiet as the excubitorium ever got. Most of the vigiles were sleeping in their barracks. A few were training. One fellow was manning the front desk, but the work of the morning—releasing the drunks brought in overnight, returning the unhappy runaway slaves to their masters, or sending the thieves to be whipped—had already finished by lunchtime, so he was really just staring at the wall. It was Manius, the littlest vigile, and he brightened when he saw us and gave Atreus what might have passed as a salute in non-military circles. I got a smile and a wave.

Atreus and I had bought stuffed vine leaves from a nearby thermopolium, and we ate them upstairs in his office. Well, the office technically still belonged to Atticus, the actual centurion in charge, but he was still on extended sick leave. I'd never even met the man. Atreus and I planted our arses on his desk, and I tried not to drip oil from my vine leaf as I ate.

"What do you think?" I asked him around a mouthful.

"About all your poets and playwrights?"

I hummed.

"I think it's worth following up," he said, his expression thoughtful and serious. "And I hope we'll have a clearer picture tonight after Otho's dinner party."

"You mean you don't trust me to relay my impressions of them, and want to meet them for yourself?" I asked, only half joking.

"No." He was still serious. "The first time you met them, you weren't thinking of them as potential suspects. Why would you? Nothing had happened yet."

"You would have, though."

"Well, as you like to remind me, I'm a suspicious-minded plebeian with a chip on his shoulder." His mouth twitched.

"A chip the size of the Tarpeian Rock."

"Shut up and eat your lunch," he said, knocking his shoulder against mine. "*Sir.*"

I knew an order when I heard one.

Smiling, I shut up and ate my lunch.

* * *

The night was dark and cold and moonless when I climbed out of my litter on the Esquiline at the house of Marcus Salvius Otho, with Atreus at my side. A little knot of waiting slaves disentangled themselves, and a pair of them hurried to us at a trot, as though they were afraid we might get lost on the way to the portico without their torchlight to help us.

I'd met Otho two nights ago at Petronius's house, and I didn't flatter myself that I'd made enough of an impression for him to extend the warm hand of friendship. No, I was here because Petronius, Nero's confidant, had decided that I should be. And whatever Petronius decided was what happened in this little group of poets, playwrights, and the man Petronius had described as a purse.

I watched with a smirk as Atreus adjusted the unfamiliar fall of his borrowed toga. Atreus wasn't a man who had much use for a toga. His idea of a dinner party was lying on his couch with a dish of olives, with his balcony door open so he could listen to the neighbours caterwauling. To be fair to him, that sounded like a more pleasant night than the one we were about to have, which would doubtless involve hours of listening to poets and playwrights try to murder each other with words. Or possibly more than words if Litus attempted to throttle Fabianus for stealing his ideas.

I pasted on a pleasant smile as a slave led us through the atrium and into Otho's formal triclinium.

The house was large. The doors to rooms leading onto the atrium were all opened, as was the custom in the evenings, and I caught glimpses of expensive, exquisite furniture as the slave led me past. The formal triclinium was no less elegant; the walls were covered in intricate frescoes that depicted the founding of Rome, and the ceiling was painted the same blue as a summer's sky, complete with soft tendrils of clouds that drifted on an invisible breeze.

We were not the first guests to arrive; the couches in the triclinium were already occupied, and slaves flitted around with wine and dishes of olives and nuts to make sure that no guest ever had an empty mouth while they waited for the main meal.

Otho rose and greeted us as we entered the room. He was around my age, possibly a few years older, and wearing a rose-coloured tunic under his toga. He was plump and cleanly shaven, his eyebrows shaped as carefully as a woman's, and he smelled of lavender. His hands, when he clasped mine, were soft. "Valerius," he said with what seemed like a genuine smile, "thank you for coming."

"Thank you for inviting me," I said. "This is Junius Atreus, centurion of the Fifth Cohort of Vigiles."

Otho's gaze shifted from me to Atreus, widening slightly before he remembered his manners and clasped Atreus's hands too. Not as warmly or for as long as he clasped mine, of course. "Atreus, how nice to meet you."

"And you, sir," Atreus said, and, if I didn't know him better, I would have thought he sounded perfectly pleasant. But I did know him better, and I knew that he already resented Otho for looking down on him for being a plebeian who actually worked for a living. It was Atreus's default position when meeting arrogant patricians, and I couldn't really blame him for it. He was one of the best men I knew—smart, diligent, hardworking, and good—but none of those were categories that counted in opulent dining rooms like this, and with overweening men like Otho.

"Did you say a *vigile?*" a woman asked. "How unusual!"

Otho's eyes shone. "Ah! Come and meet my wife."

The woman herself was reclining on the main couch her husband had just vacated, and I felt a jolt of surprise which was quickly followed by a jolt of self-recrimination. I'd spent most of my life hating dull old patricians and their stupid, outdated traditions, and yet here I was being shocked that a woman was apparently reclining with the men for dinner. She was beside her husband; it was hardly an orgy.

Otho beamed proudly as he introduced us. "My darling wife, Poppaea Sabina."

Poppaea was a beautiful woman, with a spark of cleverness in her eyes that I immediately warmed to, probably because it made me feel at home. Her hair was reddish blonde, worn in a band of tightly woven curls layered against a gold diadem at the front, and in a bun at the back. She had paired her rich blue tunic with a yellow stola that was intricately embroidered with flowers. She was a vision; I wouldn't be surprised if at least half the men here were already composing poems about her in their heads.

"Aemilius Valerius," she said, extending a hand. Her eyes shone. "Petronius promises you're a delight."

"All poets are liars," I said, and I liked to think that at least half the room laughed.

Poppaea was one of them. "Thank you for coming."

Tonight we were sharing a couch with Lucan, and we renewed our acquaintance with glasses of sweet mulsum wine. Petronius was at the main couch with the married couple, and he raised his glass in my direction, flashing me a smile that I returned. The rest of the guests were the same as

I'd met two nights ago at Petronius's house, spread out over the remaining couches. Litus, tall and thin and acerbic. Cilnius, the stammering poet. Entellus, the brash rich boy. Hosidius, the shy playwright Entellus laughed that nobody had heard of. And Fabianus, of course, with his light-coloured eyes and his oily curls, who had stolen Litus's idea of a poem about Horatius at the bridge.

Dinner was everything I'd expect from a man with a fortune in frescoes on his walls: expensive. We had shellfish, pheasant, and peacock, amongst many other dishes, and all of them were served with the finest wines. A flute player wandered the room as we ate, proving a musical accompaniment to the diners' conversations. He might have blended into the background except his sheer chiton left nothing at all to the imagination. I wondered if Petronius was taking notes for his next instalment of the adventures of Encolpius and Giton. And speaking of taking notes, Hermes, Lucan's slave, sat on the floor in front of our couch, stylus poised above his wax tablet in order to catch any impromptu poems that might fall from his master's lips. He tapped his toes along to the flute player's lilting tune.

I half expected Atreus to whip out his wax tablet too, and start jotting down his observations of our dining companions. But while he observed the scene as closely as Hermes did, he must have decided to leave the notetaking for later.

Talk turned inevitably to Nero's Juvenalia, and what each of the poets and playwrights in the room was writing for the emperor.

"Of course, I have no idea what I shall write," Litus said, shooting Fabianus a murderous look, "since I hear that someone else has decided to use Horatius at the bridge."

Fabianus, who had an expression as bland as flour, opened his mouth and poked a spear of asparagus inside. He didn't even blink.

"What about you, Petronius?" Lucan called across the space between our couch and his. "How is your play coming along?"

"The play is perfect," Petronius said, and rolled his eyes. "But don't get me started on the fucking *actors*. Well, you'd know all about that, eh, Entellus?"

Entellus lifted his lip in a lazy sneer and then turned his attention back to his wine.

Petronius waited until the laughter subsided. He transferred his sharp gaze to our host. "Still, I'm more interested in what Otho here has planned, since he couldn't pull a poem out of his arse with the aid of a team of donkeys and a rope."

More laughter, the loudest of it from Otho himself, and I saw Hermes smile as he scratched a few words onto his wax tablet.

"It's true," Otho said, face bright with glee. He exchanged a look with Poppaea. "How can men like myself hope to compare with those of you who are attendant to the Muses? I'm afraid that all Poppaea and I can offer the emperor on the occasion of his Juvenalia is a mere slave."

But his tone belied his words. Whatever slave Otho had lined up as a gift to Nero, he and Poppaea were clearly pleased about it. My interest was piqued.

"Nero has hundreds of slaves," Petronius said, his eyebrows raised expectantly.

"None like this one," Otho replied, laughter bubbling out of him again.

He was like a fisherman baiting a hook, and a glance around the triclinium showed that he'd caught every single man in the room.

"A-a slave is m-mortal," Cilnius said. "P-poetry l-lives forever."

Poppaea rested her chin in her hands. "Poetry is a shadow on a cave wall, Cilnius. I can recite Catullus's words all I want, but I shall never be able to embrace and kiss his beloved Lesbia. My blood will never heat at her touch."

I looked at Petronius, the most famous of all the artists in the group, and the smile he wore was delighted. He liked to see this little wasp's nest stirred sometimes.

"Cilnius is right," Entellus said. "Art *preserves* life. Art bestows immortality!"

"A pale shadow," Poppaea said, lifting her glass in his direction. "Life is to be lived, my dear Entellus, not just related."

"I am reminded of something Valerius said the other day," Petronius said. "He said that war isn't much like the way the poets tell it at all."

"Art preserves *beauty*, then," Hosidius said, but his tone was so hesitant he made it sound like a question instead of a declaration.

Entellus let out a bark of what sounded like startled laughter, and Cilnius fumbled with his cup and spilled wine on the tiles. A slave darted forward to clean it up.

"To what end?" Petronius asked. "You can't fuck a poem. You might be able to grope the tits of a statue of Venus, but it's not as good as the real thing, is it?"

Hosidius didn't have an answer. He made a noncommittal humming sound, and then shrank back into his couch anxiously like a turtle retreating into its shell.

"The problem with answering your question, Petronius," I said, drawing attention away from poor Hosidius, "is that the man who does will have to admit to molesting a statue."

"Oh, so you have no opinion on it, Valerius?" he asked, his eyes sparkling.

"I could not possibly take a more neutral position on the matter," I said, and laughter filled the room again. Hosidius send me a grateful look.

"If we find ourselves in harmony on anything," Petronius said, "it's that Otho and Poppaea must show us this slave who they think is a better work of art than art itself."

The triclinium echoed with loud agreement.

"After dessert!" Otho said and clapped his hands. A small army of slaves paraded into the room, with dessert fit for a bunch of hedonists. Sweet apples, cheesecake, gloti, fig cakes, and tiropatinae set into moulds shaped like seashells and garnished with glistening pearls of pomegranate. After the first three courses it was a lot, and both Entellus and Fabianus had to leave the room to throw up and make room for more, and Litus was looking more queasy than appreciative as he dug into his cheesecake.

The flute player was joined by a girl with a beautiful singing voice and a boy with cymbals, and we ended dinner in high spirits, buoyed by both the excellent food and the music.

"Idaeus," Otho said, gesturing, and the boy with the cymbals darted forward. "Go and fetch Iris."

The boy nodded, his eyes wide and his dark curls bouncing. "Yes, master."

"Well, this should be interesting," Litus murmured from the couch beside ours, sounding like he didn't believe it for a moment.

"It's a slave," Lucan replied in an undertone. "Even if it's the most beautiful creature in the world, how can that compare with..." He trailed off as the cymbal player returned with a girl at his side.

My breath caught, and my heart tried to climb into my throat.

Jupiter best and greatest.

The girl was dark-haired and wearing a plain blue tunic that fell to her bare feet. Her gaze darted nervously around the triclinium as she came to stand in front of her master's couch, and he waved his hand in a lazy circle to have her turn. No, the slave girl wasn't the most beautiful creature in the world, but apart from the fact she was twenty-odd years younger, she could have been the identical twin of Nero's mother Agrippina.

Even the flute player fell silent.

"Well, fuck me," Petronius said mildly, blinking. "Sons of Dis, Otho. That will certainly get his attention."

The cheesecake turned over in my gut, so I climbed off the couch and headed next door. A slave boy waited there with an empty basin and a jug of wine, and I waved him away. I paced the tiles for a moment, following the Greek key pattern around the edges of the room. I could still hear the boy playing the flute in the triclinium, and the sounds of conversation picking up again. The boy with the basin watched me curiously.

I sorted through my thoughts, searching for the reason for my visceral reaction to the girl.

My fear and hatred of Agrippina? No, not just that. It was the knowledge that nothing good could come from giving a Nero a slave that looked like the mirror image of his mother. It seemed cruel, not just to the girl, but to Nero as well. And I didn't know the emperor like this crowd did, but something about it felt dangerous. Reckless. And Otho and Poppaea seemed like they were too smart not to know it. The petty rivalries amongst this group of friends as they all tried to win the emperor's favour with their poems and their plays had seemed amusing up until now, even though they might have been connected to the attack on Lucan. Now I felt as though I was out of my depth, and it had happened as suddenly as though I'd been paddling along happily with my new artist friends before I'd stepped off the edge of an underwater cliff.

I didn't like this. I could barely articulate why, except that it felt dangerous. It felt like giving the most powerful man in the world the reflection of the woman he both loved and hated in equal measure, and waiting with bated breath to see if he would break the mirror or not.

I paced some more, and the boy with the basin watched silently.

"Your master," I said to him, because I suddenly needed to know the answer. "Is he a good man?"

I thought of Otho's laugh, and his expensive feast, and his soft hands.

"Yes, sir," the boy said, but hesitated just a moment before he answered.

Whether that was because he was wary of his master's odd guest, or because it was a lie, I had no way of knowing. And it wasn't as though it would have made any difference either way, because if I was to be a friend of Nero's—and he had made it clear that I already was—then I would also have to be friends with every man in Otho's formal triclinium.

And I didn't like the way that made me feel suddenly very uneasy.

Atreus came into the room, wearing a typically sombre expression that the boy must have mistaken for indigestion. The boy darted forward with the basin, and Atreus waved him away.

"Are you alright?" he asked me.

"I don't know," I said. My unease was mirrored in his green-flecked eyes. "What we just saw was..."

"Cruel," he said in a low voice, and I felt a rush of gratitude that he understood and agreed without my having to try to draw the tangled words out.

"I suppose I needn't ask your opinion of our host, then," I murmured so the slave boy couldn't hear.

Atreus's eyes crinkled slightly, but his smile was a grim one. "No," he said. "No, you really don't."

* * *

Atreus and I were in a sombre mood when we arrived back at my house at around midnight. I was ready for bed, but Atreus wanted to check in on his vigiles before heading home. As someone who had once been in charge of men, I understood the need. The moment they thought you weren't paying attention was the moment they started to slack off. Or, in the case of the men I'd been in charge with, the moment they started to plan your murder. The Tenth Legion, when I'd been in it, had been a shadow of its previous glorious self, but the general Corbulo had knocked it back into line. Eventually. It was all well and good to *say* you were in charge, but legionaries could count as well as anyone. Well, as well as regular toddlers and exceptionally smart dogs. They could count as well as they needed to, was my point. They knew they outnumbered us officers. There had been a lot of dicey moments getting the legion back into shape, that was for sure.

Atreus's vigiles were unlikely to be plotting his murder, but he still wanted to make sure nobody was sneaking in naps when he should have been out on patrol. I did get him to agree to stay for a drink, though, and we sat on the reading couch in my dark tablinum and went through what we thought of Otho and his guests.

"The problem is that they're a nest of vipers," I said. "I just can't tell which of them have actual poison in their fangs."

"Petronius does like taking a stick and stirring them up, doesn't he?" Atreus asked and sipped his wine.

"I think it's a sport of his." I dragged a hand through my hair. "So they're all jealous and petty, and possibly malicious too. Which would be laughable, because nobody in their right mind gives a shit about poems and plays—"

"Except Nero," Atreus said.

"Except Nero," I agreed, "which raises the stakes, and explains why one of them has possibly tried to attack Lucan already. Or *worse*. Jupiter, we don't even know if the men were hired to beat him and rob him, or to murder him."

"And will they try again, since they failed the first time?" Atreus asked.

I let out a long breath and gazed into the darkness.

Beside me on the couch, Atreus's body was a long line of warmth. I would have moved even closer if I could have, but just because the house was dark didn't mean we wouldn't be seen. Hursa slept close to the front door in case of visitors, and Juba patrolled the house and gardens during the night—he had been on edge since an intruder had managed to get over the garden wall a few months back. Not that I didn't trust Juba implicitly. But who knew what other slaves might be wandering around in the darkness? No, it was better for both of us that we kept those moments for Atreus's apartment, where there was less chance of someone blundering in.

Still, it didn't stop me from taking his hand, or him from squeezing mine in return.

"None of them stand out though, do they?" I asked him.

"Not yet." He was as taciturn as usual. Until I'd come along, Atreus had been a man who kept his thoughts to himself as he worked through a knotty problem. He still tried to be that sort of man, but I was slowly training him out of it. If we had to work together, then I had to know where his reason was leading him. "Except it's not Otho."

"Why not?"

"We saw it tonight," he said. "Otho can't compete with the poets and the playwrights, and he knows it as well as they do. That's why the slave girl who looks like Agrippina is such a triumph. They're all trying to beat each other at a single race, and he's already won the entire games."

I nodded. "Yes, why would he try to attack a poet when his gift is one that stands so far apart from the rest?"

"Exactly so."

"It's a solid theory," I said, "and I hate it."

Atreus turned his head in the darkness. "You hate it?"

"Yes. I would have liked Otho to be guilty."

Atreus's silent huff of laughter jostled us both. "Agreed. Well, it's just a theory. He might still be guilty."

"I'll give a small offering to the relevant gods," I said, "and see what they can do."

He laughed again, and then we settled into silence. I don't know how long we sat. It felt like hours, although I'm sure it wasn't. But it was dark enough and quiet enough, and I was close enough to sleep that I could no longer judge the passing of time. It was nice, sitting here with Atreus, a puzzle bubbling in the back of my mind, but not urgently enough to truly disturb our peace.

"I should go," Atreus said at last, and pulled his hand from mine.

"Breakfast tomorrow?" I asked. "You're welcome to bring Lucilla, of course."

It was dark, so I didn't need to see his awkward indecision. I could make life a lot easier for Atreus, if only he would let me. Of course, he would never let me. I was sure he was coming up with some excuse or another, which would have at least been more of a concession than a terse "No", but it never came.

At that moment, there was a loud banging on my front door, and my heart leapt.

It was the middle of the night, and there was a frantic stridency to the knocking that instantly told me it wasn't a social call, even though I now had friends—well, Petronius—who liked to drop in at odd hours and invite me on strange bridge excursions.

I hurried through the darkness of the house to the fauces, where a lamp was burning. Hursa slept in a small alcove nearby and was just rolling himself to his feet as Atreus and I arrived. The front door was locked at night, a heavy chain looped through the iron rings on the back of the door. It allowed Hursa to open the door a crack. When he did, torchlight spilled in from outside.

"Who is it?" Hursa asked, squinting into the torchlight unattractively.

"There's been a fire," a panicked voice returned. "At m-my master Lucan's house! He said Aemilius Valerius should come at once!"

It looked as though our mysterious attacker had answered one of our questions for us. Yes, he most certainly would target Lucan again. And tonight, he had.

Atreus and I hurried out into the darkness.

* * *

Lucan was distraught. Pale-faced, red-eyed, and holding a shaking hand over his mouth as though he was attempting to hide the sound of his hitching breaths. None of it was for the burned shelves in his tablinum, the scorch marks reaching the ceiling, and the scrolls disintegrated into piles of soggy ashes thanks to the quick work of the slaves who had doused the flames in buckets of water filled from the cistern. No, Lucan's distress was because of the body of the boy that had been found in the hallway leading to the posticum door: Hermes.

"I woke when I heard the oil lamp smash," said the door slave, a middle-aged man with a reddish tint to his hair. He darted a glance at his master, who sat hunched over on a bench in the atrium. "The door to the tablinum hadn't been closed all the way. I saw the flames. I yelled out, and the others came to help." He blinked rapidly. "It wasn't until after that we found...that we found poor Hermes."

"You sleep by the door?" Atreus asked.

"Yes, sir," said the door porter. "The front door." He frowned, his face the picture of misery. "But the posticum door—Hermes was by the posticum door. He must have let the intruder in."

I exchanged a glance with Atreus.

"Did Hermes ever let anyone in that way before?" I asked.

"Oh, yes!" the door porter said. "Well, not often, sir, but sometimes, if the master is working late, his guests might come in that way." He added, in response to my blank look: "The other writers, sir. They sometimes come and go at strange hours, but if Hermes knew to expect them, he would—" He blinked rapidly again, tears flooding his already-watery eyes. "He would wait for them outside and bring them in the posticum door, so I wasn't woken. He would—he would even fetch and carry all the wine and food so that the kitchen slaves could sleep."

The door slave dissolved into tears, and Atreus gripped him on the shoulder reassuringly.

I glanced at Lucan, and at his attitude of grief. Hermes had been his master's favourite slave, but also popular with the door slave. With the kitchen slaves too, if he saved them work. Whichever gods looked out for lowly slaves as they crossed the Styx, I hoped they were paying attention tonight.

Lucan's red-rimmed gaze followed me as I went for another look at his tablinum. Atreus joined me.

I was no expert on fires, but even I could see the smashed pieces of an oil lamp in the sodden mess that remained of Lucan's library. The shelf itself was probably salvageable, but most of the scrolls were utterly ruined. The room stank of the damage caused by the fire. Both sets of doors had been wrenched wide open by the slaves rushing to put the fire out, leaving the tablinum open to the atrium on one side, and the peristyle on the other.

I went out into the peristyle, following the light of a lamp down the narrow corridor to the posticum. A grey-haired woman, her tunic hitched up to her thighs, wept silently as she scrubbed Hermes's blood off the tiles.

Atreus knelt down beside her and murmured something in her ear.

She wiped her face with the heels of her hands and pointed to the room nearest the posticum door.

They'd laid him out on his bed. His eyes were open, his hair mussed up, and his jaw hanging. His yellow tunic was stained with his blood. He looked even younger in death than he had in life, just a gangly boy who hadn't grown into manhood yet, and now never would.

"This is his room," Atreus said. He set a lamp down on the low table beside Hermes's bed and knelt down beside the mattress. He studied the boy's face, his own serious and contemplative, in silence.

The room was spartan, and yet, for a slave, clearly spoke of his high status within the household. There was only a single mattress in the room; Hermes hadn't shared. He had a mattress of his own, the low table, a couple of scrolls standing neatly in a bronze pot in the corner, and small cabinet with an unlit lamp on top.

I opened the cabinet.

Tunics and sandals. A cloak. A belt. A bronze ring. A comb. A purse filled with copper coins and hidden in a tricky alcove at the back of the cabinet, a wooden box with more coins in it. These were also mostly copper, but there were a few glints of silver and gold in there, and the box also contained a gold ring with an emerald set in it. I put the box back, dislodging something that made a rattling sound against the cabinet. I reached in and pulled it out.

It was a little wooden horse, just a children's toy, but precious enough to Hermes that he'd hidden it with his money. It reminded me of the toys that Mouse was beginning to grow out of. It reminded me that Hermes was still only a boy. Maybe grown enough that he didn't take his horse out anymore, but not old enough to discard it. Still a boy, for all his cleverness, who had clung to a childish toy that still gave him comfort.

My chest ached, and it was a long moment before I could turn and look at him.

Atreus had closed Hermes's eyes, and his hand still lingered on his forehead. "He could have been waiting for any one of them. Any one of the men we dined with tonight."

"One of Lucan's friends," I said. "Trusted enough to be allowed entry through the posticum door."

Atreus sighed and rose slowly to his feet. We returned to the atrium. It didn't look like Lucan had moved. A slave girl knelt at his feet, her eyes wide and her cheeks stained with tears. She held out a cup of wine for her master, but he hadn't taken it.

I sat beside him on the bench, and Atreus stood close by.

"You ought to drink that," I said to Lucan, and nodded at the cup the girl held.

He turned his head to look at me. "What?"

"Drink," I said, and it appeared as though he noticed the girl for the first time.

He took the cup in his shaking hands and sipped.

"What happened here tonight, sir?" Atreus asked.

Lucan drew a deep breath, looking bewildered. "I woke up when I heard Philonik yelling about a fire." He spread his hands out in front of him, and I saw that they were stained with soot. "I—when it was out, I realised Hermes wasn't there. I found him. In the corridor."

"Outside his room? By the posticum door?" Atreus asked.

Lucan gave a jerky nod.

"Were you expecting any visitors tonight?" I asked.

Lucan just stared at me and shook his head. "Oh, Jupiter. My poor Hermes." He put a hand to his mouth. "I bought him from the market, you know? He must have been seven or eight. I just wanted a boy to fetch and carry, but he was so *clever*. He could memorise anything. He learned to sound out words by watching me work. So I taught him, properly. And he wasn't just a secretary. He was..." His voice trailed off, and when the next words came, they were faint with both wonder and sorrow. "He was beloved of the Muses."

Not just the Muses. Lucan was bereft.

A household did not mourn a slave, at least not in any public way. Hermes would not lie on a couch festooned with leaves and flowers. A cypress branch would not be placed at the front door. Paid mourners would not wail and tear their hair for him, and Lucan would not wear black. And yet Hermes would be deeply, privately mourned by his master and his fellow slaves, and his death would cast a shadow over this house for a long time. It was more than most slaves got, and at the same time, it wasn't enough.

Hermes had deserved a better ending than this.

Atreus and I left Lucan to his grief and went home.

The night was cold and dark, and misery, both old and new, swirled around me as we walked. In only a few hours, another cruel day would begin to dawn, and the endless cycle would continue. My eyes pricked, and it wasn't just the wind. I was tired, chilled to the bone, and everything felt hopeless and bleak until the back of Atreus's hand brushed mine and reminded me that he was by my side.

It was only the briefest glint of hope in the heavy darkness, but it was just enough to lift the weight from my shoulders and to see me safely home.

Chapter Five

The morning brought no surprises, only another cold winter's day and the solemn weight of melancholy. I barely knew Hermes, but he was a bright little flame unfairly extinguished, and the world was darker for it.

I sat in the peristyle as dawn bled weakly across the sky, and Juba brought me a blanket to keep off the worst of the chill. He brought me a cup of calda too, and I thanked him by asking him to join me instead of slinking off back into the darkness. The calda was hot enough to warm my hands as I held the cup, but not so hot it was undrinkable.

Juba stretched his legs out in front of him and watched the nearby fountain. Juba had said nothing when I'd returned from Lucan's house, although the single raised eyebrow had spoken volumes. I was certain he was just dying to remind me that he was my bodyguard, and that it was only possible for him to perform those duties if my body remained in his general vicinity. Which was fair, but I'd had Atreus with me, so I hadn't been entirely reckless. Of course, out of all of us, Juba was the only one who could hold his own in a street brawl with Hercules, so perhaps he didn't see Atreus as an adequate substitute bodyguard, which would also be a fair point.

"Did you ever talk to the boy?" I asked, taking another sip of calda. "To Hermes?"

Juba shook his head. "No, sir."

"I thought everyone's slaves got together and gossiped while their masters were at dinner."

That earned me another raised eyebrow. Juba was the furthest thing from a gossip. He knew all of my secrets, after all, including the one I kept closest because its discovery could destroy my reputation. He'd been right there when I'd first kissed Atreus—I'd been full of recklessness and stupid ideas that time—and I had no doubt he knew what happened on my visits to Atreus's apartment when I instructed him to take a long lunch break. And yet I trusted him. I hadn't even known him for any great length of time. There were some slaves in the household I'd known since childhood, but Juba wasn't one of them. When I'd returned to Rome from the army, he'd opened the front door to me, and that was the first time we'd met. Then, when I'd been reacquainting myself with the city's nightlife, my father had assigned Juba as my bodyguard. I suppose we proved that old rule of friendships being made in adversity, if you stretched the definition of 'friendship' to include the relationship between a master and a slave, and took 'adversity' to mean a lot of late, drunken nights which had involved Juba having to pick me up from the floor and lug me over his shoulder to get me home again. The adversity had very much been on his side of the arrangement.

"So, you never spoke to him?"

Juba let out a long breath. "No. He didn't join the other slaves. In some houses, when you eat, we might too. A friendly cook might make sure there are enough leftovers to feed the guests' slaves. You see the same faces, most of the time. But I never saw Hermes hanging around in anyone's kitchen. That boy was stuck like a limpet to his master."

"Do you think…" I cleared my throat. "I find myself wondering this in too many houses lately. Do you think he was happy?"

"That boy?" Juba raised his eyebrows. "Yes."

We sat in silence for a moment, and then I said, "You have more to say on the subject, Juba, I think."

Juba hummed. "He was just a boy, and his master clearly loved him. He was happy. If he would have stayed happy as he grew into a man, I don't know."

"You think he might have changed his mind?"

"I think when he got a little taller, he might have seen a little further."

"That's very philosophical of you, Juba."

Juba shrugged and I wondered if he was right.

If Hermes had lived, would he have found himself dissatisfied remaining under Lucan's yoke? Would Lucan's love have granted the boy freedom, or would the master have been unwilling to cast such a treasure away? He had unearthed it, after all, and had every legal and moral right to keep it.

"And what about you, Juba?" I asked him in the darkness. "You're very tall. You must be able to see a long way."

The question won me another hum.

I set my cup aside, not sure if I would be able to drink with the way my stomach suddenly lurched like the storm-tossed surface of an angry sea. "Were you always a slave?"

In life, there are many things that should go unasked and unsaid. That question was perhaps one of them. Because while I thought of Juba and I as something like friends, I wasn't a complete fool. A question like the one I'd asked would tear the skin off our comfortable relationship and expose the blood and gristle underneath.

Juba threw me a sidelong look. "No, sir, I wasn't."

I didn't ask anymore, like a coward. He told me anyway.

"My father was a trader in Axum," he said. "He had debts. When he died, I was sold to his rival. I was thirteen. My first master sold me to another, and another, and eventually I was sold here in Rome, to your father. I have seen more of the world than I imagined I would, but not in the way I thought."

It was an uncomfortable subject, and one I should never have raised. Because it was very easy to look at a slave and know he was a slave, but not as easy to ask *why* he was a slave. Why one man and not another? If my father had been in debt, could it have happened to me? Sometimes, the difference between slave and master rested on the vagaries of fate and chance, and the thread that my life hung upon could be snipped as easily as anyone else's. No, not that I would ever become a slave. Unthinkable. Even if I stumbled headfirst into political and financial ruin—and it would have to be completely catastrophic, and I would have to be completely friendless to ever have it happen—someone would put my gladius in my hand before it came to that. But if I'd been a child and my father had been ruined by his enemies? Unthinkable became not impossible.

I thought of Hermes, and of Otho's slave girl Iris, and of Juba, and of the power that masters held over the lives of those beneath them. It was the natural order of things, and yet, here in the darkness, what was the difference between Juba and me? It was a philosophical question I hated to ask because I hated the answer even more.

"Have all your masters been fair?" The wound was open already, so why not dig around in it in the hopes of finding no infection?

"No," he said frankly. His voice was low. "But I consider myself fortunate that your father bought me. He was a fair master."

"And me?" I asked. Another stupid question. An unfair one, too, because was there any way for him to answer it if the truth was less than complimentary? I reached out and put my hand on his forearm before he could speak. "Sorry. You don't have to answer that. My thoughts are leading me strange places tonight. A boy is dead, beyond all care, and I'm fretting about whether or not he was happy when the answer has nothing to do with who killed him."

"The law says that a slave is property," Juba said. "Whoever killed Hermes, when you catch him, will have to pay Lucan the cost of the boy. Like the killer walked into Lucan's house and smashed a glass vase or a statue. But statues don't have minds or hearts. You can love a statue all you want, but it will never love you back."

I thought of Petronius and his witty words at Otho's dinner party about groping statues. But before he'd dragged the conversation down into the gutter, Otho's wife, Poppaea, had said it much more poetically: *I can recite Catullus's words all I want, but I shall never be able to embrace and kiss his beloved Lesbia.* Art and statues and slaves and love. Where did property end and life begin? It was a trickier question than it appeared, and the law was not always correct. Hermes had not been a mere possession to be admired. He'd had thoughts of his own, feelings too. But the law made no distinction between Hermes and a *thing*.

A vague ember of a thought caught in the back of my mind and extinguished itself before I had grasped it. I thought of the corpse in the fountain, lifeless, bloodless, as white and still as an unpainted statue. Cold as the marble it resembled. Another thing.

"It mattered to Lucan that the boy was happy," Juba said. "It matters to you too, sir, and not because you give a shit about poetry. I think that answers the question you said I didn't have to answer."

For some reason, I couldn't name, my eyes stung. I nodded. "Thank you, Juba."

We sat together a while longer, my thoughts a little lighter than before Juba had found me, but still tangled up with Hermes, and Lucan, and that little wooden horse we'd found in the boy's belongings. He had loved and been loved, even though he might have outgrown it, but while that should have felt like some consolation, it wasn't. Not when his life was cut short. Not when Lucan was grieving.

Perhaps that's why I'd asked Juba the questions I had.

There wasn't much fairness in the world, after all, for masters and slaves and everybody in between, but I hoped that I had cultivated at least a little of it under my roof. And I hoped that it was enough.

* * *

Before dawn had even properly broken, Juba and I headed down the Caelian Hill into the city. Damos, the cook, was already awake, thumping around in the kitchen, and he sent us off with an apple each, like recalcitrant schoolboys. I figured I owed Juba more than an apple because of this early start to the day, but as we walked down the hill in the darkness, it became apparent that a good breakfast was out of the question. It was still too late—or too early, depending on which side of dawn you were viewing the question from—for anything to be open. Most of the houses on the lower side of the hill had rented their frontage to shopkeepers, but the many thermapolia we passed had their shutters pulled closed, hiding the wide counters with their earthenware dolia from view. At the bottom of the Caelian Hill, the houses gave way to close-packed insulae. We took the shortcut Atreus had shown us once, forsaking the wider street for a series of narrow, twisting alleys that deposited us close to the excubitorium. As we arrived, the first thin rays of sunlight pierced the final flimsy veils of the night.

The day was here.

There were already people at the excubitorium, waiting for the attention of the vigile stationed at the desk inside the front door. It was Manius, the world's littlest vigile, and despite his young age and his skinny stature, he was unflinchingly ignoring the waiting public with a practiced ease that he could only have learned off a much older, much lazier man. Probably Vibilus, who had elevated unawareness to an artform that was incredible to watch. Somehow Manius was aware of exactly who was coming and going, without ever looking up from his wax tablet.

"Go straight through, sir," he said, waving his stylus towards me.

I swept through, ducking between a scowling man with greasy clumps of hair sticking up from his scalp, and a stony-faced young woman clutching a basket. Juba followed me, and strident complaints followed the pair of us. But Manius knew I wasn't here to enquire about a drunk, or a runaway slave, or a thief, or whoever else had been dumped in the cells of the excubitorium overnight. The vigiles might have been firefighters in theory, but in practice, they were street sweepers, and all the human rubbish they cleared from the gutters ended up here at some point.

A man with a black eye and a cut on his cheek nodded at me as we passed him in the corridor. I didn't recall his name, but I recognised him as one of the men who'd visited my house back when Atreus had been convalescing there. That small kindness had won me a lot of goodwill with Atreus's men. If my house was ever on fire, Jupiter forbid, they might even attend at a jog instead of a leisurely stroll.

"Sir?" the vigile called, and I turned around. "Atreus is in Leander's room."

"Thank you."

Juba looked far too pleased to be getting a visit to the physician's room. I had seen my fair share of gore before—I'd been in the military, so it wasn't as though I could escape it—but I really didn't enjoy the way Leander left the instruments of his trade laid out so that a man might just stare at them and uncomfortably speculate as to their purpose. He had knives, and forceps,

and things with more teeth than an angry eel, and my skin crawled whenever
I saw them as though it was trying to remove itself from my body. Leander
probably had a specialist tool for that as well.

I knocked on Leander's door when we arrived, and Atreus opened it.

"Valerius." He raised his eyebrows. "Has something else happened?"

"Wonderful," I said. "You don't see me for several hours, and immediately
assume the worst."

He gave me a look at my teasing tone, but Juba didn't even blink, and
Leander was busy cleaning a wicked-looking bronze knife.

I breezed inside, pretending not to notice the faint smell of decay.
"Leander, good morning."

He flashed me a smile that sat a little uncomfortably on his thin, sallow
face. "Good morning, Valerius."

There was a body-shaped lump on the table, covered with a blanket.
"How's the patient? Any hope of recovery?"

"Not unless you have a few buckets of blood and a way of getting it back
in him, sir," Leander said, his smile widening. I didn't like Leander's room
much, but the more time I spent with the man, the more I appreciated his
macabre sense of humour. He needed one, I supposed, in his line of work.

Lamplight flickered on the blanket covering the corpse, almost making it
look as though the dead man was moving. Just an illusion. The only way
the corpse would ever move again would be once the worms got to it.

"He doesn't smell as bad as I thought he should," I said. There was an
odour of faint decay in the room, a staleness that was verging on something
worse, but it wasn't putrid like a corpse ought to be.

"We have the cold to thank for that," Leander said.

"The lack of blood, too?" Juba asked keenly. He loved the gruesome parts
of Leander's job. Well, most of them were gruesome, weren't they? It wasn't
as though he made daisy chains for a living.

"Yes," Leander said. "The discarded parts in a butcher's bin begin to stink
long before the carcass hanging on the hook, don't they?"

Juba nodded and slunk closer to the table. He lifted the corner of the
blanket, and I caught a glimpse of the dead man's hand. The flesh was ashen,

but not yet discoloured with true rot. I'd thought of statues earlier—statues and art and beauty. Life and death. The dead man's hand might have been carved out of faintly mottled marble.

Atreus leaned against the wall and folded his arms over his chest. "What brings you here, sir?"

"I'm seeking your advice," I said. "It was bad enough when Seneca wanted me to find out what was going on. As soon as word gets out that someone broke into Lucan's house and set fire to his library, all of Rome will be demanding to know who the guilty man is. And I'm fairly sure the emperor himself will also be asking that question. I'd very much like to be able to answer it."

My tone was flippant, but I knew Atreus understood. I liked Lucan, but I didn't give a shit about his library. This was about finding a killer—a man so brazen that he'd killed the slave who had welcomed him into the house.

Atreus nodded.

"Someone must have approached Hermes last night at Otho's dinner party," I said. "How else would he have known to be waiting by the door?"

"Not necessarily," Atreus said. "His room was closest to the posticum door. Anyone arriving in the middle of the night and knocking might have woken him without rousing anyone else. He must have been known to Hermes, though. A good enough friend of his master that he saw nothing wrong with letting him in."

His gaze darted to the blanket-covered corpse, and I felt a brief flutter of guilt. He had his own murder to investigate, and I was pulling him away from it, but in my defence this matter with Lucan was a murder now as well, and there was no way I should have been left to look into it without supervision. It wasn't just that I doubted myself—although I did—it was that I relied on Atreus to provide a different point of view when one was needed, and I trusted his opinions.

"We will need to talk to the men from dinner last night," he said, his expression hardening. "Properly, this time."

His tone made it clear that the poets and playwrights would not enjoy their talk in the least. So much for my burgeoning friendships, if Atreus was going to stick his plebeian nose in and shock them all with a magnificent show of his bad attitude. But one of them was a murderer, so fuck them. A dose of Atreus at his most prickly was the least of what they deserved.

"We'll go now," he said. "I just need to get home first and collect Lucilla from my neighbour. Leander, will you take her?"

I tried not to bristle. This was Atreus's line, and I knew better than to overstep it, even though it was ridiculous. Lucilla could easily spend the day at my house while we were busy, and there would be plenty of people to look after her. But Atreus had made it clear in the past that when it came to Lucilla, I wasn't allowed an opinion on his decisions, however stupidly impractical they were.

"Of course," Leander said. "I'm finishing up here now anyway."

A frantic knock sounded at the door.

"Or perhaps not quite finishing up," Leander continued wryly.

But, when little Manius opened the door and stuck his head inside the room, it wasn't a physician he was chasing.

"There you are, sir!" he exclaimed when he saw Atreus.

"Here I am," Atreus agreed.

"Sir! There's a woman at the desk," Manius continued, his eyes bright with excitement. "She says she saw the chalk sign near the Medusa Fountain, and she thinks the dead man is her brother!"

Atreus and I exchanged a look, and Atreus smiled.

Finally, at least something was going right.

The woman Manius brought into the room was the one I'd stepped past when I'd arrived. She wore a stony expression and clutched a basket in her arms. She wasn't old, but she looked as though she'd already lived a hard life. There were lines scoured down either side of her lips, and more that radiated out from the corners of her eyes. She could have told me she was aged anywhere between twenty and fifty, and I would have believed it. If a sculptor had carved the dead man out of unblemished white marble, capturing his high cheekbones, his full mouth, and his straight nose, then a potter had shaped this woman out of terracotta and then left her too long in the kiln. She was already starting to crack. Her expression was pinched, the anticipation of bad news lying heavily on her features. She wore a silver ring on her thumb.

Atreus stepped forward to meet her. "I am Junius Atreus, acting centurion. And you are?"

"Atia." Her voice was as rough and prickly as the wicker basket she held. "I think...I think you might have found my brother."

From outside, I could hear faint shouts and laughter, and the sound of practice swords crashing up against wooden shields. It felt almost disrespectful, as though the whole place, perhaps the whole city, should have been as silent as a mausoleum while Atia attended to her awful task.

Atia's gaze darted around to all of us—Leander, Juba, and me—before settling finally on the blanket-covered corpse on the table. She pressed her mouth into a line as hard as the rest of her. "Is that him?"

Leander drew the blanket back, exposing the dead man's face to view.

Atia's expression was stony. "That's him. My brother."

This was a grim task, and I wondered if Atia's stoicism would fail her now. She wasn't wailing—she wasn't even shaking as Lucan had after he'd discovered Hermes dead. But Lucan had been amongst friends, in his own household. Atia was in a dark room with a group of strangers. It didn't mean her grief and shock was no less profound than anyone else's. It only meant that we had no right to witness them.

Atia tightened the grip on her basket, and the wicker creaked. "What happened to him? Why does he look like that?"

"He lost a lot of blood," Atreus said, which was kinder than saying he was slaughtered and hung up to drain like a pig. He nodded at Leander, and Leander replaced the blanket over the dead man's face. "What is his name, Atia?"

"Atius."

Atius and Atia. Clearly their parents were imaginative people.

"Can you tell me about him?" Atreus asked quietly.

She shot him a narrow, suspicious look. "What do you want to know?"

"Anything that can help me discover who killed your brother," Atreus said. "We believe he often visited a friend who lived in an apartment that overlooked the Medusa Fountain. Do you know who that is?"

Her gaze flicked away from him briefly. "No."

"Do you know if he had any enemies?"

"No. He didn't."

"What about close friends?" Atreus prompted. "Someone who could tell us what he was doing before he was killed?"

"No," Atia said again. She lifted her chin. "Our parents are old. Atius went to work every day, then came home and helped with them, same as me. He didn't have close friends, and he certainly didn't have enemies."

I barely stopped myself from raising my eyebrows at that. City of a million people, and apparently poor Atius hadn't known any of them.

"What sort of work did he do?" Atreus asked, keeping his tone level.

"He was a brickmaker," Atia said. "Same as our father before he got sick."

"That's hard work," Atreus said.

Atia threw him a suspicious look, as though she was looking for the sting in the comment, and finally dipped her chin in a nod. "Yes."

"Did he have a girlfriend?" Atreus asked. "A wife?"

"No. I would have said if he did."

"Did he have any debts that you know about?"

Atia shook her head. "He worked, and came home, and we looked after our parents. I already told you that."

"I understand this is a difficult time for you," Atreus said. "If you think of anything that might be helpful, please let me know."

"I will," Atia said, although I didn't know how much help Atreus expected to get from her. I'd thought her stony when she'd walked in, but I was leaning towards outright hostile by now. Her gaze darted from Atreus to Atius and back again. "When can I take the body home?"

"Whenever you like," Atreus said.

Atia nodded. "I'll go and get my cousin. He has a cart."

Manius, who had been lingering by the door like a cat deciding whether to come in or not, showed Atia out again.

I waited until I could no longer hear their footsteps before I spoke. "Well, that wasn't useful at all."

"She's lying," Atreus said.

"Is she? She was certainly hostile, but maybe that's just because she hates the law," I said. "That's hardly uncommon. I've seen people clam up and scuttle away when you wish them a good morning, Atreus."

His mouth quirked in acknowledgement.

"The thing about not having any friends we know is a lie," I said. "The old woman in the insula said Atius visited his friend who lived there."

Atreus nodded slowly and let out a breath. "Even if Atia didn't know his friends, she knows more than she's telling us. She's definitely lying, but I don't know about what."

"About everything, probably," Juba said suddenly, lifting the edge of the blanket to expose Atius's hand. "I've never seen a brickmaker without any burns or callouses, Atreus. Have you?"

* * *

An hour later, from the shelter of the caupona across the street from the excubitorium, Atreus, Juba, and I watched as Atia and her cousin wheeled the corpse of Atius away. I regretfully left my soup on the counter, tucked my bread into my tunic for later, and fell into step with Juba and Atreus as we followed Atia to see where she led us.

The streets were busy now. The sun was up, and the day was in full swing. It wasn't difficult to keep sight of Atia and her cousin, though. The cart slowed them down, wheels catching in the road as the cousin pulled it, and pedestrians veered away from them like ships steering away from rocks. The corpse was covered, but it didn't take much of an imagination to guess what was under the blanket; who could blame people for giving them a wide berth? Let the omen be absent, as the old saying went.

We followed them into the Aventine.

I'd once scouted deep into Parthian territory, wary that every movement might give me away to the enemy. I was familiar with the prickling sensation you got between your shoulder blades when there were unfriendly eyes on you. Atia's cousin, who was broader than the Tarpeian Rock, looked to be feeling it now. A few times he stopped to look behind, but since he had to put the cart down to do it, we had plenty of forewarning.

Bad instinct, or perhaps a simple need for symmetry, told me that we were heading for the Medusa Fountain, but we turned off into unfamiliar streets before then. I joked with Atreus that all of the Aventine was a sewer filled with nothing but rats, shit, and criminals—strangely, he didn't see the funny side—but it wasn't true. Parts of the Aventine, like Atreus's neighbourhood, were decent enough. But the narrow, twisted alleys that Atia was leading us into now, with insulae tall enough to block the light? We were definitely about to be murdered. I had no idea where we were. We were close enough to the Tiber to smell the stench coming off the river, yet somehow far enough from civilisation that my family would never recover my corpse.

Atia and her cousin slowed their pace in the narrow, twisting alleyways, having to navigate the cart past obstacles and around sharp corners. Once, a beggar berated them for almost running over his toes, and the cousin raised an arm to strike at him before Atia pulled him away.

Beside me, Juba made an unhappy sound.

I didn't like this situation any more than he did, but what choice did we have except to follow and discover what we could learn?

A grubby chorus of children merrily shouted, "Fuck you!" at each other, and pelted one another with stones and rotten vegetables. We passed through the battle relatively unscathed, although I did get hit in the knee with an onion that had the consistency of watery dough. The smell was a greater injury than the impact.

We lingered on a corner for a while, looking as suspicious as everyone else in this neighbourhood, when Atia and her cousin finally stopped in the crumbling entrance of an insula that looked to be holding together out of nothing but habit, or possibly spite. We couldn't hear what the cousin said— his voice was a low rumble against Atia's strident insults, and eventually he threw his arms up in a gesture of defeat, and lifted the corpse over his shoulder like it was a sack of grain. He lumbered inside the insula with Atia at his heels, still swearing at him. They left the cart outside.

"What do you think?" Atreus asked.

"I think that walking into that building could be the stupidest thing we've done in a while," I said. I held his gaze. "I also think we're going to do it."

Atreus flashed me a grin. "We are, aren't we?"

"Never a doubt in my mind."

Juba's snort told me he agreed, and we hurried down the alleyway to the doorway of the insula.

There was an oil shop on one side of the insula's doorway, and a bakery on the other, which seemed like a disaster waiting to happen. The entryway itself was dark and smelled like piss. It opened into a central yard that was so narrow it would have taken until mid-morning for the sunlight to filter down to the lower levels. The ground was littered with broken pots, dog shit, and a couple of stringy plants strangling each other as they each strained feebly to reach the light. Laundry flapped over rickety-looking balconies that I wouldn't have trusted to hold a human being. Wooden stairs in the yard linked the levels of the insula together. Atia and her cousin were already at the third landing.

"Hold," Atreus said, and we lingered on the ground level, our backs to the stairs as we tried to see which door on the third floor that Atia and her cousin approached. If they turned and looked over the railing, there was every chance they'd spot us, but their being encumbered by a dead body, in the cousin's case, and an impatient personality, in Atia's, worked in our favour. They stopped at a door about halfway along the landing on the northern side of the insula. They were too far away for us to see much, only that they were there for a few moments while they waited for the door to be opened, and then they vanished into the apartment.

We started cautiously up the rickety stairs.

The cousin's stomping steps above us as we reached the second floor warned us that we were about to have an awkward reunion. Instead of waiting to meet them on the stairs, we hurried along the second-floor landing, turning the corner onto the eastern side of the building, and coming face-to-face with a dog chained in a doorway.

Well, I say a dog.

It was more the size of a bull.

About as friendly as one too. Its lip lifted as it let out a low, rumbling growl, showing off its fangs.

"Sit," Atreus said sternly, and, to his credit, valiantly.

The dog, who had no respect for the law, lunged instead. The three of us scrambled hastily away, only to watch the dog brought up short on its chain. From inside the dog's apartment, a man cackled at our panic.

Well, that was one way to avoid door-to-door salesmen and debt collectors. We caught our breath on the landing opposite the stairs, turned away so that Atia and her cousin didn't notice us as they clattered their way down to the ground floor. Then we went the long way around the landing to get back to the stairs, so that we didn't have to pass the dog again. Instead, we passed a small cohort of dirty, narrow-eyed children, who stared at us suspiciously from the open door of their apartment.

We climbed the stairs to the third floor.

Who in Tartarus was waiting for us in the apartment? If Juba was right and Atia had lied about everything, then who was the dead man? No brickmaker, according to his smooth hands. A heartbreaker, perhaps, going by his face alone. The mystery of his identity was overshadowed by the mystery of all the subterfuge surrounding the claiming of his corpse, but both could be solved by whoever awaited us halfway down the landing.

The apartments here were even smaller and cheaper than those on the ground floor, the doors spaced closer together. Not only did the residents here have the stairs to manage a couple of times a day, but they probably had to carry their water up from the nearest public fountain, too. The residents on the ground level might have water, and those on the second floor might also be lucky enough to get a trickle, but even the mighty Aqua Appia couldn't push water to the upper floors of the city's insulae.

The uneven wooden boards of the landing creaked as we walked along them, and Atreus's mouth pinched into a thin, unhappy line. Whoever was in that apartment had certainly heard us coming.

He didn't take long to make his move.

The occupant of the apartment burst out of the door as we approached, in a flurry of wild movement. I caught a glimpse of copper-burnished hair, a tunic the colour of dun, and then he was running, not past us to the stairs, but around the landing that hugged the central yard of the insula. Atreus and Juba sprinted after him, like dogs getting the scent of their prey. I'd been born a patrician—my natural position in any venture was at a supervisory level—and I did what any former junior tribune would have done: I used my brain instead of my muscle and backtracked to the stairs. If the fleeing man wanted to escape this level of the insula, he'd have to get past me to get to the stairs. I might have been less smug about it if I'd realised sooner that I was the only thing standing between the man and his escape. By the time I realised, it was too late to do anything except hope that it didn't end too badly for me.

The running man, now turning the final corner towards the stairs with Atreus and Juba on his heels, slowed as though he was having the exact same thought. And then, in a moment of good sense that I was glad at least one of us possessed, he turned to Atreus and Juba and showed them his palms in a gesture of surrender. Juba reached him first, grabbing his arms and twisting them behind his back. Then he marched his unhappy prisoner towards me. A pair of hazel eyes blazed from behind a curtain of copper hair, and I realised with a jolt that I knew this man.

Well, he was a boy, really.

Erastus.

He'd been blond the last time I'd seen him, where we'd met, under less than ideal circumstances, in the back corridor of the vigiles' excubitorium. Atreus had hung him on a wall bracket by his chained wrists and proceeded to torture him. In Atreus's defence, Erastus had helped Bano, the gangster, set us up to try and murder us, and the torture had been very much on the mild side. Erastus probably didn't remember it that way though.

"Erastus," I said. "Bano's cousin."

"Fuck you," Erastus said, just as charming as always.

Juba hustled him inside his apartment, and Atreus and I followed.

The place was a hovel. It was small and dark—a single room only—and we were probably wildly outnumbered by the bedbugs and fleas that infested the sagging bed. There was no balcony, only a narrow, shuttered window, and the single lamp burning had left a dark, oily patch on the wall and the ceiling. Even removing Atius's corpse from the bed wouldn't improve the place by much.

Juba pointed to the floor, and Erastus sat like an unhappy schoolboy, drawing his legs up and hugging his knees. Juba then went and loomed in the narrow doorway, effectively blocking any escape the man might try to make.

Atreus and I stood shoulder to shoulder in the narrow room and stared down at Erastus. He stared at the floor.

Atreus took a step towards the bed, and the floorboards creaked. Erastus looked up, and Atreus said, "What are you playing at, Erastus?"

"Fuck you," Erastus said, which seemed to be his standard answer. But his gaze darted to the corpse, and to Atreus, and back to the corpse again, his eyes widening for one fearful moment before he narrowed them into a glare once more.

The thing about Atreus, was that he had a chip on his shoulder the size of the Colossus of Rhodes. It was a job hazard of his. Not only did he have to deal with patricians like me who looked down our noses at him because we thought we were better than him, but he also had to deal with plebeians like Erastus who spat at him in the street because they thought he thought he was better than them. Also, he often wanted to arrest them for their criminal activity, which didn't make him too many friends in the Aventine, which had a proud tradition of criminal activity. The point was, Atreus treated his fellow citizens with suspicion, and in most cases he was right. But this time...

"Who was he to you?" I asked Erastus. A heartbreaker, I'd said to Atreus when I'd first seen the corpse, and it was obvious to me that I'd been right, and the man whose heart had been broken was sitting on the floor in front of me right now. "He wasn't Atia's brother. She didn't even know him."

He lifted his gaze. "How did you know?"

"She told us he was a brickmaker," I said, "but no brickmaker ever had hands so smooth."

Erastus rolled his eyes and huffed out a short breath. "Stupid woman."

"She almost had us," I said. "But she couldn't quite pull it off. She just didn't seem like she cared. You should have sent someone he mattered to."

Erastus clenched his jaw for a moment and then said, in a voice sharp with bitterness, "There was *no-one.*"

"And you couldn't come yourself," I said, "because you are Erastus, Bano's cousin, and you didn't have the friendliest reception last time you were at the excubitorium, did you?"

He nodded sharply, smart enough not to complain about it since he'd helped lure us into a trap that night.

"So who is he?" I asked, nodding at the corpse.

"Marsus," Erastus said, his voice hitching on the name. "He is Marsus."

Grief looked the same, whether it was present in a fine atrium where Lucan was attended to by his weeping slaves, or here on the third floor of a shitty insula in a shitty neighbourhood where the cold air was sharp with the stink of cat's piss and, on the floor below us, the chained dog barked and barked and barked.

Erastus turned his stricken gaze towards us. "Who did this to him?"

"We don't know," Atreus said. "That's what I'm trying to find out."

Erastus gave Juba a pointed look and climbed warily to his feet. Then he sat on the sagging bad, beside the corpse, and brushed his fingertips over one of the darkening slash wounds on the underside of a pale wrist. "What'd they do? Bleed him like a pig?"

We didn't answer that. We didn't have to. Erastus could read the corpse as well as we had.

He turned his face away for a moment. Fussed with one of Marsus's curls, as though it even mattered now that it was lying the wrong way, and my chest ached for him. It wasn't even lunchtime, and I was already very, very sick of grief and death and heartbreak.

Atreus crossed to the window and pushed the shutter open. Weak winter's sunlight spilled into the room, illuminating the swirling dust motes that had been disturbed by the shutters opening. Cool, sharp air came in on the heels of the light, and Atreus drew what looked to be a bracing breath. Then he leaned against the wall, his arms folded over his chest, and looked keenly at

Erastus.

"Did Marsus have any enemies?"

I could see Erastus battling every instinct that urged him to tell us to fuck off again. Finally, he shook his head. "No."

Men without enemies didn't usually get murdered and then dumped in fountains, but I supposed there was always a first time for everything.

"You do, though," Atreus said. "And no, not just me. You were living in the apartment overlooking the Medusa Fountain, weren't you?"

"Haven't been back there in a few weeks," Erastus confirmed.

"Why not?" I asked. "It's nicer than this place."

He curled his lip. "Because there's shit going on in this neighbourhood, friend, that you couldn't even begin to understand."

"Oh, why don't you try me and see?" I asked airily. "Because I imagine that it's something to do with the fact that a few months ago you were Bano's little henchman, but as soon as he went splat off that warehouse roof, suddenly you found out that not everyone loves you after all, and, in fact, a good few men would enjoy the opportunity to kill you, now that you no longer have your cousin's protection. How am I doing?"

His glare told me I was totally correct, but he still managed a derisive snort. "As if I even liked Bano, anyway. He was a prick."

"We're in full agreement there," I said. "So, he's dead, but perhaps not all of his enemies are satisfied. Did they kill Marsus and leave him in the fountain under your balcony to make a point that they hate you as well?"

My barb found its guilty target. Erastus flinched.

"How long since you saw Marsus?" Atreus asked.

Erastus blinked up at him and swallowed a few times before answering. "Maybe a week ago?"

"Where?"

"Here," Erastus said. "I didn't want him to come here, but he said he didn't care that the place is awful." He stroked Marsus's curls.

Atreus nodded. "What did Marsus do for work?"

"He was an actor," Erastus said.

I drew in a sharp breath before I could stop myself. An *actor*?

103

Erastus misinterpreted my reaction and threw me a hostile glance. "It was better than being a plasterer, like his father is. And it was good money. He was on the stage, not the street corner."

The way he was defending his choice of job, even now when it really didn't matter at all, hinted that Marsus must have argued hard for it at some point too. Against his plasterer father, perhaps. For days he'd been nothing but an empty corpse to me, but suddenly I caught a glimpse of him as a living being. A stubborn young man, on the outs with a father who just wanted him to get a *real* job, and with a boyfriend just as stubborn as he was. A boyfriend who had his back even now, even as his voice trembled.

Erastus lifted his chin. His eyes swam with tears. "He was good. He was *wonderful*. He said he was going to be in Petronius Arbiter's new play, with the emperor in the audience, and I could come and see it when it was put on for the public at the Theatre of Pompey."

I exchanged a look with Atreus as Erastus confirmed the connection my brain had only just seized upon as a possibility.

Petronius had complained about missing an actor, and it looked as though we'd just found him.

Marsus was the ideal Giton. Boyish, lithe, beautiful. Cheeky and vulgar as fuck, probably, but there was no way of telling that now. I couldn't imagine Petronius casting anyone less than perfect for the performance at Nero's Juvenalia though, and even though I'd never met Marsus, I felt a pang for his loss. His murder was criminal, but the way it had happened felt even more grotesque. Someone had taken this boy, so bright and full of life, and hadn't just snuffed that life out—they'd taken the time to drain every last drop of it away, leaving nothing but the empty vessel behind. It felt worse than just a simple killing. Murder could be the result of hot anger, but Marsus's death? It felt as though it could only be the result of a hatred that was cold beyond almost all comprehension.

"I meant no offence," I assured Erastus. "He was going to be in Petronius's new play? You're sure of that?"

He creased his brow. "That's what he said. I don't know. It sounded to me like all those writers were full of shit, making him all sorts of promises that he'd be rich just as long as he warmed their beds in the meantime. They didn't like it much when he just laughed at them."

Having seen the writers in action, I wasn't surprised they took refusal bitterly. They were a petty and jealous bunch.

Erastus narrowed his eyes. "Why are you asking about them?"

"No reason," Atreus said before I could answer. "We're just trying to learn about Marsus's life, because it's likely that something in his life led to his death."

Erastus shook his head. "Or something in *my* life."

"Probably, yes," Atreus said.

Erastus didn't tell him to fuck off again, but it was a near thing. And, with no other questions coming immediately to mind, we fucked off anyway.

Chapter Six

Petronius Arbiter wasn't at home, and so, under the advice of his door porter, Atreus, Juba, and I headed for Nero's theatre in the Gardens of Agrippina (not *that* Agrippina, but her mother). I wished I'd had a grandmother who'd left me some real estate like this. The gardens were built on the flat land between the Janiculan Hill and the Vatican Hill and stretched all the way down toward the Aventine. The vegetable gardens that had once covered the small plain had long since been removed, and the land had been bought up by wealthy families who wanted luxurious villas and gardens but didn't want to travel all the way to Baiae to get to them. The Gardens of Agrippina, with the villa, the portico overlooking the river, and the circus that ran parallel to the Via Cornelia, were, of course, among the most luxurious. The gardens were sometimes opened to the public by Nero, giving the citizens of Rome yet another place to watch the chariot racing. Perhaps in the near future the public would get a chance to see the theatre here too.

The Theatre of Nero was still under construction, but the parts of it that were built were so new that they sparkled in the sunlight. The scaenae frons was supported by a row of Ionic columns, and its walls were made of white marble and stucco covered in gold leaf. The scaenae frons rivalled an Imperial palace, from the front at least. I'd never given much thought to what lay beyond the stage.

When we arrived at the theatre, there was already action happening on the stage. Not a play, it soon became apparent, but an unscripted argument between two of Nero's favourite poets: Litus and Fabianus.

Atreus, Juba and I sat in the first row of the cavea, where the curve of the seats almost met the stage, and watched with interest.

A few workmen on trellises were doing something with the scrolling heads of the Ionic columns of the portico, tapping away with hammers and chisels. They paid no attention to the arguing poets, which gave the impression this was standard sort of behaviour.

Litus, mid-stride across the stage, gave a sudden, dramatic turn that any actor would have been proud off, and pointed an accusing finger at Fabianus. "I don't give a *fuck* if you're writing about Horatius at the bridge, Fabianus. My poem will be greater than yours ever could be! But you're a thief of ideas, and everyone should know it!"

"My friend," Fabianus said beseechingly, holding his hands out in a begging gesture. "Litus!"

"You do this every time!" Litus exclaimed and stalked towards the front of the stage like the insect he resembled. He jolted when he saw the three of us watching. "Oh, Valerius. You have caught me with a short temper."

Fabianus, his gesture of reconciliation rebuffed, threw his hands in the air and stomped away through one of the doors that led to whatever lay behind the façade of the scaenae frons.

A small child, sitting in the dust of the half-paved orchestra at the front of the stage, gave a half-hearted round of applause before the men paving the area shooed it away. One of them hauled a handcart half full of paving stones into the area, muscles bulging like an oxen's.

Litus sighed and dragged a hand through his hair. "We are all at odds today, I fear, because of what has happened with Hermes. And the work on the theatre is going slower than it ought to, and we're meant to be practising. How does one practice surrounded by bricklayers, Valerius?"

"I'm sure you will prove yourself through adversity, Litus," I said, and he snorted. "Is Petronius here? I need to speak with him."

"Yes," Litus said. "I think so, at least. It's chaos here today. Come through, and I'll show you to him."

Steps led from the dusty orchestra up onto the stage. We climbed them, and I stood there gazing out at the steep rise of the encircling seats of the cavea. I had only ever sat at the front during theatre performances, and I wondered if the people who climbed all the way to the top had creaking knees by the time they found their seats. Then I turned my attention to the façade of the palace that made up the scaenae frons. The detail was incredible. It was a three-storey façade, with columns, marble statues tucked into alcoves, a portico leading to a wide set of doors, and several other doors along the front that appeared as though they were operational. I was certain that at least one of the balconies above us opened onto the back as well. They had to lower the god who turned up to save the day from somewhere, right? The roof extended all the way out to the edge of the stage. The ceiling was gilded, just like the walls. Standing with my back to the cavea, I could have easily pretended that a full palace extended beyond those wide doors in the portico, and that it was no mere façade.

Litus strode up the shallow steps of the portico, pushing the doors open, and we followed him through to the narrow building of the scaenae that held up the intricate scaenae frons.

The palace was immediately transformed into a corridor of dark brick-work, and we found ourselves knocking shoulders with people scurrying back and forth with ropes, and fabric, and furniture, and even trees and shrubs.

"Most of the props are kept back here," Litus said over his shoulder, as he led us down the cold, gloomy passageway of the scaenae. "Usually, for one play, it's bad enough, but for the Juvenalia? It's *worse*. Everyone with a couple of stanzas to recite suddenly wants palm trees, or a dozen braziers, or an elephant."

I hoped that was an exaggeration, because there was no way they'd get an elephant to fit in any of the small rooms we passed.

Litus led us up a set of stairs at the end of the passageway. On the stage side of the passageway, I saw a balcony. The doors to it were open, letting in the light and a view of the seats of the cavea. On my other side, more brick rooms opened up. The second floor wasn't as busy as the first; real estate closest to the main stage entrance was certainly at a premium.

We passed rooms full of planks and ropes, and others full of furniture.

One door opened as we passed, and I almost recoiled as a figure hardly any higher than my knee, but with a grimacing, awful face, stepped outside.

"Nonus!" someone chided wearily, and a woman hauled the creature back into the room. She wrestled the satyr's mask off it and revealed a small, grubby-faced child underneath.

The room was hung with actors' masks: the mouthless pantomime character, the red-headed slave, the bearded old man, the grotesquely grinning brothel-keeper. They were even more off-putting close up than they were watching from the cavea.

"Petronius!" Litus called, still leading the way down the passageway. "Petro!"

A door was flung open almost in our faces, and Petronius appeared. He was wearing a russet-coloured tunic and had a cup of wine in one hand and a pen in the other. There were splatters of ink on his tunic.

"Come in," he said, and ushered us into the small room. "This is my home away from home these days."

The room contained a couch, a small, low table, a brazier, and a bunch of mismatched cushions. There were sheets of papyrus spread out all over the couch, a small pot of ink balanced precariously on the arm, and a half-eaten pastry on one of the cushions. A narrow window with open shutters allowed a view of the gardens behind the theatre.

"Litus, did you see any of my actors down there?" Petronius asked as he sat on the couch, barely missing the pastry. "I have new lines for them, if they haven't scattered like cockroaches."

"I haven't seen them," Litus said, "and I have my own work to be doing. Strangely, none of it involves being your messenger boy." He gave me a nod. "Valerius."

Then he stalked away down the passageway, hands clasped at the small of his back.

"Take a seat," Petronius said, gesturing at us, "if you can find one."

He shoved the papyrus pages onto the floor.

I sat next to him on the couch. Privileges of rank. Atreus sat on the table, and Juba leaned against the wall.

Petronius picked up his pastry and inspected it, then tossed it onto the floor with the pages. "This is about Hermes, is it? I went to see Lucan this morning. He's a mess."

Before I could correct him and tell him that we were here to speak about Marsus, his missing actor who had been found floating in the Medusa Fountain in the Aventine, Atreus asked, "Did you know Hermes well, sir?"

Petronius made a face and scrubbed his knuckles against the dark hair at his temples. "Well enough, I suppose." Then he paused for a moment and shrugged. "How well does one know a slave, Valerius?"

I thought of the conversation I'd had with Juba, about where he'd come from. Petronius was right. A household slave was a wax tablet. Unless you took the trouble to flip the boards open, you never saw what was scratched inside. And how many of us bothered?

I certainly hadn't before now.

Perhaps we were all secretly afraid that if we opened up those tablets, we'd see something written there that we didn't like.

"As much as is practicable," I said, "which is not much at all."

"One does not need to know how the broom feels about sweeping," Petronus said, "let alone ask it who bundled its twigs together in the first place."

Juba's face was as expressionless as always.

"Lucan said Hermes was clever," I said. I wasn't sure why Atreus had steered us down this path instead of asking about Marsus straight away, but I trusted his instincts. He'd had longer to hone them when it came to investigations than I had, and his were probably better to begin with anyway. I had never been accused of having the mind of a thinker. Ask anyone.

Petronius nodded. "A tongue as sharp as a blade." He let out a huff of breath that was almost a laugh, as though remembering something cutting Hermes had once said, and then grew serious again. "Gods. What a waste."

We were silent for a moment. I glanced at Atreus, and he caught my gaze, his expression sombre.

"The sun shines on all of us," Petronius said. "That's from the Satyricon, or it will be if I can ever get the fucking thing written. Do you think the gods care if a man was an emperor or a slave? I suppose they must, if they govern our lives so closely. And yet, the sun shines on all of us."

A noble sentiment, and it probably told me something important about Petronius and his moral values, but I couldn't help thinking that the slave who got up at dawn to hack away at roots and rocks as he cleared a field for planting was probably less delighted to be in the sun than the rich man being carried in a canopied litter.

Petronius shook his head. "Who would do this to Lucan?"

Juba's eyebrow twitched.

Petronius was right, though. Lucan had first been attacked by thugs the night of Petronius's dinner, and now somebody had killed his beloved Hermes and tried to set his house on fire. This wasn't about the boy. Or it was, but only in so far as Hermes was a possession of Lucan's.

"Lucan is the best of the poets, isn't he?" Atreus asked.

Petronius took a swig of wine. "Juno's tits, Atreus. You don't ask another poet that."

Atreus smiled and ducked his head.

Petronius took no real offence. Knowing what I did of the man, he was probably delighted at Atreus's lack of manners. "He will be," he said. "He's not there yet. His grasp on rhetoric is sometimes a little clumsy, but he's young. His poems will outshine mine someday very soon." His mouth quirked. "But he can't write plays for shit, so my fame there is still unthreatened."

Unthreatened.

The word caught me faster than any poetry ever had, because that was the crux of this whole matter, wasn't it?

Here we were, in a theatre that was being purpose-built for the emperor's Juvenalia, busy as a nest of ants as workers and actors and poets and playwrights all hurried to be ready in time. And for what? For the muses? Doubtful.

For *Nero.*

For Nero, and the fame and accolades—and fortune—that he could shower on his favourites.

Petronius said he wasn't threatened by Lucan, but someone else must have

111

been. This was sabotage, and it wasn't just against Lucan either.

"Your actor," I said. "Marsus. He's dead."

Petronius's jaw dropped. "What?"

"He has been for days," Atreus confirmed. "But we only just now discovered who he was."

"Fuck!" Petronius might have been a poet, but he was smart enough to know you didn't always need to use a fancy word. He screwed up his face in disbelief. "Are you sure?"

I nodded. "Yes."

Petronius huffed. "Fuck," he said again. "Well, so much for my perfect Giton." He lifted his cup to take another mouthful of wine, found it empty, and set it down with a sigh. "You didn't just come here to ask about Hermes, and it's not just Lucan who is being attacked. Unless this is all an incredible coincidence."

"I wouldn't put money on it," I said, and I'd put money on plenty of dumb things in the past. Felix, the racehorse, came to mind.

"No," he agreed unhappily. "Well then, what do you need to know about Marsus? I've written hundreds of thousands of words about him, of course. Some of them have even seen the light of day, though my critics would argue none of them should have."

"You talk of him as if he's your muse," I said. "Was he?"

"Insofar as I am Encolpius and he was the manipulative little flirt who had me wrapped around his finger," Petronius said, without a hint of shame.

"You lusted after him?" I asked.

"Of course I did," Petronius said, and laughed at what I was certain was my expression of outraged Patrician morality (and hypocrisy). "Everyone who ever set eyes on him did. He knew it too, the delightful little tease. With Marsus, the thrill was in the hunt, and not the kill." He jolted, and blanched. "A bad choice of words."

"So you never slept with him?" Atreus asked.

"No," Petronius said. "He liked to tease, and I liked to be teased. It was fun, and it inspired more than one scene with Encolpius and Giton. Besides, Marsus would never have done anything to make his boyfriend unhappy."

112

"Because the boyfriend had a temper?" Atreus asked keenly, leaning forward to catch the answer.

"No," said Petronius, looking genuinely puzzled. "Because he was madly in love with him. It drove men mad. Here they were, offering him money and fame and whatever they could think to win his favour, and yet nobody could hold a candle to his plebeian boyfriend from the Aventine."

I could tell Atreus didn't like that answer. He wanted Erastus to be as violent as his cousin Bano had been. I wondered if that was because he wanted a simple answer to Marsus's murder—a jealous boyfriend with a vicious temper—or because he was having difficulty seeing Erastus in a different light. Atreus didn't usually struggle with seeing complexities in people. Then again, from the way Leander had reacted at the excubitorium the day Atreus had 'questioned' Erastus, Atreus didn't usually torture people either.

"When did you last see Marsus?" he asked Petronius.

Petronius leaned back. "Perhaps a week ago? Maybe one and a half. He came to my house."

"Was that unusual?"

"Unusual? No. Once you open your door to an actor, you'll get an infestation in moments. They're like mice overrunning a kitchen. Anyway, he stopped by to complain about Ammenius, one of the other actors, and then left again when I said I'd deal with it."

Atreus hummed. "What was his complaint?"

"That Ammenius is such a terrible actor he'll ruin the entire play."

"And did Ammenius know that Marsus complained about him?"

"Probably," Petronius said. "Actors are always complaining about each other."

"How did you deal with the complaint?" I asked.

"How I deal with all of them," Petronius said with a shrug. "I ignored it. Listen, the Satyricon isn't even a *play*. I've rewritten a few scenes to be performed on the stage for the Juvenalia, and that's all, and Marsus was worried that Giton didn't have enough lines. And then he wanted a dance, and three different costumes. Complaining about Ammenius was just the latest of his grievances. I laid on some flattery about how he was my best actor, and how he'd turn every head in Rome—all true, by the way—and he went away as happy as a sparrow in spring."

Petronius looked and sounded like a man telling the truth, which was invariably the problem with investigating a string of murders. Everybody always looked and sounded like they were telling the truth. Nobody yet had ever said, "Oh, yes, I'm the killer!" when we asked, which certainly would have made mine and Atreus's lives much easier.

And even though Petronius appeared honest, and I liked him, I reminded myself that he was a man who had made his reputation, and his fortune, by telling stories. So had everyone in his circle.

"This isn't just about Lucan, is it?" Petronius asked. "Marsus was my best actor. There is a viper somewhere in our nest, and he has already struck at two of us."

"Who is the most jealous of all of the poets and playwrights?" I asked.

Petronius snorted. "You would do better to ask where the sky is bluest, Valerius. Every single one of them is jealous, but murder? There is such a large step between jealousy and murder that most men would never contemplate it. I can hardly imagine one of my friends has." He ran a hand over his face and let out a long breath. "Did poor Marsus suffer?"

"Yes," I said, because I knew Petronius wanted the truth. I'd seen men die of blood loss before. Even if they no longer had the senses to feel the pain, they knew they were dying. Not a single one of them had been ready to let go of his life. "It was slow."

Petronius's mouth twisted, and his eyes shone brightly for a second before he passed his hand over his face again. "He did not deserve that."

I exchanged a solemn glance with Atreus. I hated that unwarranted death was the recurring theme of our investigation so far. Because Marsus hadn't deserved his painful ending, and neither had poor Hermes.

* * *

A little brown bird hopped along the edge of the stage as Atreus and Juba and

I sat in the seats in the cavea, reminding me of how Petronius had described Marsus. Happy as a sparrow.

"The last murders we investigated weren't as grim as these," I said.

Atreus raised his eyebrows.

"There's an argument to be made that they were more important," I said, "because they were important men. But you know what else they were? Arseholes."

Juba snorted.

I sighed. "Whereas what do we have here? A slave and an actor, and nobody has so far said a word against them. They weren't the architects of their own demise. They're just collateral damage."

We'd left Petronius up in his makeshift tablinum, searching for more wine, and come back down to the front of the theatre to watch the rehearsals. Apparently Ammenius was due to practice some of his lines. The actors, just like the theatre, were all being shared for the Juvenalia, and we were about to get a sneak preview of Fabianus's play. Which, as we already knew, was Horatius at the bridge.

I wondered if Litus was watching from one of the little windows above, like a malevolent god.

I didn't like the theatre when it was properly produced; I was sure that watching a half-arsed practice of a hastily written play wouldn't change my opinion at all.

Juba had procured nuts from somewhere, and was popping them in his mouth as he watched the sparrow hop along the stage. Probably the best performance we'd see today, let's be honest.

"They were men destroyed by their greed and treason," Atreus said in that maddeningly even tone he employed when we both knew I was being unreasonable, "but we didn't know that at the time. It was only in hindsight that we knew they deserved it."

I thought of Marsus and Hermes. "Do you think we'll have a similar moment of revelation here?"

Atreus pressed his mouth into a thin line. "I somehow doubt it."

So did I. I stared glumly at the stage. The little sparrow fluttered away, and Juba's gaze followed it.

It took a while for the actors to appear. They were preceded by Fabianus, clutching a stack of papers and looking frazzled. "Marvellous," he said with what appeared to be genuine delight when he saw us sitting there. "An audience!"

Then, when his actors took the stage, he came and sat beside us.

The actors were an interesting-looking bunch. There were five of them, two women and three men. They were not in costumes or makeup, so I wondered which parts they usually played. One of the women had to be the young maiden, which meant the other was probably her harridan mother. They both looked the same age though, and similar enough to be sisters. In the natural light, and wearing their natural faces, it was impossible to tell their usual roles.

"Who is Ammenius?" I asked, and Fabianus pointed out one of the men.

Definitely the braggart soldier. He was big and burly, with a beard. He stood with his legs apart as though he was trying to remain standing on the deck of a ship in the middle of a storm, hands on his hips and his head turned so that his admirers could gaze upon his handsome profile. He also stood with his pelvis tilted forward, as though he was concerned that we might all forget he had genitalia hidden underneath his tunic, and he couldn't have that.

As far as I could tell, the practice was a disaster. The actors didn't know their lines, whoever was in charge of the costumes hadn't brought the right masks, the only musician who turned up was a boy with a single cymbal and an embarrassed expression, and Marsus had been right: Ammenius was a terrible actor. He strutted about the stage as though he was the only person on it, speaking over his fellow actors as they tried to deliver their lines, and even stepping on the toes of one of the women when she couldn't get out of his way quickly enough. He might have been perfect in the role of the puffed-up solider, but apparently nobody had told him that this was not a comedy, and that Horatius was a hero and not a braggart.

The story of Horatius was as old as Rome itself. I'd heard it hundreds of times, but this was the first time I'd hoped he'd drown.

Juba clapped politely as the scene ended with a triumphant Horatius being welcomed back, gravely injured, by the people of Rome.

I glanced at Fabianus. He had the dead-eyed stare of a man who had seen terrible things.

"It's still a few weeks until the Juvenalia," I said in what I hoped was an encouraging tone.

"Yes," he murmured, possibly calculating the costs of an urgent trip to the farthest reaches of the empire at this very moment.

I clapped him on the back and stood, making my way over to the stage. Juba and Atreus came with me. "Ammenius?"

The man himself, flushed with undeserved glory, strutted to the front of the stage and peered down at me. "Ah! Are you an admirer, sir?"

"No," I said, and gave him a moment to come to terms with that blow. "My name is Aemilius Valerius. I wanted to talk to you about Marsus."

A few of the other actors drifted closer to listen, one of the women still limping.

"What about him?" Ammenius asked.

"I heard he was jealous of you," I said, "getting all the good lines."

"That's because I'm a better actor than he is," Ammenius said. "All he has is a pretty face and Petronius by the dick." His appraising gaze took in the fine cut of my clothes and the gold ring on my hand. "Are you a patron of the arts, Aemilius Valerius?"

Translation: *How much money can I wring out of you?*

"I am not," I said, dashing his hopes on that front. "Just curious about Marsus."

His expression soured. "Take your coin to a brothel, sir. You'll get better value there."

And then he lifted his chin to show me that heroic profile, and presumably everything I was missing, and strutted away again, like a rooster through a farmyard, scattering all the other birds.

The other actors regrouped and trailed slowly after him back into the wings of the scaenae. The limping woman remained behind, her dark eyes narrow. She closed the space between us, and then sat down on the edge of the stage, letting her legs dangle over the front.

"What do you really want?" she asked me, tilting her head.

I showed her my palms. "Just asking about Marsus."

"Is he alright?" she asked. "I haven't seen him around for a while, and he's usually always here." She glanced over her shoulder. "He's the best actor in our troupe, no matter what Ammenius says."

"How long since you've seen him around?" Atreus asked.

"A week?" She shrugged. "Maybe a few days more? I'm not sure." She worried at her lower lip with her teeth. "I hope he's back before long, or Petronius might recast him."

I forced a smile and nodded.

It wouldn't be long until the actors found out the truth from Petronius, I was sure, but I was tired of being the bearer of bad news, and she didn't need to hear it from a stranger.

"How's your foot?" Juba asked, and she smiled and extended her leg towards him so he could inspect it for himself.

He shoved his paper cone of nuts at me in his haste to wrap his hands around her delicate ankle.

Fine.

But I was eating them.

Atreus and I wandered away to leave Juba to…to whatever was going on there, and retreated across the orchestra to the seats of the cavea. We climbed up a few rows and sat, the sun warming our backs.

"What do you think?" Atreus asked me after a while.

"That the theatre is overrated."

He snorted and nudged me with his shoulder.

"I think this is sabotage. I think that someone wants to be Nero's favourite, and they're prepared to kill to make it happen," I said. "They killed Lucan's slave and destroyed his tablinum, and they killed Petronius's best actor."

Atreus furrowed his brow.

I hated when he did that. It usually meant he was going to point out something I'd missed and make me feel stupid.

"Shit," I said, straightening. "They're *sharing* actors."

"They're sharing actors," Atreus agreed.

"Are they *all* using them?" I asked. "The playwrights, of course, but the poets? You wouldn't, usually, for a poem, but we already know Petronius had turned some of his prose into a play for the Juvenalia. Maybe some of the poets are doing the same."

"We need to find out who isn't," Atreus said. "We need to find a poet in the group who is reciting his own work, without giving it to the actors."

"We need to find out who's in charge of the Juvenalia," I said. "Someone has to be." And then I added, "Despite appearances."

Atreus snorted.

* * *

Antigon was a balding middle-aged palace administrator who, even if he wasn't a slave, wouldn't be being paid enough for this bullshit. He had a tiny room on the top floor of the scaenae, and from the length of time it took him to open the door when we knocked, he possibly had it barricaded against demanding playwrights, poets, and actors. When I explained that Atreus and I were none of these things, he was glad to escape the theatre with us.

We strolled through the surrounding gardens, which were beautiful despite the season.

"It's a *nightmare*," Antigon confided unhappily. "Aemilius Valerius, I helped plan the travel of the divine Claudius to Britannia *and* his triumph when he returned to Rome—do you know how many changes of wardrobe an emperor needs each day? —and it was easier than this!"

I hummed sympathetically and didn't tell him that it was probably even worse than he knew, the poor bastard. "They do seem like a handful."

"That's putting it mildly, sir," Antigon said, the corners of his mouth turning down.

"Do you have a schedule of events we could see?" Atreus asked.

Antigon studied us both for a moment, clearly deciding if we could be trusted with what I had no doubt were meticulous plans. Meticulous plans that he was probably rewriting every day, given the people he was trying to organise. But he was a palace slave—more than that, he was close enough to Nero to be put in charge of the real work of the Juvenalia. He probably knew Nero had decided I was his friend before I did.

He unhooked a wax tablet from the loop on his belt and opened it. "Here it is. So far. It will change, of course. It always changes."

"Thank you." I took the tablet and held it open for Atreus while he copied the information down. The tablet I was holding had a shiny mother-of-pearl cover. Atreus's was wooden, with the corners knocked off, and scratches and dents all over it. It looked like it had been through the wars, or at least a few late nights in the Aventine, which amounted to much the same thing. Even his stylus was bent.

Atreus asked for clarification of Antigon's shorthand more than once, translating it to his own in shallow cuts across the smooth wax surface of his tablet. His brow grew more furrowed as Antigon explained, but he didn't say anything.

He didn't have to; for once, I was following along perfectly.

I paid Antigon a sestertius for his trouble, and we watched as he strode back towards the looming theatre.

"It was a good theory," I said. "And it was worth following up, even if it didn't lead anywhere."

Atreus gave an unhappy grunt and snapped his tablet shut.

Because the only man on the list who had no need of an actor for his performance for the Juvenalia was the one man who I would swear had nothing to do with the murderous sabotage of the poets and playwrights: Lucan.

Could Lucan have murdered Marsus to ruin Petronius's play? I didn't know much about him at all, or how deep his passions were, or if any of them were strong enough to lead to killing, so possibly? But, unless I'd seen him commit the act himself, there was nothing in the world that would convince me that he'd murdered his beloved Hermes.

I clapped Atreus on the back. "Let's go and find somewhere for lunch."

He grunted again, and this time, there was fervent agreement wrapped up in that little sound.

It was probably the only win I'd get today, so I was happy to take it.

* * *

Lunch was at the wineshop I'd visited before with Atreus. It was a few blocks from his home, and the waiter was pale, skinny, and suspicious of me. I'd once asked Atreus if he was a runaway slave. Atreus was too smart to answer a question like that. The waiter gave us a private back room, looked unperturbed when Juba joined us at the table, and brought out a plain but hearty spread of bread, eggs, salted fish, and vegetables.

Juba dug in enthusiastically. "I asked Tertia about Marsus."

"Oh, your new girlfriend Tertia?"

He snorted. "I don't have the funds to have an actress girlfriend, sir. She's a sweet woman, but she's got her sights set on a callow patrician boy. She asked after you, actually."

It was my turn to snort. "What did you learn from her?"

"That Marsus was well-liked," he said. "Well, Ammenius hated him, obviously, but that was because he was jealous. Tertia said at the moment Marsus wasn't a threat to Ammenius, because he was still young enough to be put into different roles than the ones Ammenius gets, but that everyone could see the writing on the wall. And Marsus was Petronius's favourite, which gave him even more of an advantage." He broke a piece of bread in half and dipped a corner in the little dish of oil on the table. "Ammenius definitely hated him."

"Interesting that the others didn't," I said. "If they're anything like the poets and playwrights, they're a jealous bunch."

"Tertia didn't give that impression," Juba said. "Hating Ammenius is a group sport, but I think they genuinely loved Marsus. They're not like the playwrights. They're a troupe; they are hired as a group. If Marsus did well, then the whole troupe reaped the benefits. Private audiences in the houses of rich and influential men, plus the leverage to try to get more money whenever they're hired for a play in a public theatre."

"Did she say anything about Marsus's personal life?" Atreus asked.

Juba popped the bread in his mouth. "No. She knew he had a boyfriend in the Aventine but couldn't tell me his name. She said Marsus spent most of his time practicing, either at the theatre, or wherever they were working out of. She said he'd sometimes stay until after everyone else had gone home, up on the stage, saying his lines, making sure his feet were in the right place, all the things he wanted to get right."

An actor with a work ethic. And they said there was nothing new under the sun.

Juba chewed on his bread for a moment, and then said, "They're very different, aren't they? The corpses?"

"What do you mean?" I asked.

He shrugged. "Whoever killed Hermes did it suddenly, almost like he was just in their way when he was getting from Lucan's posticum to his tablinum. But Marsus's death wasn't like that. It would have taken a very long time. Do you think they wanted to look him in the eye as he died?"

A chill ran down my spine. Then, because it wasn't out of legs yet, it ran back up. "Whoever killed Marsus wanted to watch him suffer. It was personal, and it was cold. Why would one death be so cold, and the other not?"

Atreus had been listening, his chin resting in his hands. He straightened up. "Maybe Marsus was personal, but, with one death under his belt, the killer has discovered there's no moral chain holding him back from committing a second murder. He already killed Marsus, who he hated. So why not get rid of Hermes too?"

I nodded slowly, but I wasn't sold on the idea. I couldn't even say why, only that it didn't fit together as neatly as I wanted. Perhaps it was only that I thought that if I ever killed someone I hated, I'd lay low for a while afterwards, and not pivot straight to another murder. But who knew what was inside the mind of a killer?

"Or maybe Hermes wasn't supposed to be a quick death," Atreus said. "Maybe the killer intended to kill him the same way he'd killed Marsus, but Hermes struggled, and he had to stab him there to silence him."

That bleak scenario fitted much better.

I ate an olive to see if it made me feel better. It didn't, but it tasted nice enough that I ate another one anyway. "So is it sabotage against the poets and playwrights, or is it personal? Because I don't see how it can be both."

"A happy coincidence, sir?" Juba asked. "One of them likes to kill in such a manner, but also wants to undermine the others?"

"Maybe," I said, and huffed out a frustrated breath. "We're playing with the vagaries of *why* they did it, when we ought to be concentrating on *who* had the chance to do it."

Atreus nodded and flipped open his tablet. "Lucan is the only one of them who doesn't need actors for his performance."

"Of course," I said. "The others are playwrights. The only other poet is Cilnius, and of course he needs a performer, because he has a stammer."

C-C-Cilnius wouldn't be able to recite his own works on stage.

"So Cilnius wouldn't kill Marsus," Atreus said, "unless—shit." He shook his head. "Unless Marsus wasn't going to be the one who recites his poem for him. There are plenty of other actors to choose from, after all. He only needs *one*, not the entire troupe."

"Petronius needed Marsus," I said, "for his Giton, *specifically*. But what are the chances Cilnius needed him?"

Atreus ran his finger down the list he'd copied from Antigon. "It just says here that he is using an actor, not which one."

And there it was, another new path to follow in the tangled maze of this investigation. It wasn't much, and it was entirely possible it would lead to a dead-end—or, knowing our luck, the minotaur—but it was *something*. And it was more than we'd had when we'd started lunch.

The food, it turned out, was just the bonus.

* * *

After lunch I left Atreus to go back to his place and get some sleep finally, and Juba and I climbed the Caelian Hill at a leisurely pace and headed for home. There were clouds drawing in this afternoon—the night would be a dark and moonless one, let the omen be absent—but our reception at home was sunny.

"Aemilius Valerius!" Hursa exclaimed happily, as though he hadn't seen me in years instead of hours. "Octavia Junilla's cat escaped! It went straight over the garden wall!"

"That seems like bad news, Hursa, and yet you're delivering it in a way that makes me think you're absolutely delighted the cat is gone," I said as I handed him my cloak.

He gasped. "No, sir! It's not gone! I went next door and asked if I could look for it, and they said yes, and I found it. Octavia Junilla gave me a quadrans!"

That was the source of his delight then. Hursa's life was a series of such depressing misfortunes that a quadrans was a shining beacon of hope indeed.

"Well, congratulations," I said, heading through the atrium and leaving Hursa to talk Juba's ear off instead.

I passed through the house and found Octavia sitting on a bench in the garden. She had a scroll unrolled across her knees, and a long piece of grass between her fingers that she was bobbing half-heartedly for the cat. The cat took one look at me, and streaked across the garden, up a scrubby bush, and made a leap for the top of the wall. It vanished in moments. Octavia glanced up once and let the piece of grass drop to the ground. She was unbothered. Of course she was. It was a cat, and it literally did this ten times a day.

I sat down beside her. "If you're going to pay Hursa a quadrans to bring that cat back every time, you'll be bankrupt in a month."

"Oh, but he was so proud of himself, Quintus! He's campaigning as hard as a politician to be the King of Saturnalia this year and finding a hundred different jobs to do each day. I couldn't bear to tell him that the cat would be home again in time for dinner."

Something that me and the cat had in common most evenings.

"He is not going to be king," I said. I loved Saturnalia as much as the next man, but the thought of exchanging positions with Hursa for the day was too much to contemplate. Hursa couldn't even lace his own sandals without clear instructions and close supervision. If there was a way to mess up being the King of Saturnalia, and master for the day, he was sure to find it. I'd put up with a lot of silliness for the sake of the festival, but I was not going to act as a slave for the man who only last week swallowed a dupondius.

No, he couldn't explain how.

My thoughts turned to darker subjects.

"The corpse in the fountain," I said, and Octavia looked at me expectantly. "It's an actor. One of the same troupe working on the Juvenalia."

"Gods," Octavia said. "Then it all comes back to Lucan?"

"Lucan, or one of the others, or all of them." I shook my head. "At the moment we have no idea how they are connected, only that they are."

My sister gave me a look that was both wary and concerned. "I'd tell you to be safe, Quintus, but that's ridiculous advice, isn't it? There's nothing safe about hunting down a killer."

She was correct, but it was a necessary duty. Not necessarily *my* duty, but when it came to public service there weren't many other options for men of my pedigree (extensive) and experience (basically none). I had the strange fortune to have become paterfamilias young—too young to even be appointed as a quaestor. The cursus honorum, that most slippery of ladders to climb, didn't have a rung for men my age. I had to wait until I was twenty-five before I could take that first official step. Until then— since I had decided the military no longer suited me—I was functionally unemployed, but still expected to begin building a career. So here I was, investigating murders ostensibly under the supervision of the magistrate Septus Severus, but really just poking my nose into anything that interested me, with Atreus's help. And, naturally, agreeing to assist important men like Seneca when they insisted their nephew was in danger.

"Maybe when I become a quaestor I'll be sent as second-in-command to some cushy province," I said. "To make up for all this messy murder business."

"Be sure to write," Octavia said.

"Oh, you won't come and see the world with me?"

"Someone will have to stay behind and make sure Hursa doesn't burn the house down."

"That is a very good point. I suppose I'd better stay here too, then."

"I knew you'd see reason at last," she said mildly.

I elbowed her. "What are you reading?"

"Seneca, actually." She raised her eyebrows. "*Oedipus*. There's this entire section at the end of Act Four where the chorus warns against pursuing ambition."

"Sounds typically Stoic."

"It does, of course," she said, "and yet one would never accuse Seneca of having a lack of ambition, would they? I suppose all men are hypocrites to some extent." She laughed at my look. "Yes, all women too."

"This is what you and Fulvia talk about when I'm not here, isn't it? The hypocrisy of men."

"Well, not always. We also talk about how arrogant men are, thinking that everything we discuss somehow revolves around them," she said.

I was never going to best Octavia in a battle of wits. You'd think I would have learned that by now. The only way to win at all was by playing dirty.

"I'm going for a nap," I said, giving a theatrical yawn and stretch. "I think I'll just let Hursa know the cat's escaped again, and that you're offering even more reward money this time."

And then I escaped before she could stop me.

Chapter Seven

In the sort of stories that were told to growing Roman boys to make them yearn to cast aside their bullas and pick up a gladius to defend the empire, the hero never had to stop in the middle of the adventure to go to dinner with their future extended family. But that night, instead of meeting up with Atreus to track down Cilnius—I couldn't even call him a suspect yet, our reasoning in that regard rested on such shaky foundations— I was instead climbing out of a litter at Marcellus Naso's house and being welcomed inside by a polite slave.

Naso was an excellent host. He'd not only invited me and Fulvia, but also Octavia. Julia Drusilla was here too, as well as her father Silanus, but so were mad Uncle Maro and Aunt Marcia, so I hoped they'd act as a buffer between Silanus and I. And, of course Florian, Julia's happy fiancé, was here as well. As far as I could tell, despite having inherited a house on the Caelian Hill close to mine, he spent most of his time living under Naso's roof. Florian had a good heart; Naso would never admit he was lonely, but it was obvious he enjoyed his adopted heir's company and so Florian shared it generously.

It was almost a relief to dine with Naso after all the time I'd been spending lately with poets and playwrights. At least I could follow the conversations here, since they were the same ones we Roman patricians had been discussing since forever: the state of the provinces, the price of grain, and whether the Greens or the Blues were in better form at the Circus Maximus.

"Didn't you have a racehorse at one time, Valerius?" Naso asked curiously.

I picked over a dish of stuffed olives. "Just a share in one, and I don't like to call him a racehorse, since he never broke a sweat."

Naso hummed understandingly. "I owned racehorses once. Didn't breed them—I left that to the experts—but bought a few. You may as well toss all your money into the sea."

"Quintus actually made a handsome profit," Maro said proudly. "Sold his share to a fellow from Gaul who didn't know any better, and came out on top in the end. What was the horse's name again? Something unintentionally ironic, from what I recall."

"Felix," I said.

"Felix?" Naso raised his eyebrows. "Not the same Felix who just won for the Reds?"

I almost choked on an olive, and then exchanged an incredulous look with Fulvia. "No, it couldn't be. The only time my Felix got any speed up at all was when he was trying to throw his charioteer under the wheels."

Felix had been on his third charioteer by the time I'd sold my share in him. One of them had been buried on Via Appia, one of them now walked with a limp, and one of them, last I heard, was still persevering. But Felix hadn't raced for the Reds, unless they'd bought his contract. And, honestly, who would?

After dinner, Fulvia and I walked along the terraces that looked down over the river, ostensibly to chaperone Florian and Julia, who walked a little way ahead of us, but mostly because everyone else was being entertained by a poetic recital from one of Naso's slaves, and Fulvia had seen my eye twitching. I'm sure the slave was very talented, and the poem might have even been the sort I liked, packed with action and drama, but I was full to the back teeth with poetry right now.

It was a pleasant enough night, and the cold gave me an excuse to hold Fulvia's hand under our warm layers of clothing as I filled her in on everything I'd done that day. Ahead of us, illuminated by the lanterns hanging along the terrace, Florian and Julia kept a respectable distance apart.

It was strange to watch them leaning towards each other like flowers towards the sun. I had never been in love like that. I loved Fulvia, because who could not? But the only flutter in my belly I'd ever got around her had been nausea, when my father had introduced us and announced she was to be my wife. Our love wasn't built on furtive glances and stolen touches. It was built by familiarity, by practicality, and by the growing realisation on my part that public life was like a war, and there was no better woman to go into battle with than Fulvia. We had never been swooning lovers, but, Jupiter, we made a good team.

Atreus...

Well, that was everything Fulvia was not—new and undefined and complicated and unspoken. I couldn't say yet if it was anything like love, but the flutter was there.

"Are you going to see Atreus after we leave here?" Fulvia asked. Evidently, I wasn't the only one thinking of him.

I hummed. "Possibly."

"It might be a good time to try to track down this Cilnius fellow. The theatres are just getting out now, so most people are beginning to make their way home. He may be one of them."

"Or he's partaking in mad revelry in some private party anywhere in the city," I said, "and we'll never be able to find him."

She made a soft sound of agreement, and then squeezed my hand. "Also possible. Well, if you and Atreus spend all night running around the city, you must invite him for breakfast. Lucilla, too."

"Atreus gets all standoffish whenever I invite him for something," I said. "Doubly so if I include Lucilla. I'm afraid he thinks I'm trying to buy his friendship."

There was probably more truth in that than I wanted to share with my wife. Not the part where Atreus was a prickly arsehole, but the part where I'd admitted a fear regarding to him. Figure of speech or not, it cut closer to the bone than I liked.

Fulvia leaned into me. "Time works best at a stone."

It was the perfect analogy, since I was sure it would take eons to wear the sharp edges off Atreus.

Ahead of us, Florian and Julia had stopped in a dark space between two torches, so I cleared my throat loudly to keep them moving, and Fulvia hid her laugh behind her hand.

I did want to see Atreus tonight, and also try to chase down Cilnius. I honestly didn't think he was our killer—we weren't lucky enough to have the answer fall into our laps that easily, and on what evidence? The strength of him being the only man, apart from Lucan, who wasn't sabotaging his own performance by killing one of the actors? Jupiter, we didn't even know if Cilnius had been planning to use Marsus to recite his poem or not. And it was probably irrelevant. Had Marsus been truly irreplaceable to any of them except Petronius, who had been enamoured of him? For all we knew, the moment the troupe had been told of Marsus's death, they had a hundred other handsome, cheeky boys lined up to strut their way across the stage who would make more than adequate replacements. So Cilnius was probably nothing, but since we currently had less than nothing, we might as well start with him.

I hated to admit it, but a part of me was waiting for the killer to strike again, and perhaps give us something else to work with, because, at the moment, we were floundering. Which wasn't uncommon for us, sadly.

Fulvia and I gave the lovebirds a moment longer to walk together, and then ushered them back inside so that we could say our farewells and head home.

* * *

I didn't need to go into the Aventine to find Atreus, as it happened. He was waiting for me inside my triclinium when I got home, in the middle of a game of latrunculi with Cretes, my secretary. Cretes leapt to his feet the moment I wandered in, bobbing his head apologetically like an excited pigeon.

"It's fine, Cretes," I said, and, still bobbing, he backed out of the triclinium.

Atreus pushed a stool toward me with his foot. "He's a nervous one."

"He's still finding his feet," I said. I took a seat and studied Cretes's pieces for a moment. He was a decent player; I'd have to invite him to play sometime.

"He hasn't figured out how little I care what any of the slaves do as long as the house isn't falling down because of it."

Atreus slid one of his pieces into an empty square. There was a tension in his posture that he was trying his best to hide, an undercurrent of anxiety he couldn't quite suppress. "Hursa told him you wouldn't mind if I waited in here, but he didn't seem to believe it."

"Because only an idiot would believe anything Hursa said without getting the account of an independent witness." I moved one of my tokens. "There. I've won."

Atreus blinked at the board. "So you have. Well, Cretes did all the work."

There was a metaphor for Roman society in there somewhere. I'd have to alert the poets.

"Not that I'm not glad to see you, Atreus, but why the visit?" I asked curiously. There was something going on with him, and the fact he hadn't told me immediately made me wonder exactly how bad it was going to be.

Atreus turned a latrunculin piece over in his hand. "We've been invited to a party."

That wasn't what I'd expected. "What?"

"There's a party at the imperial palace tonight," Atreus said. "And we've been invited."

"When did all this happen?"

"A messenger came to the excubitorium this evening," Atreus said, and for the first time since he'd dropped the news, his calm expression shifted into one of hopeless uncertainty. "The emperor...Shit, Valerius, the emperor wants to meet *me*."

I took a moment to digest the news, and to wonder why this was the first thing I was hearing about a party at the palace. It was one mystery that was easy to solve.

"Hursa!" I called, and the man himself scuttled through the door like a dishevelled fieldmouse, nose twitching.

"Yes, sir?"

"Did you take any messages for me while I was out at dinner tonight?"

Hursa scratched his cheek for a moment, and then said, "Ooooh!"

Of course, an invitation had been left at my door as well. Of course, Hursa had forgotten about it until I asked. And, of course, Atreus, although he was trying his best to pretend he wasn't nervous as a pigeon in a room full of augurs, had come rushing to my house because he had nothing fit to wear for the occasion.

"It'll be fine," I told him as we were jostled together in a litter on the way to the Imperial Palace. "It's Nero, and it's a *party*. It'll be full of artists, and musicians, and acrobats, and prostitutes, and whoever else he decided to sweep out of the gutter tonight to make it more fun. No offence."

Atreus fixed me with a stare. "None taken, until you pointed it out."

"Sorry." I cleared my throat. "Anyway, it's not going to be a stuffy state banquet, is what I'm saying. Everyone will be wild and drunk, and you'll hate it, but it'll be fine."

He furrowed his brow. "Do you think I don't like fun?"

"No, of course not," I said. "I'm sure your face always does that when you're looking forward to something."

His face kept doing the thing it was doing.

I leaned forward and put a hand on his knee and squeezed. "It'll be fine, I promise. You're more polite than I am, and much smarter. You won't mess this up."

He nodded, and then let out a long breath. He put his hand over mine. "Thank you."

The gratitude in his voice reminded me how very far apart our worlds were. Meeting the emperor was hardly a daily occurrence for me, but neither was it totally unfathomable as it clearly was for Atreus.

Nero's party was held in a series of pavilions close to the Domus Tiberiana on the northwest corner of the Palatine Hill, amid a cluster of grand buildings that stretched from the palace towards the Forum. The buildings were linked together by colonnaded paths illuminated by torchlight. Statues of the gods stood in the spaces between the columns, their stares imperious. A slave met us and led us down a series of pathways. We passed the earthworks where Nero was building his cryptoporticus and were eventually deposited at the edges of a grand peristyle that was surrounded on all sides by expansive

132

arcades. The peristyle was large enough that the garden inside seemed as vast as a forest, and it was certainly inhabited by plenty of wood nymphs.

I had been right to promise Atreus this wasn't a formal occasion.

In fact, it was so informal it was delightfully indecent.

A girl wearing little more than a slip of sheer fabric gave us a smile as she darted across the path in front of us, and then she vanished between two boxwoods that had been grown into rounded shapes. A musician, dressed in a short chiton, darted after the girl, his lyre tucked under his arm. It ought to have been too cold for their kind of nakedness, but there were enough braziers around the peristyle—and enough of a crowd—that the chill night air barely touched us.

Unlike the paths that had brought us here, the garden in the peristyle had no straight lines. It had been designed to mimic nature rather than impose order upon it. Each bend of a path brought a new delight—a burbling spring, a stone grotto, or a secluded grove. Or, not so secluded given the number of people trampling through the place.

The party was *wild*. All the usuals from the Milvian Bridge looked to be here—the actors, the acrobats, and even the fire-juggler—and there were enough togas mixed in that I didn't feel overdressed in mine. The crowd was a mix of patricians, plebeians, performers, and prostitutes, and everyone looked to be having a great time. Nero certainly knew how to throw a party.

The man himself was in the middle of the peristyle, or, given the number of twists and turns our path had taken in getting there, what I could only assume was the middle. He was reclining on a large couch that was itself on a dais. Attractive young men and women wearing very little sat on the steps of the dais, smiling and chattering, like a flock of bright little birds gathered around a feeder. At the corners of the ornate couch, large bronze tripods held burning coals; the legs of the tripods were narrow statues of Pan, complete with hooves, horns, and other appendages erect enough to hang cloaks on.

Nero was flushed with wine and happiness, his smile broadening as Atreus, and I approached. He sat up.

"Valerius!" he called and gestured to me. Naked backsides squeaked against marble as the nymphs made space for us to climb the steps of the dais. "My friend! You made it! It was such late notice, I thought you might not."

A gaggle of musicians paraded past, dropping notes in the air behind them. I climbed the steps with Atreus at my side. "Thank you for inviting me."

"Sit," Nero said, patting a space on the couch beside him. "Both of you, sit." He looked around. "Petro was here a moment ago, but now he's vanished again. And Lucan didn't come."

That fit. Two very different men with two very different ways of grieving. Lucan was probably at home, sitting in the darkness and grappling with his loss. Petronius was at a party attempting to drown his in music and wine. I'd been there.

I sat, and Atreus sat next to me.

"And you are Junius Atreus!" Nero said, peering around me to get a look at Atreus.

"Yes, sir," Atreus said, and ducked his head respectfully.

"Petro says that you are interesting, and I must meet you," Nero said. "So consider us met!"

"Yes, sir," Atreus said, natural conversationalist that he was.

Fortunately, a youth climbed the steps with a tray of wine, saving him from having to say anything else.

"I've been asking about you, Valerius," Nero told me, his eyes bright. "You are a hero of Corbulo's Parthian campaign! You saved the general's life. Tell me about that."

And this was exactly what I'd hated when I first got back to Rome, but it wasn't as though I could refuse the emperor. Also, unlike most of the senators and patricians who'd wanted me to tell the story so that they could then interject with their own tales of military heroism in their youth, Nero hadn't spent any time in the army. It was rumoured to be something of a sore spot for him, because it was something every one of his critics could easily bring up, and often did. But so what if he'd never led a legion or two? That's what he had Corbulo for.

Nero didn't care when I told my story almost honestly—including the part where I'd tripped over the ropes of Corbulo's tent while chasing the Parthian spy who'd tried to kill him, and getting a face full of what I'd told everyone was mud but was actually horse shit.

"So it was luck that you saw the man to begin with?" he asked.

"Pure luck," I said. "The only reason I left my tent in the first place was because I needed to piss. If I'd drunk one less cup of wine before bed, Corbulo's wife might be a widow today."

It wasn't the whole truth. The whole truth would go to my grave with me.

"Who the fuck is this?" I'd demanded as I'd followed the man into Corbulo's tent, only to realise it wasn't some middle-of-the-night assignation at all, but an assassination attempt. And the reason there had been no guards at Corbulo's tent that night, or slaves inside, was because he had been expecting me. I wouldn't be a hero if that story came out. Corbulo's reputation wouldn't remain unscathed either, because one did not defile another Roman citizen, let alone a patrician, in that manner. No matter how nicely he asked.

Nero laughed loudly at the tale of my clumsy luck; fortunately, I had plenty more, and I was glad to share them. A few of the nymphs on the steps even shifted closer to listen. Petronius turned up at last, his toga trailing in a long, heavy train behind him. He ended up discarding it on the steps and staggering the rest of the way in just his tunic.

"Valerius!" he exclaimed, and then collapsed onto the couch on Nero's other side. "You made it!"

And then he began to snore.

Nero waved for some more passers-by to come up and join him, and soon Atreus and I had been pushed to the far edge of the couch. From then, it was easy enough to drop off the edge and make our way back down the steps. We found another nymph with a tray of wine and then one with oysters and cheese.

Someone clapped me on the back and greeted me by name. I'd drunk enough wine that I couldn't place him, but I smiled and said how glad I was to see him, and we chatted for a moment like old friends before his actual friends dragged him away again.

A man with a drum marched through the crowd, exhorting people to dance.

I followed the nymph with the wine.

"I haven't seen Cilnius," Atreus said as we squeezed through a knot of toga-clad senators.

"I haven't seen any of them except Petronius."

The nymph, a pretty youth with golden curls, smiled at me as I helped myself to another cup of wine and then gave Atreus a blatant up-and-down look.

"Don't even think about it," I said.

Atreus looked startled. "What?"

I pointed at the nymph. "I was talking to him."

Atreus caught me by the elbow and led me away. "You're drunk."

We had somehow reached the edge of the peristyle, close to the arched entrance to one of the arcades. Atreus pulled me down into the arcade. It was colder and darker in here, but still full of people streaming in and out of the peristyle.

A familiar face, glittering with cosmetics, caught my eye.

"Otho!" I called, and the man stopped just as he had almost passed up.

"Ah!" he exclaimed. "Valerius! I wanted to speak with you!"

His clever wife Poppaea Sabina was on his arm. She was wearing a shimmering yellow chiton. A snake made of gold with emerald eyes curled around her left upper arm. Several others poked out of her elaborate curls. In a garden full of nymphs, she was a Gorgon—and she looked appropriately stunning.

Otho ushered us into a shadowed alcove off the main gallery. We shared it with a statue of Tiberius.

"I heard about Lucan's slave," he said, "and Marsus, too! Is it true that someone is trying to ruin the Juvenalia?"

"More specifically, to ruin Nero's gifts," Poppaea said.

"It's a theory we're working on," I said, proud of myself for not sounding as drunk as I was. Well, I hoped. But no, Atreus wasn't looking censorious, so I figured I was doing a decent job of sounding at least partly sober and responsible.

"But ours is the only gift that's truly irreplaceable," Poppaea said, and threw me an imploring look. "There are thousands of actors in the city, but where would we ever find another girl like Iris?"

Iris, who looked like Agrippina, Nero's mother.

"We aren't holding any gift in reserve," Otho fretted. "If something happens to the girl, it'll ruin us."

Not as much as it would ruin Iris, but in a conversation centred entirely around the girl, somehow it wasn't about her at all.

"It's all very troubling," I said, honeying my voice with sympathy, "but I'm sure everything will be cleared up very soon, and the Juvenalia will be a success, and that your gift to the emperor will be the talk of all Rome."

For someone who'd once thought himself unsuited to politics and public works, I certainly had a firm grasp of how to say a lot of reassuring words without committing to any related actions. The wine helped, but I suspected my ability to bullshit at a senatorial level was mostly hereditary.

Otho looked mildly relieved at my meaningless reassurance, but Poppaea, who seemed smarter, pursed her mouth.

"Keep the girl secure," Atreus said. "And don't let your slaves open the door to uninvited guests in the middle of the night."

"Of course we're keeping her secure," Poppaea said. "We're not fools. But this whole situation is very unsettling."

I hummed. "It is."

Her glance was as sharp as her fashion sense. "You will find the killer, won't you, Valerius?"

There wasn't a way to weasel out of a direct question like that, which meant I could only do one thing: lie. "Of course," I said. "Without a doubt." And then I pretended to spot someone I knew over their shoulders and stepped away from them. "Oh! Excuse me, please."

"Dinner!" Otho called after me. "Tomorrow night. Both of you!"

And I darted away—fine, I lurched—letting myself be caught up in the stream of people flowing back into the garden. I didn't check to see that Atreus was behind me; I trusted that he was as I lost myself again in the little maze of groves and grottos. The crowd thinned at one of the darker, quieter sections, and a hand on my elbow drew me into a shadowed nook beside a statue of Leda and the swan.

"You're drunk," Atreus said again, and then, as though to prove I wasn't the only one, he kissed me.

I closed my eyes to savour the moment, but it was already ending.

Atreus's stubble scraped against mine, and his breath was warm against my mouth. "That was foolish."

"What was?" I blinked at him. "You, or me, or what?"

"You, running off like that," he said, "when there's a killer who knows you're looking for him."

"We're in a crowd," I said, my heart thumping because, Jupiter, we were in a *crowd,* and he'd kissed me. The darkness of this part of the peristyle offered some protection, and Leda and the swan offered a little more, but what if someone had walked past at that moment, and recognised me? The wine had made me reckless and stupid, although I'd never needed much of a push to get there, but Atreus was usually a lot smarter than me. "A killer isn't going to murder me in the middle of a crowd."

But Atreus just kissed me in one.

"How many times has someone bumped up against you tonight?" he asked, his brows drawn together. "What if one of those men had a knife under their toga?"

I leaned against Leda's plinth. "In fairness, most of the people bumping up against me aren't wearing enough clothes to hide what they had for breakfast, let alone a weapon. Besides, stop pretending you're annoyed with me when you're the one who's taking unnecessary risks."

His gaze dropped to my mouth, so I knew I'd made my point. But then, because he couldn't let me win, he said, "I'm not the one who tried to start a fight with a nymph for no reason."

"He knows what he did," I said, "and so do you, so shut up."

He leaned against the plinth with me and folded his arms over his chest. He wore his borrowed toga well. He let out a sigh. "You're right."

"I'll mark this day as an auspicious one in my calendar," I said, and then added, "About what?"

He turned his head to look at me. "About taking an unnecessary risk. I shouldn't have."

"Probably not," I said. "But I'm not complaining."

His mouth quirked.

We leaned there for a while longer in the darkness. Atreus was probably planning our next move in our attempt to find our killer; I was wondering if we could go straight to his place after this and kiss again. I vowed that the next kiss wouldn't be over before I even realised it was happening. I'd commit every detail to memory before it was done.

But there must have been a nascent spark of public duty flickering somewhere very deep inside me, because I knew we wouldn't do that. We'd end up traipsing around the city for hours instead, because that was Atreus's job, and he took his duty seriously. I couldn't even hold it against him. Not when I thought of Marsus and of Hermes.

"We'll get him," Atreus said, reading my expression.

I nodded, not because I believed he was right, but because I wanted it to be true. "Is it Cilnius we're after, though? Because of the fact he's using an actor, but not Marsus... well, it's not a lot, is it? I'm sure there's a philosophical term for the exact logical hole we've fallen into here. Some old Greek with a taste for hemlock has probably based a whole school around it."

"It's not a lot," Atreus agreed. "And it may even be nothing at all, but we have to follow it up, just in case."

I nodded again, glumly, even though I felt like we'd have just as much luck watching a bunch of chickens scrabbling for grain and asking an augur to read the omens. "Maybe I was an idiot when I agreed with Severus to work with you. I assumed there would be much less walking involved, and a lot more evaluating the evidence."

"It's all walking, I'm afraid." Atreus was kind enough not to point out that critical thinking wasn't exactly one of my strengths either. "And sometimes fighting."

"Not with nymphs, though."

He smiled at that. "Not usually, no."

I drew a deep breath and pushed myself off the plinth. "Very well. Let's get back out into the crowd and see if we can spot any familiar faces. Cilnius's, if the gods favour us."

The gods did not, the fickle bastards.

Apart from Petronius, and Otho and Poppaea, we didn't see any of the poets and playwrights. Perhaps Nero hadn't invited them, or, more likely, we just kept missing them in the crowd. The problem was that none of the partygoers was standing still and waiting to be spotted—everyone was moving and dancing and carousing, and the night would have been a lot more enjoyable if I was doing the same.

I caught sight of hundreds of faces flushed with wine and happiness, but none that I knew. I saw the same faces more than once, as though we were planets in alignment, following the same fixed path around the Earth. As the night wore on, those planetary spheres began to wobble more and more off course. A man in a toga took a tumble into a bush right beside us and was laughingly helped to his feet by a couple of musicians. A woman screeched at his predicament. She was as loud and discordant as a parrot.

On our fourth or fifth circuit of the paths, Atreus finally shook his head. "This is getting us nowhere."

A clash of cymbals nearby underscored his point dramatically.

I was more than ready to leave, so I nodded my agreement, and we headed for the entrance to the nearest arcade. It was possibly the same one we'd come down to get here, but I wouldn't have put money on that bet. Atreus seemed to have a better sense of direction than me, because it wasn't long until we found ourselves heading down a wide set of steps that I definitely remembered from the way here. We were almost at the street, and torchlight led us the rest of the way.

A pair of Praetorians stood at the wide gates, watching the people still arriving, and those of us giving up and going home early.

There was a crowd out on the street; litter bearers and attendant slaves who were waiting for their masters and mistresses to emerge from the party. It was colder out here, and most of them were rugged up against the chill as they talked, or snacked, or played dice.

My litter bearers must have been somewhere along the street, and they were obviously paying attention because we didn't have to wait long until they appeared. I climbed into the litter first and waited for Atreus to get in too.

He didn't, and so I stuck my head outside. "Atreus?"

He had one hand on the side of the litter, body angled towards the door, but his gaze was fixed a little further down the street, where two men in togas were hurrying towards the palace gates.

Brash, bold Entellus, and his usual shadow Cilnius.

I clambered out of the litter. "It's Cilnius."

I silently apologised to the gods for calling them fickle bastards, and straightened the folds of my toga as Atreus and I strode forward to intercept the two men.

"Entellus!" I called. "Cilnius!"

I honestly didn't think that Cilnius was our killer—or at least that he was only as likely to be the killer as any of the other poets and playwrights—but he was apparently determined to prove me wrong, because the little rat took one look at us and *ran*.

Ran, with no consideration for my feet, which were already sore, or my stomach, which was full to the brim with wine.

Entellus gaped, his jaw on the ground, as Atreus and I ran after Cilnius.

My litter bearers, showing the sort of initiative that I would compensate them well for once this was over, joined the pursuit, making six of us, and one of him. Litter bearers were built more for strength than for speed, though, and could apparently easily be outpaced by a wiry little playwright with a guilty conscience. So, unfortunately, could patricians.

Even Atreus gave up by the time we reached the bottom of the hill and the Forum.

Even at night, the Forum wasn't empty. The grand marble edifices appeared almost ghostly in the moonlight. At the Temple of Castor and Pollux, where Atreus finally gave up the chase, the columns seemed to stretch high into the heavens themselves. A woman and her client peered at us suspiciously before moving further into the shadows behind the columns. A couple of drunks looking for trouble took one glace at my litter bearers and veered away to look elsewhere. A dog skittered hopefully towards us, half cowering, tail wagging, and then bolted when someone whistled for it.

"Lost him," Atreus said, his hands on his knees as he caught his breath. "I thought he came this way, but there's no sign of him now."

The Forum was full of shadows, and about a thousand different places a man could slip out of sight if he wanted. Cilnius was probably watching us, waiting until the coast was clear before he dared show himself again.

I hated the sting of failure I felt, but at the same time, I tried to rationalise it. At least we knew now that our suspicions of Cilnius weren't based on nothing, right? A guilty man didn't run when an apparent friend called his name. We'd spooked him, and I could only think of one reason for that: Cilnius was our killer. And we may have lost him for now, but this was the start of the chase, not the end. We'd find him again. Every man in the vigiles and the urban cohorts would be looking for him by tomorrow once Atreus put the word out.

Because one thing I knew for sure about Atreus was that he hated to lose.

* * *

I sent my litter bearers home, and then went into the Aventine with Atreus. The Forum hadn't been empty at midnight, and neither was the Aventine. Men with jobs and families to support might have been tucked up in bed, but the drunks and the wastrels—the Aventine had no shortage of them—were still out and about. More than one thermopolium was still open too, and Atreus and I pulled a couple of stools up to the counter of one and ordered the baked cheese and lentils.

After we ate, we went back to Atreus's apartment. It was late for me, but early for Atreus, so we went out onto the balcony with a cup of wine each and a lamp, and discussed where we were with this investigation.

Where we were was still largely in the dark, but we were both certain Cilnius could tell us everything we needed to know.

The night felt quiet and peaceful after Nero's party. Well, if you could ignore the woman down in the street yelling emphatically at her boyfriend to fuck off, and both Atreus and I could.

There was a little wooden box on the table between our chairs, battered around the edges and with a busted hinge that meant it no longer shut all the way. I picked it up; everything inside rattled, and the corner of Atreus's mouth quirked in a smile. The hinge made an unhappy sound as I opened the lid. I tipped the contents into my palm. Six pebbles and a piece of chalk.

Atreus picked up my wine cup, giving me room to sketch out the rough board on the table. He shifted his long legs off the balcony, planting his bare feet on the floor. He turned his chair so that it faced mine. I slid the lighter-coloured pebbles over to him, leaving me with the darker ones. We set our pieces quickly, both of us having played often enough that we didn't have to think too much about it. Terni lapilli was no latrunculi, but with just a bit of chalk and a handful of pebbles, you could play it at any wine shop, street corner, or even a random vigile's balcony.

Well, perhaps not so random.

I watched the tendons in the back of Atreus's hand move as he placed his pebbles. Watched the way the golden light from the lamp caught on the fine hairs on his arm. Watched the faint smile he was still wearing, and the shadows under his eyes as dark as bruises because he never got enough sleep.

"After we catch Cilnius and are rewarded handsomely by the emperor, I'm going to go on holiday," I announced, just to see how he'd react.

"Hmm." He moved one of his pebbles. "On holiday from your exhausting job of doing whatever you feel like?"

"It's harder than it looks," I said, and his mouth twitched. "I have a villa just outside of Baiae, did you know?"

"Of course you do."

"Of course I do," I agreed. "We should go."

He looked up from the board. "Are you serious?"

"Well, not now," I said. "And probably not in the winter. But in summer. We could."

"Could we?" he asked warily.

"You do get time off, don't you? You must. You're acting centurion for a man who's been on leave the whole time I've known you."

"I do," he said evenly.

"Then it's settled," I said, although, of course, it wasn't. I had the feeling this was going to be one of those times when Atreus decided I was throwing money in his face and trying to buy him. I considered telling him how much Lucilla might enjoy the seaside, but there was no safe way of mentioning that without him assuming I was being manipulative. Which I was, but for altruistic reasons. But Atreus wouldn't appreciate that my motives were good. "We'll go in summer."

"Hmm," he said, which was his way of sounding as though he agreed with me, when really he was just tucking his opinion away for a later argument.

But that was fine. There was a sort of optimism in that. Murder? Bloodshed? The unavoidable dark underside of the city we lived in? And here Atreus and I were, setting things aside for a later we were both sure we had.

I could live with that.

Chapter Eight

The caupona on the corner across from the excubitorium did a good breakfast. Juba was already eating his when Atreus and I arrived.

"Juba, what are you doing here? Have you developed powers of the Oracle of Delphi?"

"Possibly, sir," he said. "Or you're just very easy to predict."

He had a point. Where else would I be, except with Atreus, and where else would Atreus be except here?

We'd been up with the dawn, giving Atreus time to check in with Lucilla at the neighbour's place before negotiating what sounded like a terse agreement that the woman continue to watch her until he sent Leander to collect her later.

"Her husband's back," he'd told me as we walked to the excubitorium. "Whenever he dries out and comes home, he fills her with promises that this time he'll support her, and she doesn't need to watch someone else's kid for money. But in a couple of weeks, he'll fall into an amphora again, and be gone again for a while."

"Lucilla is always welcome at my house," I'd replied, but the worried look he gave me made me wonder if he thought I was just as unreliable as that drunk husband, or perhaps our friendship was.

I joined Juba at the counter.

"Ledo says Cilnius got away from you last night," he said.

"Are you insinuating I should have taken you with us last night, and it never would have happened?" The thought had crossed my mind too.

Juba gave me a look that would have crushed the spirit of a lesser man than me. "I would never presume to question your decisions, sir."

"And yet I sense that's exactly where this conversation is going," I said, craning my neck to see what was on offer from the dolia set into the counter.

Juba gave me a flat stare. "I am your bodyguard, sir. And it is much easier to guard your body if it's in my general vicinity."

"Point taken," I said, and meant it. "But I did have Atreus with me, so I wasn't being entirely reckless."

Juba didn't look impressed, because, unlike him, Atreus couldn't give Hercules a run for his money in a street brawl. I also suspected he was unimpressed because it went against all his best interests to be advocating for his position as my bodyguard. He deserved better, and we both knew it. It was his own fault for being so good at the job.

"I need to check in on my men and put the word out that we're looking for Cilnius," Atreus said, nodding towards the excubitorium.

"Then what?" I asked.

"Then I want to talk to the poets and the playwrights," he said, his expression hardening, "and find out which one of them can tell us where Cilnius is."

His tone made it clear that the poets and playwrights would not enjoy their talk in the least. So much for my burgeoning friendships, if Atreus was going to stick his plebeian nose in and shock them all with a magnificent show of his bad attitude. But Cilnius was probably a murderer, so fuck propriety. It wasn't as though they wouldn't survive a dose of Atreus, even at his most prickly.

"I'll come with you," I said. "And of course Juba will too."

Juba didn't smile—Juba rarely did—but his mouth quirked in a barely-there movement that still managed to convey his immense sense of smug satisfaction.

Atreus went and spoke with his men, and then we set out across the city for Nero's theatre, which was the one place we could be almost certain the poets and playwrights would attend at some point in the day. It was too early for them when we arrived, so Atreus and I sat in the third row of the cavea and watched the builders scurrying around the scaenae frons. It was impossible for my untrained eye to tell if they were doing any actual work or just trying their best to give that impression in case anyone looked in on them.

There was no sign of the actors either, and after a while I grew bored of sitting there staring at an empty stage, so I crossed the orchestra, climbed the stairs to the stage, and headed to the back of the scaenae frons. I went upstairs, and the same boy in the same grotesque mask accosted me as the first time I'd been here, and the same woman chided him in the same tired tone: "Nonus!"

"Hello there," I said to the grinning satyr. I took a bronze quadrans out of my purse and held it out. "Have you seen Cilnius, the poet, here today?"

My attempt to bribe the child was pointless. Even if he'd known who Cilnius was, he probably couldn't see a damn thing when he was wearing that mask. But I'd caught the attention of the woman, who was sitting on a stool stitching red wool to the head of the slave's mask.

"Did you say Cilnius?" she asked, straightening up. "Which one's that?"

"The one with the stutter."

The woman snorted. "Oh, yes. The poet with a stutter. Ridiculous, isn't it?"

I stepped inside the room properly, while Nonus tore off down the narrow passageway to presumably frighten anyone else he could find. The room was small but well lit. Masks hung on hooks on the wall, and bundles of fabric—costumes, perhaps—were stacked along the floor underneath them.

"I'm Valerius," I said. "I'm a friend of Petro's."

"Fabia," she said, stabbing the mask with her needle. "And I already know who you are."

"Do you?" I heard footsteps in the passageway, and I glanced around to see Juba move past the door. I hoped he and Atreus were discreet enough not to lurk in the doorway, and instead stand a little distance away and eavesdrop politely.

Fabia flashed me a quick grin that revealed a missing tooth. Despite it, she was pretty. I especially liked the cheeky gleam in her eye. "Ammenius was telling everyone he had a new patron."

It was my turn to snort.

"Ammenius is thick as pig shit." The gleam in her eye faded as her expression grew serious. "Everyone else knows that you're here because Marsus was murdered."

I sat down on the empty stool across from her. "Did you know Marsus well?"

"I've been with the company for the past five years," she said. "I know all of them well. Some of them better than I'd like, if you catch my drift."

I wondered if we were talking about Ammenius again. But before I could ask, Fabia continued.

"Marsus was a sweetheart," she said. "You wouldn't think it, to look at him. He was beautiful, and popular and confident and had so much talent on the stage it was like Melpomene herself had birthed him." She sniffed, and her voice wavered when she spoke again. "You'd expect someone like that to be an arsehole, except he wasn't. He was very kind."

"I heard Ammenius didn't like him," I said.

"Ammenius doesn't like anyone more talented than he is," Fabia said, and rolled her eyes. "Which is *everyone*."

"I don't think anyone else has called Marsus kind yet," I said.

Fabia stabbed the mask again, threading another strand of red into its scalp. "That's because no other arsehole in this place gives a damn about kindness. They're blind to it because it doesn't get them anything. But Marsus wasn't like them. Last year when Nonus was sick, I couldn't afford a doctor, and he gave me the money. I was going to pay him back, but he told me not to. Told me that he could afford it. It wasn't much, but it was more than I could pay at the time." She shook her head. "None of the rest of them thought to offer."

I thought of Marsus, and of Hermes, and how I much preferred it when I was investigating the murders of men I didn't like. "He sounds as though he was a good man."

"He was, and I hope you find the man who killed him." She ran her fingers through the tangle of red hair on the mask's head, and then asked, "So why are you looking for Cilnius?"

"He might have some information that can help us," I said, and her dubious look told me that she didn't believe that bullshit for a moment. "What do you know about him?"

"He's quiet," she said at last. "Well, you would be, wouldn't you, with the way he talks?" She shrugged. "I don't know him much."

"Do you know which of the actors was going to recite his poem for the Juvenalia?"

She shrugged. "No. But I'm always the last to know. I only have to provide the costumes. It's not as though I need any forewarning for that, is it?"

Her sarcastic tone could have curdled milk.

She furrowed her brow. "I think Tertia slept with him a few months ago, and said he lived with one of the others? Entellus? As soon as she realised he was penniless, she moved on to better prospects. She's screwing some senator now, and good for her."

"Good for her," I echoed. "Did she mention anything about Cilnius to you?"

Fabia snorted and bit off a piece of wool. "Just that if his spine was as hard as his dick, she might have given him a second chance."

That seemed like the sort of brutally honest assessment I'd always suspected women gave about men, and the reason men were trained as soldiers and women were not. Women were born knowing how to go straight for the throat.

"She thinks he was a coward? Do you know why?"

"No idea," Fabia said, tugging lengths of wool through her fingers. "We just laughed about it and went on to talk about something else. I got the impression it wasn't any one thing, just that he was, you know, weak. It's always some drama with Tertia and her men. She wouldn't know what to do with herself if she ever found a decent man." She raised her eyebrows contemplatively. "Not that there's much chance of that, I suppose."

I hummed at her bleak pragmatism because I felt that if I said anything aloud, I would only incriminate myself along with the rest of mankind. "Do you know where Entellus lives?"

If Cilnius was sharing a place with him, then we needed to go there.

"No," she said.

I reached into my purse and drew out a sestertius. I handed it to her.

"Still no," she said as she took it. "And Tertia won't be here until at least noon, probably." She chewed on her lower lip for a moment. "But Antigon might know."

"Thank you," I said, and stood.

I left her to her masks, sidestepped her hellion son in the passageway, and joined Atreus and Juba to go and hunt down Antigon.

* * *

Antigon informed us that Entellus lived in an apartment in a decent neighbourhood on the Quirinal Hill. Entellus's neighbours must have been solid middle-rankers carving out comfortable lives in a neighbourhood bustling with honest industry. The doors in the courtyard of the insula were spaced a good distance apart, hinting at the decent size of the apartments inside, and Entellus lived on the second floor. A slave woman, middle-aged and neatly dressed, opened the door for us and showed us through to a sitting room to wait for her master.

It was all very respectable.

I'd never heard of anything Entellus had written being famous, but someone in the family was doing very well if he was able to live like this.

The man himself appeared shortly afterwards, wearing a rumpled tunic, bags under his eyes, and the aroma of last night's wine.

"I'm so sorry," he said. "I was asleep still." He sank down onto a couch. "What's going on?"

"Have you seen Cilnius since last night?" I asked.

"No! We were going to the party, and he just ran off!" Entellus shook his head, and then winced as it must have rattled his tender brain. "Ow. Well, you saw what happened. What was it about?"

"We were hoping you could tell us, sir," Atreus said.

Entellus scoffed. "I have no idea. He rents a room from me. Idolises me a little too much, if I'm honest with you, but I don't know him very well. He's not exactly talkative." And then he laughed, the sound hoarse, as though he suddenly remembered why. "Anyway, he didn't come home last night, so I have no idea where he's got to. What did you want to talk to him for anyway?"

"About Marsus, mostly," I said.

Entellus's face twisted, and then he laughed again. "About *Marsus*?"

I nodded.

"As in, he had something to do with all that? Jupiter, sorry, but the thought of Cilnius as some kind of mad killer?" Entellus made claws out of his fingers, and growled, and then laughed again. "No, that's ridiculous. He's timid as a dormouse."

I exchanged a look with Atreus.

"This is a nice place," I said.

Entellus's bleary gaze followed the progress of mine around the room. "My father does something with grain and shipping contracts." He waved his hand. "He is adjutor to the prefect."

That pricked my interest. A boring job, from the way Entellus was so dismissive of it, but certainly a powerful one. The prefect and his adjutor were equites responsible for the delivery, storage and distribution of grain within Rome. No wonder the adjutor could afford to buy his son his own apartment in a very nice neighbourhood, and to bankroll his lifestyle while he wrote plays and poems.

"With a father in a job like that, I'm surprised you need to sublet a room," I said.

Entellus leaned back, as though he was in danger of falling asleep again at any moment. "I didn't do it for the money. I thought it would feed the muses to be in company with other writers, that's all."

"And has it?" I asked.

His mouth turned down at the corners. "I mean, it might have, if I'd picked anyone other than Cilnius. He's very boring."

"I don't know much about plays," Atreus said. "You said that Cilnius idolises you. Are you a better writer?"

"Oh, much better," Entellus said, without a hint of false modesty. "Next year I'm going to put on a play at the Theatre of Pompey. My father has agreed to pay for it."

"It's good that he's so supportive," I said.

"Oh, he isn't." Entellus gave a snort of laughter. "He thinks I need to get it out of my system, and this is the quickest way to do it. Wait until he finds out how much it'll cost him! It'll be like the luna marble argument all over again." He caught my curious look. "I wanted to be a sculptor at one time, which my father said was fine for a hobby, but not a *job*. I didn't talk to him for *months* until he paid for the luna marble. He wanted me to work in terracotta, can you believe, until I could prove that I was serious." He rolled his eyes as though the suggestion was a personal insult.

Perhaps it was, and perhaps it wasn't. Maybe Entellus's father was an unreasonable bastard who enjoyed depriving his son of the things he needed. But more likely Entellus was a spoiled brat with a new and expensive idea for an artistic career every month, and Papa was getting tired of paying for it. He'd probably thought he'd got away lightly with the playwright thing, but Entellus was right—the bill for the Theatre of Pompey was going to be a shock.

I would have bet any money that Papa had a couple of blocks of luna marble stashed somewhere that he was going to have to sell at some point because Entellus had already moved on to the next shiny idea that had caught his attention.

It was certainly becoming clearer why he lived in this apartment, instead of at home. His father was taking practical measures to prevent filicide.

The slave woman brought in wine and bread and olives, and Entellus brightened as he was given the chance to feed his hangover.

"So you went to the party last night without Cilnius?" I asked.

He nodded, and then said around a mouthful of bread, "I wasn't going to let his strange behaviour spoil the night for me. Nero throws wonderful parties."

That was certainly true.

"Did you stay at the party long?"

"It was dawn by the time I got home," Entellus said. He squinted at us. "Is it still morning?"

Atreus ignored the question, and asked, "Can we see Cilnius's room?"

It was an unusual request, and probably an impolite one, but Entellus was unbothered by it. He shrugged, and then rose unsteadily to his feet, grabbing another piece of bread on his way. "It's through here."

We passed the slave woman on the way, and she gave us all wary looks.

Cilnius had a modestly sized room, with windows set high in the wall. The scent of something warm and savoury haunted this part of the apartment; there must have been a shop right underneath the window that sold pastries and pies. The frescoes on the wall were bright and new, but blandly pastoral. Birds and fields and animals, as though the artist had been trying to evoke a world miles away from the busy city just outside.

Cilnius's room contained a bed, a small table, a chest, and a cabinet. There was a brazier underneath the high-set window. I went and inspected it, but the coals were cold. Entellus wasn't lying; Cilnius hadn't been here last night.

Atreus and Juba were more intrusive than I was. Juba went straight to the chest and lifted the lid, while Atreus opened the cabinet.

I wasn't sure what the personal belongings of a killer ought to look like. Bloodstained, perhaps. But there was nothing that stood out amongst Cilnius's things. His clothes were neatly folded and repaired in a few places that suggested he was nowhere near as rich as his roommate Entellus. He had very few pieces of jewellery, hardly any trinkets, but he made up for it in the volume of scrolls and sheets of paper stashed in the cabinet.

It was just what I'd expect to find inside a playwright's room.

Entellus, leaning in the door, said, "What are you looking for anyway?"

"Nothing," I said, which was exactly what we'd found. "Did Cilnius know Marsus well?"

Entellus's expression narrowed for a moment. Then he huffed. "Everyone knew Marsus, if you know what I mean."

I did, but I wanted him to spell it out for me. "I'm not sure I do."

Entellus rolled his eyes. "All actors are prostitutes, Valerius. Every single one of them."

I exchanged a look with Atreus, finding my own doubts mirrored in his gaze. Nobody else had described Marsus that way. Fabia had said he was kind, although that certainly didn't disqualify him from also being a prostitute. And, if he was, it was possible that his boyfriend Erastus didn't know, or at least didn't want to tell us. But Petronius had been adamant Marsus had been a flirt but nothing more—he'd made a point of telling us they'd never slept together despite initial efforts on Petronius's part, when, if they had, it seemed like the sort of thing Petronius would have joyfully shouted from the rooftops. Either Petronius was lying, or Entellus had gotten the wrong idea about Marsus somewhere along the way.

"I doubt there's anyone at the theatre who didn't sleep with Marsus," Entellus continued airily, "and that includes the slaves who scrub the bird shit off the seats." He grinned. "It's how actors are. If you open your purse, they'll open their legs. Simple."

"He was a pretty young man," I said, forcing a lecherous smile. "I'll bet he was worth the price."

"I wouldn't know," Entellus said. He snorted again, his signature reaction. "I have *standards*."

And, having got that final dig in at a dead man, he wandered back towards the sitting room.

Juba hummed.

Atreus let out a long breath.

"You don't like him, do you?" I asked in an undertone. "Because he's rich and spoiled."

Atreus flicked through a few pages of Cilnius's writing. "If I didn't like men for those reasons alone, I'd detest half the city."

Juba turned away to hide his smile, while I only nodded gravely and didn't point out that Atreus *did* detest half the city, and that was exactly the reason why. He worked hard, so there must have been some element of jealousy or at least mild resentment in his dealings with those who barely worked at all but would still rise above him in every one of their interactions—I'd figured that much out the very first night we'd met—but it was also the result of his strong sense of justice and fairness. Nobody knew better than a man with Atreus's job that the world was unjust and unfair, but that didn't mean he had to like it. He wasn't here because Seneca had asked him, or because a rich man like Lucan was being threatened, or because this investigation involved friends of the emperor. He was here for the man who had been dumped in the Medusa Fountain—before he even knew who he was—and also for the slave boy who had been killed when he opened his master's posticum door. Plebeian, actor, prostitute, slave, or senator; none of that mattered to Atreus, which was why I admired him as much as I did.

So no, he didn't like Entellus because Entellus was a rich, spoiled brat in a world that only ever rewarded rich, spoiled brats, and he was right to feel that way. Some might have thought him cynical, but I thought him almost idealistic; he didn't like that the world was the way that it was, and life hadn't quite knocked the sting of that injustice out of him yet. He did his job to the best of his ability because it was the right thing to do, but that didn't make him blind to the unfairness he saw every day in Rome, and in the rich, spoiled brats he met. And if the stoic, hardworking vigile happened to have a soft spot for one particular rich, spoiled brat—one who teased him about owning a villa at Baiae, for example—well, that was nobody's business except his.

We spent a few more moments going through Cilnius's things, but there was nothing there to find. On our way to rejoin Entellus, I noticed a locked door on what should have been another bedroom and nodded at it to make sure Atreus saw it too. Maybe it was where Entellus kept his money box, and he was afraid of burglars. But it was enough to cause me to wonder what might be behind the door.

Entellus was reclining on the couch when we got back to the sitting room, not in a position to eat, but with a cushion shoved under his head as though he was about to doze off at any moment.

I picked over the olives. "Do you live here alone?"

He gave a grunt, which I took as agreement.

"It's a big house for an unmarried man."

"Well, I live with Cilnius, obviously," Entellus said. He covered a yawn with his hand. "So not technically alone. But, yes, I suspect my father has plans to find me a wife, but again, he's waiting until I 'outgrow' writing plays."

"Like you did with the sculpture?" I asked.

"Well, I still do that," Entellus said, wrinkling his nose. "It's part of the reason my father bought this place for me. He got sick of the noise and the dust."

I didn't see any evidence of dust in the apartment—maybe his studio was behind that locked door—and I doubted that Entellus would be hammering away at a block of marble today with his hangover.

"He's right that there's no money in it though," Entellus mused through another yawn. "But you can be famous *and* rich if you're a writer. Look at Petronius. He came from nothing, and now he's one of the most influential men in Rome. And to think that my father claims I lack ambition!"

There was no real outrage in his tone, though. He was too hungover for that, bleary and half-asleep.

I steered the conversation away from Entellus's fraught relationship with his father, and back to the matter at hand. "Did Cilnius ever sleep with Marsus?"

"I don't know," Entellus said with a lazy shrug. Then he seemed to contemplate the question for a moment longer, and brow creased. "He panted after him like a dog, though. Bought him little gifts, wrote him poems, all the usual stuff."

We'd seen no evidence of love poems in Cilnius's writings, but perhaps he'd sent them as soon as he'd written them.

"And how did Marsus respond to that?"

"How do you think?" Entellus asked. "He was a prostitute, like I said."

I chewed on an olive. "I wasn't aware they took poems for payment."

Atreus's mouth quirked.

Entellus let out a long, gusty breath. "Well, then I suppose he paid him as well. I don't really know, Valerius. It's not as though I'm Cilnius's keeper or anything. I only invited him to live here because I thought he might be interesting to get to know better. That was a mistake."

Atreus said, "Do you know of anywhere he might go? Does he have family or friends he visits?"

"He's from Cumae or somewhere. As far as I know, he doesn't really have any friends, except for us." He squinted at the ceiling as though the answer might be there, amid the goddesses and nymphs that danced across the plaster. "Maybe Lucan would know? He's about the only one who ever got more than a few words out of him."

Who didn't laugh at his stammer, most likely.

Which raised the question of why Cilnius had apparently killed Marsus and Hermes, and not the whole damn bunch of playwrights and poets instead.

I'd have to make sure to ask him when we found him.

* * *

We didn't find Cilnius at Lucan's house. We didn't find Lucan either. A wet-eyed slave told us in a croaking voice that the master was staying with his uncle, Seneca, until the tablinum could be cleaned up. He recognised us, though, and let us in.

I exchanged a look with Atreus and Juba as we treaded into Lucan's house. Such a trusting slave, when look at what happened to the last one who opened a door to someone he thought was a friend of his master's.

In the atrium, a girl was weaving wreaths in front of the household shrine, a stark reminder that Saturnalia was fast approaching. I wondered if there would be any laughter at all in this house by then. Not if the slaves followed their master's cue, probably.

The doors to the tablinum were open, allowing in the light from the atrium. It still smelled of damp and of charred papers and scrolls. Two slaves were sitting cross-legged on the soot-smeared tiles, carefully unrolling scrolls to see what could be salvaged.

"We're not to throw anything out," one cautioned the other. "The writing might still be—" He stopped talking when he saw us, bobbing his head respectfully and making to rise.

"No, stay there, it's fine." I stood behind them, peering at the mess on the shelves. "I hope you can save some of it."

This wasn't my library. Mine, if it burned, could be replaced eventually with a series of judicious visits to the Saepta Julia or the Emporium, where, with enough time spent sorting through the boxes of scrolls for sale, I could recover my losses. But I was a reader, not a writer. There was nothing in my library that wasn't in hundreds of other libraries across the city. Looking at Lucan's fire-ravaged shelves, I wondered how much was lost forever.

"I hope so too, sir," the slave said. "It is of no consolation to the master now, but perhaps in the coming weeks..."

He trailed off as we all contemplated the depth of Lucan's grief.

"I suppose that whatever can't be saved, there is at least a chance Lucan will be able to create it again," I said. I meant it as a platitude, but the slave seized on it eagerly.

"I hope that as well, sir!" And then his face fell into an expression of even deeper sorrow. "But he won't be able to rewrite Hermes's poems."

"Hermes wrote his own poems?"

"Oh, yes," the slave said. "He could make up little ones right off the top of his head—he did it as a trick at parties—but he wrote long ones too, almost as good as the master's!" He blinked rapidly and dropped his gaze to the charred scroll in his hands. "And now they're all gone."

I felt like a heel. "I'm so sorry."

The slave sighed, tapping his fingers on the end of a charred umbilicus and then, more carefully, touching the blackened verso, as though he was afraid even that scant amount of pressure might cause the thing to crumble.

We left the slaves to their dismal task.

Outside in the street, in the shade of a tree, I said, "What do we think? Do we need to go hunting Lucan down at Seneca's house just on the off chance he'll know if Cilnius has any other friends?"

"As well as helpfully be able to tell us exactly where they live," Atreus said with a rueful smile, and I let out a relieved breath. I'd been on plenty of wild goose chases with Atreus before, and I really didn't have the energy for another one today; I was happy that he didn't, either. Atreus closed his eyes for a moment. When he opened them again, his expression was weary.

"Let's find somewhere for lunch."

For once, we were in accord.

The place we found was in Lucan's neighbourhood, and unfamiliar to all of us, but there was a long line at the counter, which boded well. The queue meant there were no seats at the caupona, so we bought our lunch and sat on the edge of the footpath to eat with our feet in the gutter. We weren't the only ones doing it; the pair of lads closest by even had a game of dice going on.

"It's strange how one of them is sabotaging the Juvenalia," I said, "when the only thing everyone we've spoken to so far can agree on is that they're the best writer in the group. You wouldn't think that the best writer would have to sabotage anyone at all."

Atreus smiled and shook his head. "They all say they're the best, but I don't know if any of them really believe it."

"Petronius might."

Atreus tilted his head, considering. "He certainly has a healthy amount of pride."

Which was a nice way of saying that he was full of himself. I liked Petronius, though. He carried his pride in a way that was somehow more amusing than annoying, which was a rare gift indeed.

I folded my flatbread more firmly around the melted cheese and olives inside it, unwilling to lose the filling to the hopeful sparrows that hopped around my feet. "It's not unearned, though. Petronius is Rome's most celebrated writer, whether of poems or plays, despite the grizzling old moralists who claim he's just writing filth."

"Isn't he?" Atreus asked.

"Well, yes," I said. "But they just don't like it because it pokes fun at them much as it does everyone else. We patricians are used to being the subject of serious works, all about Rome's glory, not side characters in a dirty story about a man trying his hardest to screw a flirtatious boy."

Atreus hummed. "It's not hard to see it's about Marsus, isn't it?"

"The *Satyricon*? It's not, though," I said. "At least, not exactly. Giton is clever and handsome, yes, but he's faithless whenever it suits him, and

Petronius said Marsus was loyal to his boyfriend. He also seemed to think getting Marsus into bed would have robbed him of all his inspiration for Encolpius and Giton. Marsus and his flirting stoked a fire that Petronius claims he didn't want quenched. If we believe that, perhaps the *Satyricon* only exists because Marsus *wasn't* a whore."

"Entellus doesn't think so," Atreus said.

Juba paddled his feet on the road. "There are only two reasons you call someone a prostitute. One, if they're actually a prostitute. And two, if they won't sleep with *you*." He shrugged. "If your pride is that fragile, at least."

Well, Entellus certainly fit the portrait of a man who, if he heard the word no, felt the need to publicly disparage the person who'd had the audacity to refuse him. It was hardly a peculiar trait in wealthy young men, but I liked to think that most of us outgrew it. Eventually.

"It probably doesn't matter," I said, "but the discrepancy bothers me. I'd like to get a look inside Entellus's locked room and see what he thinks is worth hiding away."

"Me too." Atreus nodded, staring fixedly at the sparrows, as though they might hold the answer to this whole mess. "And it's not the biggest question in this entire matter, but you're right; the inconsistency in the way Marsus is described makes no sense." He shook his head. "It doesn't matter to us—we're trying to find the killer, not whether Marsus was a prostitute or not—but it matters to either Petronius or to Entellus that we view him in a particular way. That's what interests me."

"My instinct is to believe Petronius," I said, "because I like him more. But I've stumbled into that trap before."

Atreus raised his flatbread in a sardonic toast. "As have I. More than I'd like to admit."

We both looked at Juba, and he looked back at us.

"I don't know what you're talking about, sirs," he said at last, barely wrestling his grin under control. "I'm an excellent judge of character."

He was such an excellent judge of character that I made him go and wait in the line to get me a second serving of lunch.

* * *

At some point in every investigation—well, this was only my second investigation, but so far it was proving true—I felt the need to visit mad Uncle Maro and seek his wisdom. It also helped to know what, if anything, the gossips were saying about our progress. Mad Uncle Maro was always the first to know.

Juba stood beside the door in Maro's tablinum as Atreus and I took a seat on one of the two reading couches. My mad relation sat on the other one, resting his forearms on his knees as he leaned forward and regarded us worriedly. The screens to the tablinum were closed, and there was a brazier burning in the corner, filling the space with warmth and soft light. Maro lifted a hand to tug at some of his remaining hair, leaving it standing up like a bird's crest, and then clicked his tongue at me as though I was five years old, and I'd disappointed him with my behaviour.

"To begin with," he announced, "nobody really cares about a slave. An actor is a little more important—it's a low profession, but actors are popular. As soon as people notice Marsus was supposed to be in Petronius's performance for the Juvenalia, it won't be long until people are asking if this is an attack against Nero, will it?"

"It's not," I said. "It's an attack *for* Nero. Well, for his favour."

"Ah," Maro said, nodding. "Someone is damaging their competition's chances." He clicked his tongue again. "So Seneca was wrong. It was never about Lucan specifically."

Seneca was wrong.

There was a phrase you didn't hear every day.

A plump slave brought us wine and snacks. Maro's slaves were the fattest in their neighbourhood, but against all popular opinion, it had never caused them to be lazy or disrespectful. This was a happy household, and one I was always glad to visit.

Maro took a sip of his wine. "It's not important enough that Severus is being asked any questions, *yet*. But it has the potential to spin out of control at any moment, I would think. You are starting to build a good reputation,

Quintus. More importantly, you're starting to be known as a friend to the emperor. So it's in your best interests to tidy this thing up as quickly as you can."

"It's not for lack of trying that we haven't," I told him, rolling my eyes. "We've been running around the city for days and getting nowhere."

"At least you know it's not Agrippina," the old man said sagely.

For which I couldn't be more grateful.

"It's not Agrippina, and it's not an attack against Nero," I said. "But there's still a killer on the loose."

Maro hummed thoughtfully, and then said, "Well, I'm at a complete loss, boys." He straightened up and said, brightly, "Who would like a honey cake?"

Alright, so perhaps it wasn't Maro's wisdom I'd come here seeking. Perhaps it was just the comfort of knowing the old man was as flummoxed as me, but still completely on my side. I could have got similar support at home, except there was a chance I might run into Julia. We had a better relationship now than we'd ever had, Julia and I, but she was deeply invested in all the details of her upcoming wedding ceremony, and I didn't want to be caught in any discussions about exactly what shade of yellow her hairnet ought to be. I loved my womenfolk, but there was no denying that sometimes Maro's house felt like a softer place to land when I was feeling a little battered by circumstances.

"The Juvenalia is much more important than it seems," Maro said, as he dug into a honey cake. "It's not just celebrating Nero leaving his boyhood behind and becoming a man, it's the first significant celebration that hasn't had his mother at his side. If his enemies wanted to harm his reputation and suggest that he is ill-omened, what better way to do it than try to ruin the Juvenalia? But you're certain that's not it?"

"We're not certain of anything," I said unhappily. "Only that we have two dead bodies, one runaway poet, and no clear suspect. Someone attacked Lucan in the street, and then Lucan's slave was killed. Someone killed the actor, Marsus, to ruin Petronius's play, and we thought that it might be Cilnius, though our reasoning on that was shaky at best—"

"He did run, though," Atreus said.

"He did run," I agreed. "But until we find him and ask him, we can't be sure why. The only certainty—well, probability—is that it's doubtful that either Lucan or Petronius are our killer, because they've both been targeted."

"Unless Lucan killed his own slave, or Petronius his own actor, to divert your attention from them as suspects!" Maro declared, his eyes shining.

I groaned and closed my eyes briefly. "Don't even say that, please. I'm already confused enough as it is."

"You should have a honey cake," Maro suggested sympathetically. "While you do, tell me again about all these other writers in the group, and what you know about them. Perhaps it will rattle something loose in that blob of wet plaster you call a brain." He popped the last bite of his cake into his mouth and then reached behind him for a tablet and a stylus from his desk. "I shall be your secretary!"

I groaned again. "Maro, please, we—"

"It wouldn't hurt," said Atreus, the treacherous bastard.

Maro, delighted, flipped the tablet open and said poised with the stylus. "Go on then! What are you waiting for? It's like your Greek lessons all over again, when you just sat there with your mouth open, catching flies."

"That was almost twenty years ago, Maro!"

My mad relation cocked a bushy eyebrow. "I'm not seeing much improvement."

"Fine. Petronius, then." I rubbed the back of my neck. "The most famous and influential of them. The most talented, too, if you believe him."

"Do you?" Maro asked keenly.

"I think so," I said, and then shrugged. "I don't know. He's the most successful of the group, which means the others may be jealous of him. Absolutely infatuated with Marsus, but claims sleeping with him would have silenced his muse."

Maro looked dubious as he scratched a few words on the wax.

"Then Lucan," I said. "Second most successful. Snapping at Petronius's heels, perhaps?"

Maro made a dissenting sound. "Except Petronius is better known for his prose than his verse, whereas Lucan is making his name for his poems."

"Well, the first attack was on Lucan, so do we assume a poet and not a playwright?" Atreus asked.

"I don't think it's relevant for the Juvenalia," Uncle Maro said. "I only mean to say that ordinarily Petronius might not worry about Lucan stealing his thunder, because usually there are enough accolades to share between plays and poems, but in the case of the Juvenalia? There will only be one crown of laurel leaves for the best writer, I assume, whether it is a poem or a play he presents."

"So Petronius might usually be unbothered by Lucan's success," I said, "but this time it threatens his own."

Maro sucked on the end of his stylus. "Although I've *met* Petronius." Of course he had. Maro had met everyone. "His weapon of choice is the stylus, not the blade."

"And, of course, Petronius has also been targeted," I said. We were going around in circles. "It's possible he is our attacker, but it feels unlikely to me. Which leaves us the rest of them. Cilnius, who already looks guilty for running. Litus, then, Lucan's friend. I've seen him giving Lucan tips on how to properly stand on stage and project his voice to the audience, so I can't say I'm convinced he's trying to end Lucan's career."

"Poet or playwright?" Maro asked.

I thought hard for a moment. "I'm not entirely sure, but I know he's writing a poem for the Juvenalia. It was to be about Horatius at the bridge, but Fabianus stole the idea. Fabianus seems to do that a lot."

"Strange nobody has murdered him then," Maro said, and then tilted his head. "*Yet*, anyway."

"Maro. The last thing we want is another body."

Atreus nodded grimly.

"Fabianus," Maro said, tapping the stylus against the tablet.

"Steals ideas," I said, and looked at Atreus helplessly.

"That's all we really know about him," Atreus agreed. "Hosidius, a playwright. Petronius described him as having no confidence. He said he folded like a piece of wet straw."

"He said the same about Cilnius, too," I said. "And so did Entellus."

Maro wrote with quick strokes of the stylus. "Entellus?"

"Not telling anyone what he's writing about," I said. "Which, given Fabianus is in the group, is probably a smart idea. Entellus is rich, and spoiled, and looks down on everyone else. He seemed particularly disdainful of Cilnius, even though he let him stay at his apartment."

"Ah," Maro said, nodding sagely. "Even the weasel likes to be worshipped by the flea."

I didn't know where Maro found his weird aphorisms, and I was honestly afraid to ask. He always presented them as though he was imparting ancient wisdom, when I suspected that he instead just pulled them out of his arse and hoped nobody noticed.

"And we don't know much about Cilnius," Atreus said.

"We know he can run like Leonidas of Rhodes," I pointed out, and Atreus gave me an unimpressed look.

Maro stared avidly at the tablet for a moment, as though the answer lay somewhere in the words scratched into the wax. Then he snapped the boards shut and tossed the tablet onto the couch beside him. "Well, that probably didn't help at all, did it?"

Atreus threw me a confused look, even though by now he should have known Maro well enough to realise he was insane. And it *had* helped, in a way. We still had no idea who our killer was, but I was feeling a lot more relaxed about it than when I'd first arrived, and wasn't that the most important thing?

Probably not, but it had to count for something.

"We should go back to the theatre," I said. "And speak to the actors, and the builders, and Antigon, and everyone who is there all the time. They will have perhaps noticed tensions between our poets and playwrights that the men themselves might not admit to."

Juba straightened eagerly, and I wondered if he just wanted to get his hands around Tertia's shapely ankle again. From the looks she'd given him the last time, she wouldn't be opposed.

"Wonderful," Maro said, clapping his hands and rising to his feet. "Give me a moment to call for a litter."

"Excuse me, sir?" Atreus asked at the exact same moment I said, "What?"

"I'm coming with you, naturally," Maro said, beaming at us. "Unlike you, Quintus, you uncultured dog, I *love* the theatre."

And he swept out of the tablinum past a startled Juba, calling for a litter.

* * *

When we arrived at Nero's private theatre in the Gardens of Agrippina, the actors flocked to mad Uncle Maro like pigeons to a dropped crust of bread. He delighted in their attention, and in particular Ammenius's smarminess, and somehow managed to convince the man, without promising a single quadrans, that he was just desperate to throw his money at the arts. Knowing Maro, it was probably true. He'd spent most of his life keeping every insane painter, plasterer, and sculptor in employment, thanks to his never-ending home renovations, so why not branch out into an even more spectacular way to piss his fortune up against the wall? Jupiter knew he couldn't spend it all in a single lifetime otherwise. As his presumptive heir, I supposed I was entitled to some opinions on his extravagant spending, but whatever made Maro happy generally made me happy too. And it wasn't as though any of us Aemilii were crying poor.

Maro allowed the actors to pull him up onto the stage, chuckling with delight when a throne was carried in from behind the scaenae frons and they set him upon it. A few musicians were rustled up, and the actors danced for him. Maro clapped along to the music in delight.

Over in the cavea, I paced up and down the first few steps, and watched the stage.

The music and dancing brought a plump figure to the edge of the stage: Hosidius. He leaned on one of the columns in front of the fake portico that led to the rear of the scaenae frons, looking almost wistful as the actors cavorted around a delighted Maro. He gave the impression of a lonely child who hadn't been invited to play.

"Hosidius!" I called in a friendly tone and waved my arm to get his attention. He looked surprised as he spotted me. "Come and join us!"

He shook his head and gave me an apologetic smile, and then darted up the steps and off the stage.

I shared a look with Atreus and Juba, and then we followed him.

I had half expected a chase like Cilnius gave us, but we found Hosidius easily enough, tucked away in a small room on the second floor of the narrow building. He was seated on a stool, a scroll unfolded on his lap. Fabia's little boy, Nonus, was sitting cross-legged at his feet, a corn dolly in one hand and a thick chunk of bread in the other. He was chattering away happily to Hosidius.

"Hello again," I said to the pair of them.

Nonus shoved the corn dolly in his mouth, not the bread. Interesting choice, but who was I to correct him? If he wanted to learn the difference between bread and toys the hard way, that was his business.

Hosidius rolled up his scroll and said, caution tightening his tone, "Hello."

"Working on your play?" I asked, nodding at the scroll.

"No, this is Cicero," he said. "I, uh, I finished my scene weeks ago."

"Well, congratulations. What are you doing hanging around here then?"

"Oh." His flushed. "They're...the actors are supposed to be rehearsing it now. Well, sometime today, I suppose, but...but they seem to have gotten distracted."

Too busy fawning over mad Uncle Maro and his money.

I wondered if Hosidius had been here all day, waiting.

I saw what everyone said about Hosidius and his timid nature. I couldn't imagine Petronius letting the actors get away with any bullshit—at least any that he wasn't personally in the middle of—when they were supposed to be rehearsing the scene he'd written for Juvenalia.

"What is your play about?" I asked him.

"It's about Jupiter and the bee," he said, hunching his shoulders as though he was hoping he could disappear into the space between them. "The bee speaks to Jupiter, and he gives his judgement, and the chorus then warns of the consequences of the bee's request."

I knew the story. Every Roman child knew it. The queen bee, angry that people keep coming along to steal honey from her hive, petitions Jupiter to give her means of attacking the thieves. And Jupiter gives her a sting, with the caveat that if she ever uses it, she will die. I supposed that it was a story about either being aware of the consequences of your actions or being careful what you wished for, but it was hard not to see it as yet another example of the gods being bastards just because they could.

"Interesting choice," I said.

"Everyone else is telling stories of heroes and the glory of Rome," he said, his expression faltering. He let out the slow breath of a man coming to an unhappy realisation. "Perhaps I should have done the same."

I was suddenly glad that all I'd ever had to do for the emperor was to stab Parthians. At least that had been straightforward.

"Did you hear about Marsus?" I asked him.

"Yes." His brows drew together. "How sad. He was very talented."

"Did you know him well?" I asked.

"No. Not really." He blinked at me, as though willing me to believe him.

I did, strangely enough. Hosidius did not strike me as a social butterfly as much as a social silverfish; he'd much rather be burrowed away somewhere quiet and dark.

"What about Hermes?" I asked.

"Oh, he was very clever," he said, "and poor Lucan is so distraught, isn't he?"

"He is," I agreed. "But did you know him well?"

"I…" He shook his head, and Nonus, perhaps sensing his discomfort, patted his knee. Hosidius's gaze fell on the grubby little boy and softened. "It seems silly now, to say that, in some ways, I was afraid of him."

"Afraid?" Atreus asked, before I could, his tone incredulous.

"Silly," Hosidius repeated with a faint smile. "The fault was mine, and not his. I am very sensitive to criticism—I'm in the wrong line of work, I know—and Hermes had a talent of pulling these little verses from the air that could just skewer a man. They were very funny, like an after-dinner trick Petronius insisted that Lucan let him perform, and I don't think Hermes himself was mean-spirited, just…" He shrugged. "I always thought that if he made one up about *me*, that I would embarrass myself by not being able to laugh it off. Or by laughing *too* loudly and sounding false."

Hosidius wasn't just lacking confidence; he was the sort of socially awkward fellow who would worry himself into an early grave over things the rest of us didn't spare a thought about, like calling someone the wrong name, or asking a man how his wife was when you forgot he'd just been through a scandalous divorce, or accidentally insulting your plebeian friend by offering to buy him things.

Fine. I worried about that last one, too.

There had been a time when I'd returned to Rome after my military service where most of the city had thought I was nothing more than a drunken idiot. Perhaps most of the city still thought that; I didn't know. Crucially, I didn't care that much either. I'd always secretly known I was better than that, and sooner or later everyone else would too. And, if they never figured it out, what did I care? My family knew I was better than my reputation, and I had a burgeoning career and the friendship of the emperor. I didn't lose sleep over the opinions of others. It wouldn't surprise me to learn that Hosidius stayed awake all night worrying over every social interaction he'd had since the moment he was born.

We asked after Cilnius, but Hosidius didn't have much to tell us. He hadn't seen him today and couldn't think why he would have run away from us last night.

We left Hosidius babysitting Nonus and fretting about his bee play, and his distracted actors, and probably a million other things that gnawed away at him every waking hour. We tramped down the stairs to the stage again to where Maro, beaming with delight, was still being enthusiastically feted like a king. It was loud and crazy and ridiculous, but then so was Maro, so instead of rolling my eyes and chiding him for his disreputable behaviour, I rolled my eyes, grinned, and let him enjoy his moment on centre stage.

Chapter Nine

W hile Juba, Atreus and I had been hard at work getting nowhere, the urban cohorts—the diurnal brothers of Atreus's vigiles— had actually been doing exactly the same as they usually did (not much, according to Atreus) with much better results. Well, depending on your point of view. When we attended the excubitorium after lunch, one of them had left a message for Atreus to come and visit them on their side of the building. The vigiles and the local Urban Cohort shared the excubitorium, but from what I could tell, didn't have a lot to do with each other apart from some sneering if they crossed paths in the dusty training yard. Their gods might have smiled at each other from their shrines on either side of the arched entrance to the premises (Neptune for the vigiles, and Mercury for the Urban Cohort), but that was where the goodwill began and ended. There was a long history of their respective prefects being political adversaries, which filtered down as a kind of lazy mutual contempt in the lower ranks. The contempt didn't extend to withholding information, though—the man behind the counter stood up when we walked into the Urban Cohort's building and said, "Mugo the Fish thinks he has something for you, Atreus."

Now, there was an expression you didn't hear every day, whatever in Tartarus it meant. By Atreus's suddenly grim expression, it wasn't good tidings. He thanked the man behind the counter and strode outside again with Juba and me at his heels.

Mugo the Fish, Atreus informed us as we headed towards the Transtiberina, was not, unsurprisingly, an actual fish. Instead, he was one of the many boatmen who plied his trade along the Tiber. He transported cargo and passengers up and down the river, dragging a net behind him to catch his nightly dinner. But he also caught more than fish.

We caught up with Mugo on the banks of the river, in the Transtiberina, just south of Tiber Island. He was ancient and grizzled and baked nut-brown by decades of sun, and he had a beard as damp and tangled as an old net. He was sitting beside his boat, which was pulled up onto the muddy stones, repairing a net with the day's catch dripping beside him.

Today's catch was a couple of fish and a corpse.

"Junius Atreus," he said gruffly, nodding. His gaze narrowed as he took in Juba and me.

"Mugo." Atreus returned the nod, and we went forward to inspect the corpse.

We weren't the only ones doing it. A dog and a couple of grubby kids were already there. One of the kids was poking the dead man in the cheek with a pointy stick and swore at Atreus when he wrenched it off him.

Mugo laughed under his breath as the kids retreated under the weight of Atreus's stare. The dog stuck around, though it seemed more interested in Mugo's fish than the corpse.

My soles slipped on the muddy stones as I moved closer to see.

It was Cilnius. He'd lost his toga somewhere between last night and now, probably in the churning currents of the Tiber. His face was pale, his mouth was open, and his hair and his tunic stuck damply to his skin.

I'd spent most of the day thinking that we would either find Cilnius at some point, or we wouldn't. That we might find him dead hadn't even crossed my mind. The last time we saw him he'd been running, and now…now, I had no idea what had happened to him last night, but I hadn't expected this.

"It's him," I said, and Atreus gave a grim nod.

"You family?" Mugo the Fish asked me, and I shook my head in response. "Good. I'll have that tunic before the libitinarius comes to get him. Shame he's only got the one shoe left."

"Where did you find him?" Atreus asked.

"Just on the top tip of the island," Mugo said. He scratched his beard, the sound rasping in the cold air. "He must have gone in upriver from there, sometime overnight by the look of him."

"Guilty conscience?" I asked Atreus.

Suicide was the morally correct thing to do in order to avoid dishonour. Plato and Aristotle might have thought that to commit suicide was to do oneself an injustice, but we Romans were more practical than that: if the wolf was at your door, why give it the satisfaction of the kill? Well, that might have been the cynical take on things. But if you had the choice of either publicly facing your crimes, or taking them to your grave—and, bonus, preserving your fortune and your reputation for your family's sake—then I imagine that suddenly your gladius started to look very tempting.

At least for me it would be a gladius, because I was ex-military and had one at home. For a poet like Cilnius, perhaps drowning had seemed the best choice, despite the fact he'd had a perfectly good brazier in his room. He couldn't have been much of a dramatist if he'd never read the story of Brutus's wife Porcia.

"Guilty conscience?" Mugo huffed as he deftly knotted his netting back together. "Maybe so, but he's got a knock on the back of his head."

My stomach clenched. "Shit."

Juba squatted down beside the body, and put one hand under his head, and one on his shoulder. He pushed him, and the body shifted enough that we could all see the dark, sticky stain in the matted hair at the base of Cilnius's skull.

"Couldn't it have happened as he went in?" I asked. "Or perhaps a boat hit him when he was already dead?"

"I've seen a lot of bodies come out of that water," Mugo said, and shrugged. "Sometimes there's not much difference between a murder and a suicide, especially if he's been floating a while. Your fancy Greek doctor might want to take a guess, but I'll wager he's no more certain than I am."

I saw from Atreus's sombre expression that he trusted Mugo's assessment.

"Sons of Dis," I said, as Juba let the corpse roll back onto the stones. I let out a groan. "Why is everything always as clear as fucking *mud*?"

This could still be suicide. I *wanted* this to be suicide.

Atreus and Juba were silent.

Mugo the Fish combed his fingers through his beard. "Well, if it's any use, I can tell you where he went in the river based on the tides and the currents."

That got my attention, and I fumbled for my purse and tossed the old man a coin.

He caught it as deftly as a fish snapping at a piece of bait. "If I'm any judge of the river, and I've lived every day of the last fifty years on it, then last night your man hit the water somewhere very near the Milvian Bridge."

* * *

Atreus and I didn't make it back to the excubitorium. We had a dinner to get to, and so we hurried to my baths on the Caelian Hill, and raced through the process so quickly that our footprints probably still hadn't dried by the time we were halfway up the hill on our way home. We sent Juba to the excubitorium to get a message to Leander to let him know that Atreus wouldn't be back for Lucilla tonight, and asking that he either keep her with him or take her to Atreus's neighbour. It was an annoyance, an extra concern that I didn't begrudge Atreus, but could have been avoided in the first place if only he brought Lucilla to my house more often. I had an entire household who could make sure she was fed and looked after and put to bed someplace where someone's angry husband wasn't going to start an argument about it. But I didn't say anything because I was learning how to pick my battles. Slowly, yes, but I was learning.

"Quintus," Fulvia said as Atreus and I strode through the atrium. "Are you staying for dinner?"

I crossed the tiles to kiss her on the cheek. "Sorry, no."

"Be safe," she said, knowing better by now than to tell me not to get into any trouble. She squeezed my hand before looking over my shoulder. "You too, Atreus."

He ducked his head respectfully.

I headed up the stairs to my bedroom, with Atreus following. We changed into fresh tunics and togas. One thing I could do better than Atreus was a toga, and I enjoyed making him stand there, a divot digging into his forehead between his eyebrows, as I adjusted the fall of the fabric.

"I should be happier about this," I confessed. "It was Cilnius, wasn't it? And he ran away from us because he was guilty and threw himself into the Tiber."

"It fits," Atreus agreed, but he wasn't smiling either.

I drew a breath. "It's because we don't know his motive. Why Marsus and Hermes? Or I suppose the real targets were Petronius and Lucan. But it still—"

Atreus silenced me with a kiss. When he drew back, he cast a wary look at the door, but there was no sign of anyone around, and then looked back at me. "It could have been any one of them. They're a nest of vipers, and we know they mocked him for his stutter. Maybe he finally got so angry, he decided to hurt them back."

"It fits," I said, echoing his own words back to him.

It fitted, but it didn't feel like a victory. It felt hollow, like a vessel with nothing inside. But if there was one thing working with Atreus had taught me, it was that luck guided our actions more than reason, so perhaps this was Fortuna showing us her mercy, and we needed to stop questioning it and be thankful.

Except, both Atreus and I were too cynical for that. The wound on the back of Cilnius's head might have been accidental, as he'd struck something hard in the river, but it also might have been murder. And, if it was, then we both had the exact same thought as to who the killer must be: Entellus, the only man besides us who'd seen which direction Cilnius had fled in the night before.

It was still early when we left the house, wrapped in togas and ensconced in my litter. Juba led the way, his torch as yet unlit. It was too early for dinner, in fact, but we had somewhere else to attend first.

We ditched the litter and our togas a block away from Entellus's insula, and I instructed my litter bearers to wait at the nearby caupona. I left them a handful of coins so that they could more happily pass the time, and then Juba, Atreus and I headed for Entellus's apartment. There was enough pedestrian traffic in the street that we didn't look to conspicuous as we lurked outside. The appearance of a hired litter as dusk began to fall alerted us to Entellus's imminent departure. One of the litter bearers went inside the entrance to the insula and was back a few moments later. A little while after that, Entellus appeared. I caught a brief glimpse of him fiddling with his hair with his beringed fingers before he climbed inside the litter and was carried away.

"She's not just going to let us in," I said as we entered the interior courtyard of the insula and headed towards Entellus's door.

Atreus threw me a look I couldn't quite decipher and knocked on Entellus's door. The slave woman answered, and he gave her a respectful nod. "My name is Junius Atreus. I was here this morning, and your master gave me permission to look at Cilnius's room."

The nod she gave him in return was wary.

"I'm a vigile," he said.

"I remember." The woman's voice was softer than her suspicious gaze. "Do you want to look again?"

"No," Atreus said. "I want to look in the room your master keeps locked."

The woman flinched back, and I thought she was going to slam the door in our faces.

"Wait, please," Atreus said. "Your master's friend Lucan had a slave. A sweet, smart boy. I'm trying to find out who killed him."

The woman wavered.

"If you let us in, and we find nothing," Atreus continued, "then your master will never know we were here. If you let us in and we find something, then tomorrow I'll come back with a magistrate, and with vigiles, and he will never know that wasn't the first time I knocked on his door."

It seemed as though Atreus was taking a gamble in asking for the woman's cooperation, but it was a safer bet than it first appeared. Entellus had a shitty personality. It was hardly likely to be *better* in private, was it? If we disliked him after only knowing him such a short time, then chances were this woman truly hated him—and with good reason. The gamble wasn't on whether or not she would be loyal to her master, but whether or not she trusted Atreus to keep his word.

Unsurprisingly, she looked to Juba. He was a stranger too, but since she was balancing her chances, it was probably less likely a fellow slave would fuck her over than a free citizen would.

Juba nodded at her, and she stepped aside and let us in.

"I know where he keeps the key," she said, and went off to fetch it. Then, when she returned, she said, "There's nothing in there. Just statues that the master makes."

"Why does he keep it locked?" I asked.

"I don't know." The woman led us to the locked door and handed the key to Atreus.

Atreus opened the door.

Jupiter best and greatest!

I had no idea if Entellus was much of a writer, but he was certainly a gifted sculptor. Except it wasn't admiration that made my jaw drop and my breath catch in my throat as I stepped into the room and found myself surrounded by his creations. It was horror. Because each intricately detailed, unpainted marble figure—and they were *incredible*—was Marsus.

Here he was, caught with the smile on his face making the skin around his eyes crinkle. Here he was with his errant curls caught in an invisible wind. Here he was, reaching out to touch something, the muscles in his arm cording. And here he was reclining, his eyes closed in sleep. I wouldn't have been surprised to see his heart beating in his marble chest. There must have been ten different sculptures, each in a different state of creation, and each of them Marsus. He looked more human here in Entellus's workshop, carved from stone, than he had when we'd fished him out of the Medusa Fountain. In death, his skin had been white with pallor. But this luna marble? Oh, it was bloodless, too, but it caught the light and it *shone*.

Petronius might have cast Marsus as his Giton and might even have been inspired by the actor's flirtatiousness, but he'd laughed knowing that he'd never possess him. Entellus though… Entellus had told us sneeringly that Marsus was a prostitute. Entellus had hated him, but it was very easy to see that his hate was based on a very twisted sense of love.

176

What had Juba said? The only reason you called someone a prostitute was either they were…or they wouldn't sleep with *you*. Were we standing in the heart of a man's sickening obsession with a youth who had spurned his advances? It certainly felt that way. Why else would Entellus keep the door locked, if not the realisation that anyone who saw these sculptures would immediately know the depths of his obsession?

I caught Atreus's gaze, and saw my own certainty reflected there.

Entellus had worshipped Marsus and then, when that worship hadn't been returned, had killed him. And now, with the man dead and burned on a pyre, Entellus still worshipped him here, in this secret room, carving the curve of Marsus's mouth into marble over and over again.

※ ※ ※

Dusk was fading into darkness as we arrived at Otho's house, and slaves with lanterns met us to usher us to the door, as though they worried we might get lost on the way otherwise.

"Stay close," I murmured to Juba, and he nodded gravely.

Atreus and I were shown into the formal triclinium.

Dinner with Otho and Poppaea Sabina was a more subdued affair than last time, but no less opulent. Lucan had dragged himself along. I wondered if Uncle Seneca had given him a lecture on the stoic virtues of self-control, or at least reminded him that it was unseemly to be seen to mourn a mere slave in a way that interfered with his social obligations. Petronius had a place on the main couch with our hosts, and Atreus and I were on the second couch with Lucan. Litus, Entellus, Fabianus, and Hosidius were squeezed together on the third couch. It was lucky Litus was a stick insect. As it was, they'd be in trouble if one of them rolled over; they'd all end up on the floor in a tangle of togas.

I watched Entellus carefully. He smiled half a moment behind the conversation, and his eyes were glazed. He was either already drunk, or a very good actor.

The conversations that floated through the tablinum weren't as bright as the last time I'd been here either. Hermes and Marsus were dead, and Cilnius was missing—at least as far as everyone here knew—and it was clear that there was a very black cloud hanging over Nero's Juvenalia. I had never been happier that I wasn't a poet, my melodramatic, adolescent scribblings notwithstanding.

The meal began with stuffed sardines and eggs, and then we moved on to chicken cooked with mint and fennel seeds, oysters in a pepper, lovage, and garum sauce, and beets and artichokes and squash. I ate well and drank sparingly for once.

In the corner of the room, a man plucked a cithara gently, and sweet notes hung in the air.

"The theatre is looking good," Otho said, sucking sauce off his thumb. "I wasn't certain it would be ready in time, but the architect and the builders have done well."

"Are we talking about the bricks and the plaster because everything else related to the place is an unmitigated disaster?" Petronius asked curiously.

Otho jolted. "Not at all, Petronius. I was making conversation, that's all. I've seen your plays before. Everything always appears to be a chaotic mess, but then, somehow, it all goes perfectly on the night."

"I wonder how many actors can be murdered before that fails to be true," Petronius mused, a sharp, mocking edge to his voice. "Perhaps we'll get lucky, and someone will strangle Ammenius."

Otho looked baffled. "I meant no offence."

Petronius opened his mouth, and then, in what I was sure was a first for him, shut it again. He had the decency to look abashed. "I apologise, Otho. The fault is with me, and not with you. I've been on edge these last few days." He looked around the triclinium. "I think that perhaps we all are."

"I would rather talk about happier things," Lucan said.

Entellus murmured something in agreement.

Poppaea Sabina, ever the graceful hostess, turned the conversation towards the new year and how she and Otho planned to hire a barge and hold a dinner party on the Tiber once the weather turned warmer. It might have been a pleasant topic of conversation, except all I could think of was

Mugo the Fish, and Cilnius's open mouth full of dirty river water. But I faked a smile and shoved more food in my face.

The young man with the cithara was joined by a boy with a flute, and they played a sweet tune that filtered through the golden glow of light in the triclinium. Such pleasant music was supposed to allow us a respite from the season, and to forget for a moment the cold, gloomy weather outside.

Still, it was comfortable, and I was beginning to know these people and I didn't hate their company. Otho and Poppaea were witty and generous, and Petronius's wit had a sting in the tail. Lucan was quieter than usual, which wasn't unexpected. Litus was quiet too and kept casting worried glances at Lucan. Fabianus was oblivious to the others' scorn whenever he brought up writing about Horatius, and Hosidius was silent and anxious.

The viper in the nest was Entellus; spoiled, drunk, rich boy Entellus who peered blearily around the triclinium, and whose gold rings caught the light whenever he raised his hand to drink—and it happened regularly.

On our way over here, Atreus and I had discussed whether or not to confront him in front of everyone else. We'd decided against it—these were his friends first, not mine, and we couldn't be sure how it would play out. We'd decided to follow him home after dinner instead, where it would be three against one. Until then, we could at least enjoy the company and the food.

Well. The food.

Roman dinners, at least Roman dinners like these, weren't quick affairs. Food was made to be browsed over, not eaten quickly, and unlike the simple, basic meals that the majority of the people in this vast city would be eating tonight, this one was meant to last for hours. We might have taught our children that the empire was steered by the debates in the senate, but it was all bullshit. It was nights like these where decisions were made, in the company of friends, wine, and music. Not that any of us here tonight was interested in the way the empire was run—only in the man who ruled it.

Petronius was talking about how Nero liked to come to him for advice on matters of not just literature, but of fashion too, and the others were hanging on every word. I wondered which of them were just enjoying the story, and which of them were secretly seething with jealousy.

"But of course, even though I know a thing or two about fabric," Petronius said, and winked at me and raised his glass, "I've never killed a Parthian spy for the empire. Or beaten that bitch Agrippina."

There was sudden silence in the room; even the musicians faltered.

I sipped my wine. "I wasn't sure exactly how much you were told, Petronius. Apparently, everything."

"Have I been indiscreet?" he asked. Like he cared about that. "My point is, every single one of us here showers Nero with gifts of poetry and art and flattery, but there's only one of us who's actually done anything *useful*."

I waited for the barb.

Petronius's smile grew, like he knew exactly what I was thinking. "No, it's a compliment, Valerius. Have I become so cynical that nobody even believes in my honest flattery nowadays? Otho? Lucan?"

Otho rolled his eyes.

"Your honest flattery is so buried under everything else that comes out of your mouth that nobody hears it," Lucan said, his tone both exasperated and fond in equal measure. "Plus, you're drunk."

"I'll drink to that," Petronius said, and did.

The slaves came in to clear away the dishes from the main course, and I took the opportunity to go and piss. Entellus came with me, bouncing off a wall. If he came out the other side of this operation with dry feet, I'd be shocked. Still, I was wary that his drunkenness might all be an act. I'd watched him raise his cup a lot of times, but I couldn't be certain he swallowed. I made sure to keep distance between us as we relieved ourselves.

When a slave had to hurry in and swab the floor with a sponge when we were finished, I was forced to admit that if Entellus was acting, he was certainly committed to the role.

When we got back to the triclinium, Petronius had somehow gotten the cithara off the musician and was strumming it.

"Here he is!" he announced as I returned. "Valerius, come and hold this. I need to piss too, and I don't want anyone to steal it."

I perched at the edge of the couch he vacated, hugging the cithara.

"Petronius has had a little too much to drink," Otho confided in me. "But we bear it, because he is grieving poor Marsus."

Grieving him loudly and quite obnoxiously, but I understood it.

I strummed the strings of the cithara, making them vibrate under my fingertips, and said, "They say there's no cure for grief except time."

Guests moved in and out of the triclinium in the gap between courses. Someone else had to piss, someone had to vomit, and someone had to wash his hands. All the while a stream of slaves darted in and out of the room, taking away dishes, refilling wine cups, presenting napkins so that we could wipe our greasy fingers. There was more traffic here than the Via Sacra on market day.

"Where is he anyway?" Petronius asked as he tramped back into the triclinium. I wasn't sure who he was asking. Us? The gods? Bacchus, probably. Bacchus was an excellent conversationalist when you'd fallen as deeply into your cups as Petronius had. "Most famous fucking writer in Rome, and *C-C-Cilnius* snubs my company!"

I looked across to my couch and found Atreus was looking back at me steadily.

I pressed my mouth into a tight line, a last line of defence in case the truth tried to burst inconveniently free. I stood up and held the cithara out to Petronius. "Give us another song, Petronius."

Petronius sat back down on the couch beside Otho and Poppaea, setting the cithara down on the floor. "I'm too drunk. Is there dessert?"

Poppaea Sabina clapped her hands, and an army of slaves paraded into the triclinium

Dessert was honeyed quinces, pears, and pancakes so delicate that they melted on the tongue. The music picked up again, and so did the conversation.

And then, because I was sure that we'd found our killer, and just when I'd started to feel comfortable with the warm sense of victory slowly beginning to enfold me, the gods decided to punish me for my hubris.

From the depths of the house, there came a loud scream.

* * *

The woman who screamed was middle-aged, thin, with her greying hair worn in braids. She was still screaming when we found her, clutching the doorway of a narrow room somewhere close to the kitchen as though she was afraid that if she let go, her legs wouldn't hold her.

Screaming in front of me, and a cacophony behind, as Otho's entire guest list tried to push towards the sound to see what in Tartarus was going on. Luckily, I was with a man who'd dealt with crowds in the Aventine; Atreus not only managed to keep everyone else back, he also firmly shifted the grey-haired woman out of the way without even breaking his stride.

Whatever he saw in the room pulled him up short though, but only for a moment.

"Get cloths! Quickly!"

I followed him in.

There, lying on a narrow mattress on the floor, was a girl I didn't recognise. I should have, because who else could it be but Iris? —but I didn't, because I couldn't even make out her features underneath the bloody tendrils of hair that were stuck to her face, and the deep, horrible gash that cut through her cheek like a wet ravine. Her lower lip was trembling, and she held her shaking hands in front of her face, as though she was afraid to touch herself. Blood pooled out from underneath the mattress, creeping down the shallow channels between the tiles.

Atreus went to his knees beside Iris, and I did the same.

The slave woman finally stopped screaming, but then it was Poppaea's turn: "Otho, we're ruined!"

"Jupiter," Petronius said, sounding suddenly, shockingly sober.

A boy managed to squeeze himself through the bottleneck of onlookers at the door. He was clutching an armful of cloths to his chest, and he froze in horror for a moment as he took in the sight in front of him, before Atreus snapped, "Hurry up!"

The boy scuttled forward. He was a skinny boy, barely even a teenager; the same boy who'd played the cymbals the first night I'd dined here: Idaeus.

Iris's eyes rolled in her head, and she reached out a bloody hand to the boy.

Dropping to his knees beside us, he caught it.

Atreus and I bundled the cloths quickly, and I pressed the first one against the gash in Iris's cheek. She moaned, as though even screaming took too much of her rapidly dwindling strength, and her fingers tightened around Idaeus's.

The first cloth bled through quickly. I dropped it on the tiles and Atreus held a second one against the girl's face.

"Idaeus?" I asked, and the boy jolted, tearing his fearful gaze away from Iris and staring at me. "I need you to get a doctor."

He blinked at me.

"Otho?" I called, without looking behind me. "She needs a doctor."

"A doctor," Otho said, as though he'd never heard the word before in his life. The charitable interpretation was that he was in shock. The less charitable one was that he'd never even considered the possibility of paying a doctor to come and see a mere slave. I leaned towards the first, not because I thought Otho was a compassionate man, but because Iris was no mere slave. She was Nero's birthday gift.

"Go to the excubitorium of the first century of the Fifth Cohort of Vigiles," Atreus told the boy. "Tell Leander to come at once."

The boy looked torn.

"Go!" Atreus said.

The boy scrabbled around on the floor for a moment, grasping the bloody cloth we'd already used as though he couldn't bear to think of leaving it on the floor and retreating again.

Strange the way the mind worked while it tried to process the unthinkable. Otho not reacting to the word 'doctor.' The boy picking up a discarded cloth even in the middle of this bloodbath. And now, Petronius saying, "I need another drink."

Well, the last one wasn't too strange. I had the same urge myself.

"Hold the cloth," Atreus said, and I leaned forward on my knees to do as he said. Iris whimpered under the pressure of my hand, her eyelids fluttering, as Atreus checked her over for other wounds. "Nothing."

I nodded grimly. She might survive this then, if the boy got Leander here in time.

"She's worthless," Otho said from somewhere behind me. "She's *worthless.*"

Iris whimpered again.

The low heat of rage build in me, and I struggled not to lose my control on it now, when I was needed to help keep the girl alive. We had been wrong, Atreus and I, which was certainly nothing new, but the attack on Iris just when we'd decided that Entellus was our man? That felt like an attack on us too, as though the killer was mocking us, laughing while he did it, even though he couldn't have known we'd thought we'd solved it.

Not the killer mocking us then, but the gods themselves, those capricious bastards.

I concentrated on keeping pressure on Iris's wound. Nothing I hadn't done before, thanks to my military service, but usually the faces that looked up at me in pain and terror weren't as young as this one. And somehow, I didn't think my old speech about how they'd fought well for the glory of Rome would give courage to a frightened girl who had done nothing to deserve this except look like Nero's mother.

"It's fine," I said instead. "You will be fine, Iris."

She whimpered again, her hand clutching at the air where Idaeus had been, and Atreus put his hand in hers.

"Otho," I said, twisting my neck to look over my shoulder. "Take your guests back to the triclinium. Atreus and I have this under control."

Otho, his arms around Poppaea, threw me a wild look, but had the decency to not call me a lying bastard to my face. I was sure it was a topic he'd touch on later, and at length, once he came back to himself.

He ushered the guests out of the doorway, leaving only the grey-haired slave woman behind. She had stopped screaming, at least.

"Come in here," I said to her. "You are the one who found her?"

"Yes," the woman said. "Yes, sir." She stepped gingerly inside the small room. "I came to get her bowl from her."

Atreus was kneeling with his knee almost in a wooden bowl. A spoon lay on the tiles beside it. The thin remains of something that looked a little like puls still clung to the sides of the bowl.

I glanced around the room. Apart from the mattress and the bowl, it was empty. There wasn't even a lamp. Just a depressing little cell of a room.

"Was the door kept locked?" I asked.

"Yes, sir," she said. "Well, latched from the outside."

"And she was fine when you brought her dinner?" Atreus asked, and Iris moaned and clutched his hand more tightly.

"Idaeus brought her dinner," the woman said. "I only came by later to get the bowl."

The bowl that Iris had finished. So Idaeus came, left the food, which Iris ate, and the next person who entered the room should have been the woman. Except someone else had come in here, with a knife, and tried to kill the girl.

"Thank you," Atreus said. "Can you fetch more cloths, please?"

The woman nodded and slipped away.

"Well, the one thing we know for sure was that it wasn't Cilnius," I said dourly. "Or *Entellus*, because we were watching him! Our one fucking suspect, and we know it wasn't him!"

Atreus shook his head and swore under his breath.

I wondered if Iris would be able to name her attacker. I tried to ask her, but the poor girl was barely conscious because of the pain and shock. So I kept the pressure on the wound, hoping to stem the flow of blood before she lost it all, and Atreus squeezed her hand.

Leander, when he finally arrived, was accompanied by Juba. They were both damp with sweat, despite the cold weather outside, and Leander was a little out of breath. It didn't slow him down at all. He slung his bag at Juba, who caught it, and then elbowed Atreus out of the way to kneel on the floor beside me.

"How many cloths has she bled through?" he asked.

"This is the fourth," I said. "It's slowing, I think."

Iris's eyes were closed now, her eyelashes fluttering weakly. Her hand lay open on the floor, knuckles resting in a pool of her own blood, fingers twitching.

"Light," Leander said. "I need light."

Atreus hurried away to find something.

"Juba, come and take over from Valerius," Leander said, and flashed me an apologetic smile. "She doesn't look like she has any fight in her now, but that might change when I put the stitches in."

I nodded, my stomach clenching, and did an awkward shuffle on my knees to exchange positions with Juba. Then I climbed to my feet and leaned in the doorway as Leander got his needles and his catgut ready. By the time Atreus got back with a lamp in each hand, Leander was ready to begin work.

This time it was Iris's scream, weak and thready and fading, that echoed through the house.

* * *

The mood in the triclinium was an unhappy one. Only Entellus was reclining, and that was with an empty bowl cradled against his chest in case he had to throw up. Everyone else was seated. The musician had left, but his cithara was still leaning against the wall. The slaves who attended the guests were silent. One or two had to pause to wipe their faces as they worked, and their teary gazes were fearful. And why wouldn't they be? One of the men in this room had cut Iris open as though he was a butcher, and she was nothing more than a slab of meat.

I helped myself to a jug of wine on the central table, waving away the slave girl who belatedly darted forward to help. I poured myself a cup and swished it around in my mouth to try to remove the stench of blood from my throat. I drank the cup, poured a second one, then went and took my seat on the couch beside Lucan.

Everyone stared at my bloodied toga as I did.

Atreus didn't sit. He leaned against the wall, one foot propped up behind him, and crossed his arms over his chest. He tilted his chin up as his gaze travelled slowly around the room, stopping on every single guest. He might have been wearing a toga, but he appeared every inch the Aventine shitkicker he was right now, and he was clearly spoiling for a fight. He studied each of the guests with the calculated expression of a man sizing up which one of them would break first—a man who hadn't decided yet, but who was certainly going to get some grim satisfaction from the violent process of finding out.

"Valerius," Petronius said at last. His tone was low, his voice taut with tension, but never let it be said that Petronius let the circumstances get in the way of a good verbal jab. "Well, thank Jupiter you and Atreus are looking into things. Otherwise, a man might consider tonight's events and find himself very unsettled."

Litus coughed into his hand in a vain attempt to hide an incredulous sound.

"Your point is well taken, Petronius." I raised my glass at him in a mocking toast and gazed around the room.

Which one of them was it? My gaze found Entellus, simply because I didn't like him, and because I'd been certain, an hour ago, that he was the killer. His drunkenness, I'd thought a ruse. Perhaps he wasn't just a playwright, I'd told myself, but also an actor of sorts. Then again, the same could probably be said of any man in the room. Which one of them craved success at the Juvenalia so desperately that they were willing to kill for it?

I suddenly hated every single one of them.

Fuck pleasantries. Fuck manners. Fuck every sharp barb disguised as convivial conversation. I was tired, my toga was sticky and heavy with blood, and misery and defeat had carved a hollow space out inside me that I wanted to crawl into and wallow until I felt better. This might have been the moment when a more career-conscious man would have tried to brazen his way out of the situation, knowing that the emperor would know of his failure before morning, but fuck that too. Hadn't Corbulo taught me the value of a tactical retreat in order to regroup? Because sometimes when you were surrounded by barbarians, you needed to find a defensible position and catch your breath.

The same was true of poets and playwrights, apparently.

"I'm going to talk to the slaves. Try not to kill each other in the meantime," I said, and strode out of Otho's lavish triclinium.

Atreus peeled himself off the wall and followed me.

"Valerius! Please!" Poppaea Sabina caught us in the atrium. She looked fragile and distraught, and she reached out and caught my hands. Her eyes swam with tears. "Please, you must find out who did this! Otho and I are *ruined!*"

That was hard to imagine, given the luxury of this house and all its furniture and decorations. But perhaps she meant their friendship with Nero would be ruined if they couldn't give him the best gift for his Juvenalia. They had enough money; it was status they craved.

"Is Nero so petty?" I asked her, and she faltered for a moment as though she didn't know how to answer that. It was a question worthy of Petronius—a trap that she had to be careful not to spring.

"Nero is most generous and benevolent." She tugged her hands away from mine as she reclaimed her composure, and said, primly, "It is Otho and I who will not forgive ourselves."

Who said only men ought to be politicians? With a brain as sharp as hers, Poppaea would run rings around half the senate.

I inclined my head, conceding her victory. "I need to speak to your slaves."

Poppaea glanced at Atreus, and then back to me, and I wondered if I imagined the flash of confusion in her expression, as though she couldn't fathom a man of my pedigree lowering himself to talk to the slaves when there was a plebeian I could delegate the job to right there.

I probably should have.

The slaves were no use. Most of them had spent the night darting back and forth between the kitchens and the formal triclinium, run off their feet attending their master and his guests. Iris's room, the door in a shadowed alcove on the other side of the kitchen, had been out of sight and out of mind. Nobody had noticed anyone going there who shouldn't have, but nobody had been watching out for it either.

The grey-haired woman was Iris's keeper, and I didn't know if her tears were for her charge or for herself, and I wondered how Otho and Poppaea would punish her failure. She was sitting on a stool in a corner of the kitchen, and the other slaves studiously avoided her as they worked, as though she had an illness they were afraid of catching.

"She was a good girl," the woman said. "Barely spoke a word of Latin when we got her and the boy, but she's a fast learner."

"The boy?" Atreus asked, raising his eyebrows.

"Idaeus," the woman said. "Her brother. The master gave them Greek names, and then beat them because they didn't speak Greek either."

One of the kitchen slaves gasped and moved away from the conversation.

The grey-haired woman lifted her chin, defiance shining through her tears. "What? He did. As though calling a cat a dog will teach it how to bark!" The sudden silence in the kitchen told me that the woman was stepping onto dangerous ground. So did her suddenly upturned lip. "Why should I care what I say? I'll be beaten too, even though I kept the door latched like I was ordered."

Atreus crouched down and took her hand. "You care for Iris."

The woman darted him a wary glance. "Someone had to. The girl was cursed by the gods for looking the way she does."

There was no arguing with that.

"And the door was locked?" I asked. "Well, latched?"

She'd told us as much already, but I wanted to be sure.

She nodded. "Yes, sir. Idaeus took Iris her dinner earlier, and the door was latched again when I went to collect her bowl. Whoever hurt her, he closed the door again when he left."

"And you saw nothing?" I asked her. "Nobody near the door who shouldn't have been there?"

"No," the woman said. "Nobody."

Atreus nodded, releasing her hand and rising to his feet. "Thank you."

She hunched over on the stool, wrapping her arms around herself.

Atreus and I walked down the short corridor, stopping in front of the storeroom door between the kitchen and Iris's room. Three paces in either direction, and I'd be back in the kitchen, or watching Leander tend the girl. I caught Atreus's gaze and saw my own uncertainly reflected in his eyes: the distance between the kitchen and Iris's room was nothing. Even if the attacker had been lucky enough not to be spotted by one of the slaves, how had nobody from the kitchen heard her scream?

We'd heard the grey-haired woman scream all the way from the triclinium.

"It makes no sense," I said, dragging a hand through my hair. "What do you think? Entellus?"

"Entellus only left the room once," Atreus said. "And you went with him."

"He pissed all over the floor and then went straight back into the triclinium," I said.

Atreus leaned against the wall and let out a long breath. "Mugo the Fish wasn't sure about Cilnius, if it was suicide or murder. And Entellus had seen which way Cilnius ran. He would have known where he was going."

"But he also would have expected him to conveniently come home at some point," I said.

"If I was going to kill a man I lived with, I wouldn't do it at home," Atreus said. "It made *sense*, and then the statues on top of it all..."

"It was a good theory," I said, "until I gave him an alibi tonight."

Atreus's mouth twitched in the ghost of a rueful smile. "No, it was never even a good theory. He was *there*, that's all. And any one of them might have been; Entellus was just the one we saw."

"I was trying to make you feel better."

This time, his smile lasted a moment longer. "Thank you."

I shook my head. "You're right, though. *We* were right. Entellus was obsessed with Marsus, and he hated him."

"And is the only man here we know for sure didn't attack Iris."

We stood listening to the bustle of the kitchen while our minds ran in circles and got absolutely nowhere.

"Last time I was here," I said, "I wondered what kind of master Otho was. I think I know the answer now."

Atreus made a sound of unhappy agreement, and we returned to the atrium.

Poppaea was seated on a bench, a slave girl standing in attendance with wine. When Poppaea saw us, she lifted her chin. "Have you found the attacker?"

"No. And I would strongly suggest that you and Otho send your guests home and lock your doors."

"You're leaving?" She clutched her bosom and then, like a true Roman wife, steeled herself against fear. She rose to her feet, gathering the folds of her stola around herself as though it was armour. "Wait. I'll send your doctor with you."

"He's still with Iris," I said.

Poppaea threw me an exasperated look. "I do not believe in throwing good money after bad, Valerius."

So, no medical treatment for Iris after tonight, then, even though if she lived, she was in danger of infection.

"How much do you want for her?" I asked. The last thing I needed was another slave, especially one who might drop dead on me by morning, but the thought of leaving the girl in this house where she would be ignored was too cruel. I told myself I was being practical—if Iris survived, she might be able to tell us who attacked her. Leaving her in the same house as the man who had tried to murder her would be recklessly stupid. I should know; I was closely acquainted with reckless stupidity.

"Ten thousand," Poppaea said.

"What skills does she have that are worth ten thousand?" I asked.

Her mouth narrowed into a thin line.

"Just her face, then," I said, "and it's no longer pretty. Five thousand."

"She's a virgin," Poppaea said.

"Six, then," I said, because Poppaea couldn't have known that I had no interest at all in a slave girl's virginity. "Six thousand denarii, for a girl who is entirely worthless to you."

"Very well," Poppaea said, and we regarded each other suspiciously, both of us trying to work out who had swindled the other.

Atreus slipped back toward Iris's cell near the kitchen, and a moment later he returned with Leander and Juba. Juba was carrying Iris. Her head lolled against his shoulder, half her face obscured by a bulky bandage.

Idaeus hurried along with them. "Wait! Where are you taking—" He stumbled to a halt when he saw Poppaea. "Mistress?"

Poppaea spun on her heel and strode back towards the triclinium, and the rest of us swept out into the night, leaving a tearful Idaeus staring after us.

We walked home, following my litter bearers as they carried Iris. Leander spoke to Juba, telling him how to monitor Iris for fever, and how often to change her dressing, and how to apply honey to the wound to prevent infection. Juba nodded and asked questions in return.

Atreus and I slowed our pace and fell behind the others as we began the familiar climb up the Caelian Hill.

"You're soft-hearted," Atreus said, but his tone made it clear it wasn't an insult.

I pretended I thought it was anyway. "Bullshit. That girl might be our only chance of identifying the killer. We were already humiliated enough tonight, Atreus, and in front of Nero's closest friends. How do you think that will impact any career I'm trying to build? We need to grab every chance Fortuna tosses our way."

He smiled faintly in the moonlight. "Of course."

I knocked my shoulder against his and, under the cover of the folds of our blood-stained togas, our fingers brushed.

Perhaps I was soft-hearted, but I didn't mind Atreus knowing it.

I took a breath of cold night air, gladder than I could say to be standing here in the street with him, taking a moment to just breathe. Tonight had not gone as planned. The killer had effectively destroyed my reputation in front of Nero's closest friends by attacking Iris. It wasn't much of a reputation, but it was better than any of the others I'd acquired since coming home to Rome from the military. I'd had hopes it would survive a little longer.

Still, it wasn't the blow to my pride that stung the most. I hated being wrong, but, more than that, I hated not being able to prevent harm to Iris. She was only a slave, as Hermes had been, and Marsus was only an actor. They were the lowest of the low, and society at large wouldn't even miss them—they weren't even a wrinkle on the surface of the vast ocean of the city—which was exactly why they mattered. Barely anyone else cared, so I had to. I'd always been a contrarian at heart. Ask anyone.

Ask *everyone*.

Ahead of us, my litter climbed the hill in the moonlight.

Atreus scraped his shoe against the road, the sole making a gritty sound against the stones. This street was quiet, but I could hear the creak and rattle of carts somewhere in the neighbourhood, the sound rising up from further down the hill. The shout of a carter, the clop of hooves, the complaining bellow of an ox, and the answering snap of a whip. These were the sounds of night in the city.

Atreus brushed his knuckles against the back of my hand, and then caught my fingers. He squeezed them and then let go again. He nodded at the litter. "We should catch up."

I nodded, and we began to climb the hill.

It was a sombre procession that finally arrived home. The womenfolk were in bed, and Hursa was blinking sleep out of his eyes when he opened the door to us. The gasp he gave when he saw my bloody toga was theatrical enough to make Ammenius seethe with envy.

"Sir!"

"I'm not injured. Go and help Juba," I said, "and for the love the gods, Hursa, try not to get underfoot."

It was like telling a dog not to eat its own vomit; you had to try, even though you knew your words wouldn't do a thing to stop it.

Juba could, though, and would.

Hursa scuttled after Juba as he carried Iris through the atrium and deeper into the house, and Leander strode after them.

I stood for a moment in the atrium. There was a lit candle by the lararium, and I hoped those little household gods were watching over me now. I hoped, too, that they could spare some protection and good fortune for Iris, who would need it to survive the night.

I thought Atreus would leave with Leander, but he didn't.

He went into my tablinum and returned a moment later with the box with the latrunculin board and pieces in it. And we sat in the atrium, the night slipping slowly toward another cold winter's morning, moving the latrunculi pieces around in silence, both of us taking what solace we could in a game we at least had a faint hope of winning.

Chapter Ten

Seneca swept into my house the next morning as though he was my career's personal harbinger of doom. He found me eating breakfast with my family, and he was as gracious and polite as a man who built a life balancing art, philosophy and politics could be. I listened to him exchanging pleasantries with Fulvia, and wondered if he'd be so courteous when we were alone.

I invited him out to the peristyle to find out.

He inspected the winter-dormant rosemary unhappily, and then, letting out a sigh that might have been heard from the most distant corners of the world, he said, "Lucan tells me that you have not yet found his attacker."

"No," I agreed, tucking my hands behind my back in what was probably a vain attempt to appear as cool as the weather, and a man in total control of this rapidly unravelling situation. "Not yet."

Lucan raised his eyebrows. "Not *yet*? How many more chances will the man have to destroy my nephew's career, as well as the emperor's Juvenalia?"

Rhetorical questions with no answer were annoying enough. When they came from a philosopher, they arrived wrapped in an added layer of intellectual condescension that was as thick as butter but nowhere near as palatable.

Seneca huffed, and thankfully didn't wait for an answer. He picked a sprig of rosemary, crushed it between his thumb and forefinger, and then sniffed the remains. "I told you when we first spoke that an attack against Lucan may have been an attack against me."

"Sir, I don't believe—"

He didn't give me the chance to finish. "I have many enemies in the palace, Valerius, but I also have friends I can still rely on. If this *were* an attack against me, my friends would have a sense of it, no? But Anicetus tells me there is no whisper of it in whatever low places he hears all his whispers, and so I trust that this is not about me." He shot me a look that was almost wry. "And contrary to popular belief, there are certain things I care about more than myself."

Calliope entered the peristyle, bearing a tray of wine. Seneca shook his head, and I waved her away.

"Lucan is too far sunk in his grief to grasp that he is in danger," Seneca continued at last. "I would spirit him out of the city if I were able, but to snub Nero at the Juvenalia would be fatal to his career."

I could have pointed out that staying in Rome could be fatal in a much less metaphorical way, but I didn't. Seneca and I both understood what was at stake here. Leaving the city might save Lucan from an attack, but what sort of life would he live after it? His reputation would be destroyed, and all his friendships and influence lost. It was the same for every other man in the circle of poets and playwrights—if they left, there would be nothing to come back for. There were very few second chances in public life. None, if you lost the friendship of an emperor.

I knew exactly what facing that scenario felt like—I was certain Nero wasn't hearing nice things about me from Petronius and the others right now—and it wasn't pleasant.

No, Lucan was caught in the sticky web of Roman public life just as much as I was. And as much as the killer was too, and every other man in Nero's circle of friends.

Seneca and I studied the rosemary a little while longer, and then he said, "Maro speaks highly of you, Valerius, and I think you know as well as I do that he is not as crazy as he likes to pretend."

I smiled at that, feeling a rush of warm affection for the old man. "Not quite, no."

Seneca's gaze held mine. "Can you do it? Can you find the man who is threatening harm to Lucan?"

"I'm trying," I said, but I was a man trapped in a completely dark room; I could either stumble around and hope to find the exit (this was the strategy Atreus and I had been employing so far), or I could stand still and at least save myself from walking face-first into any more walls. Last night's wall, although entirely metaphorical, had left me bruised and battered and wary of making another painful misstep. "And whatever happens, I'll keep trying."

Seneca wasn't foolish enough to ask me to guarantee Lucan's safety, and I wasn't foolish enough to promise it. We both understood the gravity of this situation, and we both knew exactly how empty platitudes were.

After Seneca excused himself from my company, I leaned against a column for a while, my head tilted back as I stared up into the sky. It was another hazy day. A sparrow darted down into the peristyle and landed on the lip of the gently bubbling fountain. It tilted its head and stared at me curiously, and then flew away again. The sound of the fountain was soothing. Between that and last night's lack of sleep, I might have dozed for a moment.

So much for telling Seneca how much I was trying.

"Sir," Calliope said.

I jolted back into alertness.

"Juba said to tell you the girl is still alive," Calliope said tentatively. "And Junius Atreus is here."

I nodded at her and peeled myself off the column. I found Atreus in my tablinum, looking as sleep-deprived and haggard as I felt. It had been stupidly late last night when we'd finally parted, and he'd loped off into the darkness. This morning, he was sitting on one side of my desk, and had my latrunculi board out. He was scowling at the pieces as he pushed them around the squares in total violation of all the rules of the game.

I flopped down in my chair and put my feet up on my desk.

His scowl softened into his usual pensive expression as he pulled the latrunculi board out of my way. "Morning."

I grunted in response, and then said, "Did you sleep? You look like shit."

"Not much," he said, and narrowed his eyes. "And thank you."

"You missed breakfast," I said.

Atreus nodded at an empty plate on the end of my desk. My slaves had remembered to be hospitable, at least.

He slid a few more pieces around the board until he had one piece on its own in one corner, two in another, and the rest jammed into a third corner.

"What are you doing?" I asked.

He hummed and shook his head. "I don't know. Did the girl survive the night?"

"Yes."

We sat there in silence for a long while. Atreus kept pushing the pieces around, and I kept watching him, and both of us, I suspected, waited for inspiration to strike.

It didn't.

It persistently, maliciously didn't, and I got tired of watching him frowning at the board. I stood. "I'm going to talk to the girl."

Atreus left the latrunculi board and followed.

Iris had been housed in a small, private room behind the kitchen. It was a luxury not usually afforded a slave—they generally shared—but this room was Juba's. He'd earned it not through being a fine cook, like Damos, or a competent secretary, like Cretes, but because he'd saved my life, and Atreus's, when Bano the gangster had tried to push us off the roof of an Aventine warehouse. He was sitting on a stool outside the door, quiet and watchful.

"Is she awake?" I asked.

Juba stood. "She had some fish soup."

Damos made a fish soup that could raise anyone from their sickbed. Their deathbed, too, probably. I hoped it was working its magic on Iris.

I opened the door.

Iris was lying on her side on Juba's mattress, his blankets pulled up to her chin. Her face was obscured by the bulky bandage, and her dark hair spilled over it in tendrils matted with dried blood. She shifted when I entered the room and turned her head to see who it was. Then she sat up, pulling the blankets with her.

I crouched down so that I wasn't looming over her, and Atreus and Juba waited in the doorway. "My name is Aemilius Valerius. I bought you last night from Otho and Poppaea Sabina."

The one eye that was unobscured by the bandage was dark and wide.

"How are you feeling?"

"I am fine, master." Her voice was a little muffled by the bandage. She had an accent I didn't know, and ended her words on a slight upward note, as though she was asking a question. That was probably due to her uncertainty at finding herself in a new household. Everything in her life was a giant question right now.

"That's Juba," I said, nodding my head at him. "If you have any questions, he's the man to ask. If he's not around, ask anyone except Hursa, the door slave. You won't have any work to do until the doctor says you are healed, but you're welcome to go and meet the other slaves whenever you feel well enough to get out of bed."

Iris jerked her chin in a shaky nod. "Yes, master."

"Do you remember what happened last night?" I asked her. "Can you tell me who attacked you?"

She looked down, and her hair fell in front of her face like a ratty curtain. When she looked up again, there were tears in her uncovered eye. "It was dark, master. I—I was asleep. I don't remember."

"Idaeus brought your dinner," I said. "You ate it. And then you fell asleep?"

"There was..." Her voice hardened for a moment before it wavered again. "There was nothing else to do in that room, master, except to sleep." She drew a shaky breath. "I ate my puls, and fell asleep, and when I heard someone, I thought it was Lucida."

The old woman, I guessed.

Iris clenched her hands in blankets. "It—it was a man. But the light was behind him. I could not see. He cut me, and I... I don't remember anything else, master."

It was not the answer that I wanted to hear. It was a waste of six thousand denarii, probably, but I couldn't bring myself to regret getting Iris out of a house where nobody cared if she lived or died. Nobody except a couple of other slaves anyway, and it wasn't as though they could afford a doctor for her.

I looked to Atreus to see if he had anything he wanted to ask. His forehead was pinched, his brows pulled together as he puzzled through something. It was an expression he wore at least a dozen times a day, whether he was trying to track down a killer, or deciding what to order for lunch. He caught my gaze and shook his head slightly.

"You're safe here," I told Iris, and stood up.

She nodded, staring at her lap again, and murmured something that might have been her thanks.

Then, with nowhere else to go except where our playwrights and poets would eventually turn up, Atreus and I went to Nero's theatre in the Garden of Agrippina, with Juba in tow.

The morning was cold but bright, the sun working hard to burn away the chill that lay over the city. The air was sharp with the smell of woodsmoke. People bustled through the streets, doing whatever it was they did to pay the rent and fill their children's bellies, and I thought of men who were scrambling just as hard for the approval of the emperor, and the desperate, murderous lengths that one of them was taking.

And we still didn't know which one.

We arrived midmorning at the gardens, having fought off the chill of the air with our brisk walk. It had only been a day since we'd last been here, but the theatre had undergone something of a transformation overnight. Wasn't that the way with construction? For weeks nothing happened, and then you blinked and suddenly it was almost done. The orchestra in front of the scaenae frons was finished, and there were fewer tradesmen and builders wandering about the place today. In their place, a contingent of slaves swept and scrubbed the dust of construction away, polishing the theatre's marble surfaces to a shine in preparation for Nero's Juvenalia.

Litus was pacing in the orchestra, thin and pinched and severe looking. On the stage, Ammenius was delivering an impassioned monologue. By the look of intense displeasure on Litus's face, it was his words the actor was currently butchering with his bombastic delivery. Not every word needed to be shouted, or drawn out into more syllables than it contained, but apparently nobody had told Ammenius.

"Dress rehearsal?" I asked Litus, nodding at Ammenius and his soldier's garb. I wasn't sure Aeneus had worn quite so many peacock feathers and cosmetics on his flight from Troy, but I was no historian.

Litus stared at me blankly for a moment, and I wondered if he was evaluating whether or not to speak to me after last night, but then he gave me a grim nod. "I should have written a poem instead of the scene from a play, and then I could have recited it myself. Or at least found someone who was..." He snorted.

"Not Ammenius?" I asked.

Litus acknowledged me with a pained nod, and then drew a deep breath. "I didn't expect to see you here today, Valerius. Your exit from Otho's party last night was so dramatic, and here you are ruining it with a sudden but lacklustre reappearance."

I exchanged a glance with Atreus. "Not everything's a play, Litus."

"That's the shame of it," he agreed. "At least on a stage, a tragedy can be beautiful. In real life, they're often just mundane and grubby."

And wasn't that the depressing truth?

We left the rehearsal and went behind the scaenae frons, then climbed the stairs of the narrow edifice to the rooms above. Petronius's room was empty, but I didn't read too much into it; it wasn't even lunchtime yet, and Petronius, a devotee of Bacchus, was probably still sleeping off last night. I wished that I was too. It seemed that none of the poets or playwrights, except for Litus, was at the theatre yet, if they even intended to make an appearance today at all.

Antigon, the harried administrator, was having an argument with a plasterer when we found him in his office. Something about how he was not paying for the plasterer's missing equipment. He dismissed the man when he saw us, and the grumbling fellow turned to leave. He looked as though he was prepared to start a fight with the next person he saw—but the next person was Juba, and the man gave him a startled look and quickly adjusted his attitude before stomping away.

Antigon sat down behind his desk again, picking up his stylus and making some notation on his wax tablet.

"Antigon," I said, "it's looking good outside."

"Well," the man said, looking up at me with his head tilted, "it might all just come together for the Juvenalia as long as no more actors die!" He huffed. "And no more workmen try to get their sticky fingers in the coffers of the imperial treasury! Because the state is funding the Juvenalia, suddenly marble costs twice as much, or tiles have been mysteriously broken and must be replaced with more expensive ones, or they expect me to reimburse them for a missing handcart they failed to lock away! They would argue down to the last quadrans, some of them!"

I knew something about dealing with tradesmen from Maro and his eternal home renovation projects, so the sympathetic face I showed Antigon was both practiced and genuine. "And, of course, nobody will give you any credit when things go well."

He gave me a wry smile. "But they'll remember me when it comes to passing out the blame, yes. Still, that's the nature of life, isn't it? Was there anything I could help you with today?"

"You're here a lot," I said. "You must see all of the poets and the playwrights interacting, even if they barely notice you."

He snorted. "They are waspish and petty to a man; only the actors are worse. But if it's singling one of them out for *murder*... well, I am at a complete loss there. They are friends. You know the sort. A little gang of schoolboys who may fight amongst themselves, but if some neighbourhood bully tries to cause them trouble, suddenly they're a united front." His thin brows tugged together. "At least, that's what I thought until all of this. I suppose I misjudged them, and that at least one of them wears a better mask than even Fabia could make."

Antigon was as much in the dark as we were. I thanked him for his time, and we were just about to leave his office when Fabia's little boy, not wearing his satyr mask today, barged past us into the room.

"Nonus," Antigon said mildly, and the little boy eyeballed him, and then the small pile of coins on the desk. "No, that's to pay for my lunch, not yours."

The little boy strode forward and tried to grab the coins. Antigon caught him gently by the wrist in a move smooth enough to suggest he'd done it a thousand times. The coins went flying onto the floor, scattering all over the place, and Antigon sighed and let the boy's wrist go.

"Pick them up and put them all back, and I'll share my lunch with you."

Nonus hurried to obey, while I wondered at what sort of odd relationship the imperial slave and the tiny guttersnipe had. Antigon looked fondly exasperated at the little thief's antics, and clearly he'd never even raised his voice at the boy if Nonus was unafraid to walk right in and take whatever he wanted. When I was the same age, the adults in my life—my tutors, mostly— had very much been fans of rapping me across the knuckles, or any other body part they could reach, with a switch. Moralists, and parents the world over, would tell you that was the proper way to raise a child, but they also probably wouldn't want to use me as an example of the finished product.

Nonus got down onto his hands and knees to collect the coins, while Antigon pinched the bridge of his nose and looked more annoyed than his actions suggested he felt.

"That's not all of them," he said when Nonus put the coins back on his desk. "Where is the—where did it get to?" He leaned back on his stool to check first, and then stood up to come and scan the floor. The coin had vanished. And then Antigon laughed. "You're standing on it, you sneaky little monster!"

Nonus giggled and lifted his grubby bare foot to reveal a coin.

A neat little trick, and it lifted my spirits a fraction. We spoke with Antigon for a while longer, wished him well with his tradesmen and their creative accounting methods, and then went down the stairs again. The sunlight was blinding as we stepped back into the daylight, walking down the side of the stage to the orchestra.

I thought Atreus was with us, until I realised he wasn't; I looked back and saw him standing on the stage still, near the ornate portico that led to nothing. He was staring at the narrow columns that lined the portico, his head on the angle of that of an inquisitive bird, and as I watched he took a few steps back, and then forward, and then back, as though he was puzzling something out.

On one hand, I hoped it was a solution to this entire mess we'd found ourselves in. On the other hand, I had no idea what he could possibly have found in a row of columns that could in any way relate to the murders of Marsus, Hermes and Cilnius. I highly doubted our killer had erected a memorial plaque on the base.

I planted my arse on the lowest row in the cavea, Juba beside me, and squinted at the stage. Atreus joined us, dodging around Ammenius to get to the steps that led down into the orchestra.

"He's not happy," Atreus said, nodding back at Ammenius. "Cilnius was meant to be here to give him the final revisions to his poem, but he's not."

"So word hasn't got around yet," I said. "I don't know if that's to our advantage or not. What was so interesting about those columns, anyway?"

"Give me your purse," he said.

"Why?"

"Because mine's empty."

I unhooked my purse from my belt and handed it over.

Atreus tipped the coins out into the space between us, and Juba leaned behind me to see. "Two coins here. One here. And the rest..." He made a separate pile.

This was what he'd done with the latrunculi pieces earlier. "I have no idea what you're doing."

"Two coins," he said, tapping them. "The only ones we're sure of. Over here, a bunch of them. We're not sure of how many, but it doesn't matter. And here, one." He caught my befuddled expression, and his mouth twitched in a grin."

He still wasn't making any sense.

"When I was up on that stage, I was standing so that I could only see one column. But then, when I took a step sideways, I saw the entire row of them."

"That's not making it any clearer."

"Perspective," he said. "We have one investigation, but four different attacks, and, according to our witnesses, at least three different groups of attackers. If we take a step sideways..."

"Juno's tits," I said on a breath. "We have *four investigations.*" I nudged my fingers against his, where they still hovered over the two coins. *"Two* men killed Marsus, because the old woman with the crush on Juba *saw* them. Two men with a handcart, who dumped his body in the Medusa Fountain."

"Two men," Atreus agreed.

I pushed the single coin towards him. "One, we presume, for Hermes, and one for Iris. Maybe the same man, but maybe not."

"And a whole bunch who attacked Lucan on the street that night," Atreus said.

And then it was Juba's turn to take a sideways step and see everything from an entirely new perspective. He reached around me and claimed the single coin. Dropped it into the pile. "Except they didn't attack Lucan, did they?" he asked. "Lucan didn't have a mark on him."

His words hung there in the air for a moment, and then, wrapped around the sudden realisation, they landed like a ton of bricks.

Lucan hadn't had a mark on him.

But *Hermes* had.

But who would want to hurt a lowly slave instead of his important master?

Before I had a chance to even ponder the question, a commotion at the entrance to the theatre alerted me to the arrival of some familiar faces. Petronius swept into the theatre like a conquering hero, with his loyal generals at his side. Well, two loyal generals: Lucan and Fabianus. I had no idea where meek Hosidius was. Probably anxiously rewriting his bee play. And Entellus? My money, if I hadn't just given it all to Atreus, would have been on hungover.

"Litus!" Petronius cried cheerfully as he strode across the orchestra. "How goes rehearsals?"

On stage, Ammenius dropped his helmet, and it crashed against the floor. His sense of timing would have been perfect for a comedy—he answered Petronius's question just as succinctly as Litus's put-upon expression. It was a shame they were rehearsing a dramatic piece, then.

Petronius clapped Litus on the back, and Litus's expression soured even more. "Oh, cheer up, Litus. You have no sense of humour." Then it was Petronius's turn to look sour, as he turned and noticed me sitting in the front row. His smile vanished faster than a false friend at a wine shop when it was time to pay the bill. "Valerius."

I didn't bother wasting time being offended at Petronius's sudden change of demeanour. Instead, my brain was caught on the words he'd said to Litus, variations of which I'd heard since I'd first met the man.

You have no sense of humour.

It wasn't true, not strictly. Litus could be funny. He could be hilarious, in a dry, mordant way. But he didn't like being the brunt of the joke, did he? I'd seen that myself the day I'd met with him and Lucan on the Campus Martius. I'd thought I'd seen true hatred in the glance he'd shot Hermes's way, but then Lucan had laughed, and I'd dismissed the idea. But what if I hadn't been wrong, and Lucan had, and I'd seen an unintended glimpse of his true feelings that day?

"It wasn't Lucan who was attacked that night on his way home from Petronius's house," I said, low enough for just Atreus and Juba to hear, "and it wasn't only Lucan's poems that were destroyed forever in the fire."

Lucan's poems could be rewritten; Hermes's couldn't.

"This wasn't about Lucan or the Juvenalia," I said, having my own moment of shifting perspective and inwardly reeling from the dizziness it brought with it. Dizziness first, but, once I'd found my feet again, sudden, stark clarity. I stared at Litus as he made his way up the steps at the side of the stage, presumably to give direction to Ammenius and the other actor. "This was about Hermes, and his party trick of ridiculing his master's friends. And whatever Hermes came up with last Saturnalia, it was funny enough that they're all still talking about it, and Litus was *humiliated*."

Not humiliated the way Hosidius would have been—awkwardly and excruciatingly and obviously. And he wouldn't have been able to laugh it off like Petronius or ignore it like Lucan. Litus's humiliation was the sort of emotion that burned with a cold flame, invisible to his friends, and fed a secret desire for revenge.

"All this time we've been asking who hated Lucan," Atreus said, "and the question was who hated *Hermes*."

We didn't have a plan—we never had a plan—but the three of us rose to our feet as one and began to cross the orchestra towards the stage.

"Valerius," Lucan said, "What are—"

I shouldered past him and jogged up the steps with Atreus and Juba.

"Litus!" I had no idea what I was going to say, but fortunately my tongue had never waited for instructions before. "Hermes didn't know, did he?"

Litus tilted his head. "Didn't know what?"

"How much you hated him."

Litus clicked his tongue like a disappointed tutor. "Valerius, please. We're rehearsing."

"You were one of his master's closest friends," I said. "And I do genuinely mean that. You helped Lucan learn how to stand correctly on a stage, and how to project his voice. You actually want him to succeed at the Juvenalia, which is why it took us so long to see it. We thought—*everyone* thought—that this was all about Lucan. But it never was, was it? It was about some upstart little nobody of a slave boy who had the audacity to compose insulting poems about you."

Litus snorted. "This is ridiculous."

Ammenius and the other actor took a couple of steps away from him, because I'd never met an actor who didn't have an amazing sense of self-preservation. Down in the orchestra, Petronius and the others had drawn closer to the stage, watching what I really hoped was the final act in this drama. Or, since I was involved, Atellan farce. Lucan's face was pale, his expression uncertain. And why wouldn't it be? Litus was his friend, whereas he barely knew me, and I hadn't done anything except persistently fail in the brief time we'd been acquainted.

"But Hermes didn't know you hated him," I said. "Of course he opened the posticum door to you. It was nothing he hadn't done a hundred times before, even in the middle of the night. Did he even have enough time to be surprised before you killed him?"

"Ridiculous," Litus said again, but his voice was strained. "Even if—" He shook his head. "He was a *slave*!"

"A slave," I said. "Just a slave. It's not even a crime, is it? According to the law, you only have to pay Lucan for the cost, but Lucan never saw Hermes as *just* a slave. And that's the problem, isn't it? Lucan will never forgive you for it."

Litus risked a look at Lucan, and so did I. Lucan's expression was one of horror. His was the face of a man who wanted to deny everything he was hearing, yet couldn't, because on some level, one I was sure he'd never had to examine before, everything I was saying made terrible sense.

"You have no proof," Litus said, and he was absolutely correct—but it was still the wrong thing to say. He should have stabbed my accusation through the heart with an outraged proclamation of innocence, instead of going for the mere evidentiary flesh wound. For someone whose job was literally words, he'd certainly fumbled them when it counted.

It wasn't an admission, but it didn't have to be one. There was only one man here we had to convince, and he was smart enough to see Litus's guilt in that weaselly answer.

"Litus." Lucan's voice cracked on his friend's name. "How *could* you? For a *poem*? He was just a boy!"

I was sure that Litus had years' worth of justification that he could have poured straight from his bitter heart into his words, but he didn't. Instead, he took a sideways step, pulled Ammenius's soldier's gladius out of its scabbard, and ran straight for me.

If I'd had more than a moment to think about it, I might have been amused at how this was the worst possible thing he could do to convince his friends he wasn't a killer. But I didn't. I didn't even have time to sidestep him. I *tried*, twisting away, my heart hammering fast as I felt the blade scrape against my ribs. I pushed back against Litus, hard, expecting to be flooded with a warm gush of blood just before my knees gave out, but beyond the heat of this unexpected fight, I only felt the burning sting where my unhappy skin had been split open. Maybe it wasn't so bad, or maybe my brain hadn't caught up to my body yet. I'd seen it plenty of times before in the military, men who only noticed they were gravely injured once they stopped fighting.

It wasn't as though I had time to contemplate it. Not with Litus struggling to pull the gladius far enough back to get another hit.

He wasn't a soldier, and that was to my advantage. But he also had nothing to lose, and he was the only one with a sword. That was *not* to my advantage.

I reached for his fist, trying to wrestle control of the gladius away from him. A dangerous move, given that if I misjudged I'd find myself gripping the blade—not for long, though, before I lost my fingers!—but in close quarters like this, my options were limited.

Atreus was beside me, and the three of us were a muddle of hands, elbows, and knees as we struggled for control of the situation. No Roman stage had ever seen a fight as dismally realistic. There were no dramatic speeches, suspenseful pauses, or sweeping movements a dancer would be proud of. This was messy, ridiculous, and actually dangerous. Litus, for all that he was built like a stick insect, was surprisingly strong, and the longer we struggled, the more it occurred to me that, despite having the numbers on our side, Atreus and I might actually be in very real trouble here.

Killed by a playwright.

My family would be so embarrassed, and so would my ghost. Jupiter! I hoped I wasn't fated to suffer the indignity of haunting this theatre. I'd have to watch plays for all eternity.

And then, abruptly, Litus grunted and fell backwards onto the stage, revealing Juba standing behind him, the other actor's sword in his hand and a murderous expression on his face.

It suited him, and I appreciated it more than I could say.

Especially since, at that moment, I discovered I couldn't say anything at all. When I drew a breath in order to speak, a wave of pain buffeted me, and I bowed like a sapling in a howling wind.

Right.

That whole gladius to the ribs thing.

I stumbled to my knees onto the stage floor beside Litus, and at least had the pleasure of seeing him twitch for the last time, a pool of blood spreading out beneath him, before I pitched forward and joined him, and then rolled over onto my back to catch my breath.

At least one of us still could.

The wound wasn't too terrible, I hoped, but I also didn't want to test it by getting up right now. So I lay on the stage, stared out at the winter's sky above the theatre, and breathed in the coppery scent of too much blood. At least most of it wasn't mine. I could hear excited voices all around me, and a lot of yelling, but I ignored it as I caught Atreus's gaze.

He was still breathing heavily as he knelt beside me. "Sons of Dis."

"They were probably involved, yes."

Atreus took the nearest gladius and made quick work of the neckline of my tunic, ripping it open so that he could peel the fabric down and we could both get a look at the damage. I craned my head to see, and Atreus slapped my questing fingers away.

"It's not too bad," he said. "You'll live."

Above me, from the windows and balconies of the scaenae frons, people peered down. One of them was a grotesque, grinning face framed by a shock of bright red hair. Little Nonus, wearing the slave mask.

Atreus's green-flecked eyes said more than his stony expression did as he called for vinegar and cloths to dress my wound, and I wondered if I'd scared him.

"It's fine," I said.

He pressed his mouth into a thin line but didn't voice his obvious disagreement. Not here, at least, but I was certain I'd hear all about it later. The thought of that warmed me more than it should have.

"It's fine," I said again, and then Atreus was elbowed out of the way by Fabia, who pressed a vinegar-soaked cloth against the cut, and suddenly it wasn't fine. It was agonising, but I grit my teeth and thanked the gods I was still breathing. If I'd been a little slower on my feet, or if Litus had actually known how to properly wield a gladius, the outcome might have been very different.

And, of course, if Juba hadn't been with us.

"Thank you, Juba," I said. This wasn't the first time Juba had saved my life. It was becoming an expensive habit of his.

Juba nodded, and then folded his arms over his chest and stared at the gathered spectators in the orchestra as they stared back at us.

I clapped a hand to my ribs and sat up with Atreus's help. The flap of my ruined tunic exposed more of me to the cold air than was comfortable; I felt like one of the nymphs from Nero's garden party, in a flimsy chiton pinned only at one shoulder. Atreus held his hand down, and I pulled myself to my feet with my good arm.

Litus's body lay a few steps away. He was face down, so I didn't have to look him in the eye. I wasn't sure if I was glad of that or not. It might have been satisfying, but death so often wasn't, even when it was justified.

I shuffled through his blood towards the edge of the stage, the soles of my sandals leaving smeared footprints behind me.

"I don't understand," Lucan said. He sounded as bewildered as he looked. "All this over his wounded pride?"

"Not just the wound, I think," I said, "but the fact that it came from a slave. It was a wound that festered instead of healing, and I think he just couldn't bear the thought of another wild Saturnalia where he was made to serve the slave who'd humiliated him. It was never about you, Lucan. I believe Litus truly thought he was your friend. Perhaps he was even jealous that you loved Hermes so dearly. Just another thing that fed his hate."

"And then what?" Petronius asked from the midst of the small audience of slaves, actors, and playwrights who had gathered to watch the spectacle. "He killed Marsus as well?" His handsome face screwed up in confusion. "No. Why would he do that?"

"He didn't," I said, still catching my breath. "Marsus died first, and in any case, it had nothing to do with Litus. The thing with cultivating a literary nest of vipers, is that more than one of them might bite."

Petronius tilted his head thoughtfully. I liked to think he was ruminating enviously on my clever viper metaphor, but probably not. He blinked a few times. "So who's the other snake, Valerius? Is it Cilnius?"

I looked to Atreus, to make sure that we were of one mind on this.

"Cilnius is dead," I said. "Entellus?"

Atreus nodded grimly. "Entellus."

And then we climbed down from the stage and pushed through the little crowd before an astonished Petronius could delay us with any more of his questions. Or, worse, expect us to clean up the corpse. And I reflected, as we escaped the theatre into the surrounding gardens, that if I never had to stand in front of that stage again, or on it, that I'd be a very happy man indeed.

* * *

We sent a messenger to the Aventine, and then headed for Entellus's house on the Quirinal Hill. We detoured briefly to my house on the Caelian Hill, where Hursa shrieked at the sight of me, which in turn brought my womenfolk and most of the slaves running. I assured everyone loudly that everything was fine, and then limped up the stairs to get away from them all. It was only partially successful. The slaves milled at the bottom of the steps, discussing me over their brooms and brushes, and Fulvia and Octavia followed me up them. Fulvia bandaged my ribs while both she and Octavia pecked at me like hens attacking a mouse.

"So you barely survived one encounter with a killer, and now you're going after another?" Octavia demanded her brows set in disapproving arches.

"Truth hates delay, as Seneca himself says."

Octavia looked unimpressed.

"Besides, this is hardly a wound at all." I winced as Fulvia tugged unnecessarily hard on the bandage. "It's a scratch. It doesn't even need stitches. It only pissed out blood because it's a long cut, but it's not deep."

Fulvia and Octavia exchanged the sort of unhappy and conspiratorial look they did when they hated that I was right. In fairness to them, it didn't happen very often, but when it came to battle wounds, I knew more than they did.

"Anyway, we'll have Atreus's vigiles with us, so we'll be fine."

"Will they smother Entellus with their fire mats?" Fulvia asked drily.

From where he was leaning in my bedroom doorway, Atreus coughed into his hand.

"I know you're concerned," I said, trying to placate them. It was probably as useless as the senate trying to placate the mob any time either of the Gracchi brothers stirred things up with some new and exciting idea for the republic, but I had to try. "But I will be *fine*."

Of course, it didn't help that I was saying it while wearing a bandage. My womenfolk weren't stupid, to begin with, and we all knew I couldn't guarantee nothing would go wrong. But they also knew I couldn't be dissuaded. Jupiter, they knew I had no choice but to follow this through. My reputation rested on it.

I stood, careful not to wince, and crossed to the chest in the corner to find a clean tunic. I pulled it on, not enjoying the way my shifting muscles pulled at the wound on my ribs, but I'd had worse—the scar on my thigh thanks to a Parthian blade could attest to that. I would have reminded Fulvia and Octavia of that, except I suspected it wouldn't have been any consolation. They were going to worry, like it or not, until I was safely home again.

I felt like an idiot when it came to getting to the Quirinal Hill, mostly because I took a litter. But Fulvia and Octavia had insisted, and I was already sore, so why tire myself out on the way there when there was a chance that Entellus would give us another fight? Juba and Atreus walked ahead of the litter, and I pulled the curtains closed so that nobody could see me. I was way too young and way too sober to be spotted using a litter in the middle of the day. At least the curtains kept the cold air at bay.

Entellus's neighbourhood was as bright and bustling as the first time we'd visited. I climbed awkwardly out of the litter a block away from Entellus's insula, where three of Atreus's vigiles, Vibilus and Gaius and Manius, were waiting. I might have implied to Fulvia and Octavia that there would be more than three of them, and they might have fairly assumed that one of them wasn't going to be the littlest vigile in the world, but it was the middle of the day for the rest of the city, so it was the middle of the night for the vigiles. They should have been at their homes or their barracks sleeping—or, in Manius's case, in the care of his mother. We were lucky three of them had turned up. We also had three of my litter bearers, which boosted our numbers well; we'd left the fourth guarding the litter.

And so, it was nine of us who strode into the courtyard of the insula, looking intimidating enough that a few of the neighbours who were standing around in the sunlight suddenly remembered they had urgent business inside their own homes, behind their very firmly closed doors. I tried to take the lead, but Juba and Atreus got in front of me, and it was Atreus who approached Entellus's door and knocked.

We waited.

Atreus knocked again.

We waited again.

Atreus knocked a third time, and a more courageous neighbour stuck her head out of a doorway on the other side of the courtyard, and yelled, "He's gone! Moved out!"

And then she slammed her door.

Atreus tried Entellus's door, and it opened. We poured inside to discover that it was empty. Oh, the furniture was all still here, but there was no sign of Entellus or the woman who had previously answered the door to us.

"Turn it over," Atreus said to his vigiles, and they headed off happily in different directions. My litter bearers followed them eagerly. Who knew they'd been harbouring ambitions to ransack random houses this whole time?

I followed Atreus and Juba to the locked room, except it wasn't locked anymore. The door was wide open, the room was full of sunlight, and every single marble statue of Marsus lay shattered into rocks and dust on the floor.

"Well, fuck," said Atreus, and he was absolutely right.

Because what else was there to say?

Chapter Eleven

When we visited the magistrate Septus Severus at his home, he was working in his tablinum, with at least two secretaries, two clerks, a boy whose job it was to produce the correct scroll or codex when it was called for, and another who stood there with a jug of wine at the ready. Severus was a magistrate and jurist who spent his days writing legal opinions for those who consulted him, giving advice to the senate on the formulation of edicts, and complaining to his friends and acquaintances whenever the vigiles bothered him with news of actual crimes. I liked Severus, but Atreus didn't. Then again, I was offered a seat in Severus's tablinum and given a cup of wine. Atreus was expected to stand.

Severus sent his assistants away, and listened carefully, his elbows propped on his desk and his round chin resting in his hands, as I explained that Entellus had killed Marsus—and probably Cilnius—and then vanished when we'd gone looking for him.

"And this Entellus is the son of the adjutor to the prefect?" Severus clarified, his eyebrows scaling his creased forehead.

"Yes," I said, and raised my cup at him in a cheeky toast. "That's why we brought it to you instead of going and knocking straight on Papa's door."

He made an unhappy noise in the back of his throat. "Jupiter, Valerius."

Well, those didn't sound like the words of a man who had a plan we could immediately put into action.

Severus made that noise again. "Do you have any evidence, apart from some smashed statues? Because I think you will agree that even intact, a couple of statues of a man are not evidence that whoever carved them is a killer."

"Yes," I said. "But Entellus and Cilnius were late to dinner the night Marsus's body was later found. A neighbour saw two men dumping the body in the fountain."

"And there was a handcart missing from the theatre, sir," Atreus added.

"A handcart missing…" Severus levelled Atreus with a withering stare, and then looked back at me. "I'm not doubting you, Valerius, but Jupiter knows it's not enough to bring a prosecution. He's just going to deny it, and you have no evidence to prove otherwise." He shook his head. "Nobody cares about a dead actor."

"What about Cilnius? He might have killed him, too."

"Or he might have jumped into the river of his own accord," Severus pointed out. "I believe you, Valerius, I do. You have quite a nose for this kind of thing."

Actually, Atreus did, but why split hairs? Severus hated dealing with the vigiles at all. He would never be able to bring himself to acknowledge one of them in a complimentary manner.

"So, there's no way to bring a prosecution?" I asked.

"You've given me nothing to prosecute." Severus straightened up and pinched the bridge of his pudgy nose. "I'm sorry, Valerius, I truly am. The thought of a man facing no repercussions for murder is abhorrent, but there just isn't any evidence. And it's not as though we can send someone to threaten the son of the adjutor to the prefect until he confesses!"

He was right. The adjutor might have only been an equite, but he wielded the sort of political power that most patricians could only ever dream of. To control the flow of grain into Rome was to control the people. Hungry people were angry people, and then they were an angry mob. And once a mob entered a story, it never ended well.

I thanked Severus for his time, and his wine, and then we left.

Juba, waiting for us out on the street, didn't look surprised at our solemn expressions.

"It went as well as expected then, sir?" he asked.

I nodded.

"The woman must have told him," he said thoughtfully.

I let out an exasperated huff. "We told her she would be safe!"

"Would she, though?" my astute bodyguard asked. "He already killed a man, maybe two men. It wouldn't take much for him to kill a slave as well, and, like you told Litus, it wouldn't even be against the law."

He was right, and I hated the weight in my gut as I pondered his words. I hated that Entellus was a free man, and that there was very little justice in the world for men like him, just because he had money and a politically influential father. Most of all I hated that it made me a hypocrite, because I was just as rich and spoiled as Entellus was. It had never even occurred to me that we might have put Entellus's slave in danger; I'd been too selfish to even consider it. Perhaps a neighbour had seen her let us in the door, and Entellus had found out that way. Perhaps she hoped her master would reward her if she warned him. Or perhaps she'd just been so terrified of being found out that her fear had overcome her, and she'd blurted out the secret. I doubted I would ever know her reasons, and I really didn't want to know them. Whatever the answer was, it was a miserable one.

We were not the conquering heroes when we returned home. We were dispirited, gloomy, and defeated. Also, my purse was lighter three denarii, since I'd rewarded Manius, Vibilus and Gaius for turning up to Entellus's apartment.

The afternoon light was beginning to draw the long shadows out. It would be evening soon. I invited Atreus to stay for dinner, but he declined, so I invited myself to dinner at his place in the Aventine instead, and we set off again for another trek across the city. I walked this time; Juba was the only slave I trusted to keep all my secrets. Not that I shared them with him, but he was a clever man. He spent too much of his time sitting in the hallway outside Atreus's door not to guess at what was going on inside. Not that I expected anything of that nature tonight—I doubted either of us was in the mood—and so when we stopped to buy something for dinner, I made sure to get enough for Juba and Lucilla as well.

I climbed the stairs of Atreus's building slowly, holding my side. Atreus went to his neighbour's to fetch Lucilla, and Juba and I let ourselves into his place. I sat on the reading couch in the main room, and Juba pottered away in the little makeshift kitchen in the corner, searching for plates and cups. Then he went and brought the stools in from the balcony.

Lucilla, always shy with me, was delighted to see Juba, and insisted she sit on one of the stools beside him. Atreus sat on the couch with me, our thighs pressed together in a comfortable way that Juba pretended not to notice.

We talked of everything and nothing much at all; none of us wanted to discuss the murders in front of Lucilla. Outside, the afternoon softened into dusk, and then into night. The air was cold, and sharp with smoke. I ate my vine leaf slowly, not relishing the idea of walking back across the city to go home, but not sorry that I'd come. Victory could be celebrated with anyone, but defeat? That was a private commiseration. There would be wine and self-recrimination involved, and outsiders weren't invited. Jupiter, I probably would have avoided going home at all in the first place—Octavia and Fulvia's concerned looks had rankled more than appeased when I'd told them that Entellus had fled—except I hadn't wanted my womenfolk to think I was lying dead in the gutter somewhere.

"How much wine do you have?" I asked Atreus when he came back from putting Lucilla to bed in the other room.

"Some," he said. "Probably not enough."

I unhooked my purse from my belt and tossed it at Juba. He caught it with one hand and a wry grin, and then stood and left.

"How's your side?" Atreus asked me softly.

I grunted. "Uncomfortable."

He rubbed my leg, which did nothing for my ribs. "What are you grinning about?"

"I was just thinking that you'd make a terrible physician."

His eyes crinkled when he smiled. "I'd elbow you for that, but..."

"Oh, so *now* you know where my ribs are?"

"Shut up," he said, still smiling.

We were silent for a while, listening to the sounds of Atreus's downstairs neighbours having an argument. They argued most nights. Sometimes, they screamed and threw things, and that was when Atreus usually went

217

downstairs and threatened to drag them both to the excubitorium's cells for the night. It didn't sound too fraught tonight, so far at least. I could hear someone singing drunkenly down on the street. It seemed early in the evening for that level of drunkenness, but this was the Aventine. I could also hear children shrieking with laughter as they played, despite the darkness. Again, the Aventine. It wasn't quite the shithole the Transtiberina was, but I pretended I thought it was because it annoyed Atreus, and annoying Atreus could be fun. Not tonight, though. Tonight, I hurt, and Entellus was a free man, and I hated that there was nothing we could do about it.

Juba came back with an urna of wine in a large jar. On one hand, I admired his immediate understanding that I needed to get very drunk tonight. On the other hand, getting me back home might be a problem. It was also his problem, though, so I assumed he'd already decided he could manage me.

We didn't bother mixing the wine with water; we dipped our cups straight into the wide mouth of the jar to fill them.

On my second cup, I said, "What do we think of Cilnius? That he really idolised Entellus enough to help him move Marsus's corpse, or Entellus threatened him or blackmailed him or something?"

"I don't think we'll ever know the answer to that, sir," Juba said.

"We don't even know if he killed himself or Entellus did it," I muttered. "Fuck Severus. Why can't we beat Entellus up until he tells us the truth?"

"Because his father, the adjutor, has powerful friends, sir," Juba said. "Maybe even more than you do."

"We don't know that."

"And we're not betting our lives on it either," Atreus said firmly.

They were both smarter than me, even when I hadn't had wine.

"I just hate that he gets away with it," I said. "I hate it."

And as much as I attempted to prove otherwise as the night wore on, there wasn't enough wine in the world to numb the sting of our defeat.

* * *

The rest of the night was a drunken blur. I had vague memories of falling off

Atreus's couch, and Atreus berating me for my clumsiness while inspecting my bandages. Then I think Juba must have hired a litter, because mine didn't smell like mouse droppings, and the next thing I knew it was morning, and I was lying face down on my mattress with Mad Uncle Maro looming over me.

"Quintus! It's lunchtime. Get up!"

Perhaps not morning then.

"Why do I have to get up?" I mumbled into my mattress.

"Because I am here to visit you, not listen to the women make wedding plans," Maro grizzled. "This is an *emergency*, Quintus!"

I relented and rolled out of bed. Everything still hurt from yesterday, and today I had a throbbing head as well. Also, someone had poured gravel down my throat while I slept. Still, I managed to pull on a clean tunic and splash enough water on my face to more or less revive me.

It was a full family affair when I got downstairs: Fulvia, Octavia, Aunt Marcia, and Julia Drusilla. No wonder Maro had felt outnumbered.

"Where's Aulus?" I asked.

"With his tutor," Fulvia said, rising to greet me with a kiss on the cheek. "Come and have some lunch with us."

Aunt Marcia clasped her hands to her bosom, and her bright gold curls bounced with the movement. "Quintus! Maro tells me you stabbed a man to death yesterday at Nero's theatre!"

"That was actually Juba," I said, sitting down and inspecting the spread of food in front of me. I selected a boiled egg garnished with pine nuts and garum sauce. I hoped it would play well with my hangover. "I was busy trying not to get stabbed."

Aunt Marcia gasped.

"Julia," I said, "have you found the right hairnet to wear for your wedding yet?"

There was a time, and not that long ago, when distracting my stepdaughter with an inane question about fashion would have kept her busy talking for hours. And, as she started discussing different shades of yellow with the room, I got the impression it still could. But she showed me a knowing smile, as though she knew she was rescuing me, and was happy to. She'd grown up a lot in these past few months. She might even be generous enough to say the same about me.

Uncle Maro shot me a murderous look at all the wedding talk. I grinned and then, because the first egg had settled well enough in my stomach, I risked a second one.

While I ate, and nodded along to Julia's hairnet lecture, an idea slowly came together in the soggy, hungover remnants of my brain. At first, it was as nebulous as softly forming clouds, losing shape whenever I tried to grasp it. But then, suddenly, it struck me as hard and fast as a thunderbolt, and my heart raced.

"Excuse me," I said to my family, and rose. "I have to go out for a while."

I went upstairs and opened the trunk by my bed. The temptation to grab my gladius was strong, but I chose my pugio instead. It was much easier to hide under my cloak than a gladius. I was no expert with a dagger, and I was very much hoping I wouldn't have to use it, but after yesterday's encounter with Litus I didn't want to be caught unarmed again.

I went downstairs and called for Juba, and we headed off down the hill into the city.

It was a cold day, but a busy one. It was a market day, which meant the narrow streets of the Aventine, when we reached it, were packed with vendors and with shoppers, haggling and bartering.

Juba gave me a look when we turned off the usual well-trodden path to Atreus's insula.

"Shouldn't we get Atreus, sir?" he asked as we progressed into narrow alleyways both darker and colder than the wider streets they fed off, but no less crowded on a market day.

"Atreus isn't welcome where we're headed."

"I'm not sure we are either," Juba commented.

He was probably right, and I steeled myself as we approached the familiar shoddy insula, with its courtyard filled with weeds and rubbish, the vicious dog chained on the landing, and the foul air that was rank with the stench of cats' piss. If Atreus had known where I was going, he certainly would have objected. Sometimes it was as though he forgot I outranked him. But while I wasn't expecting a warm welcome, I knew it would be a whole lot less friendly if Atreus was with me. After all, I'd never tortured Erastus, so I hoped he was slightly less inclined to want to murder me.

The steps creaked as we climbed them.

Juba stepped in front of me to knock on Erastus's door.

When he opened the door to us, he regarded us suspiciously. "What the fuck do you want?"

I'd forgotten how pretty he was, even wearing a sneer.

"The man who killed Marsus is called Entellus," I said. "He's a playwright, and the son of the adjutor of the procurator. He's untouchable. To us." I let the words hang in the air.

Erastus's hazel eyes glittered in the sunlight.

He understood.

Of course he did. He was a gangster.

"Entellus was obsessed with Marsus," I said. "But Marsus turned him down, because he was in love with you. And he must have told Entellus about you as well, or Entellus followed him to the Aventine at some point, because he dumped his corpse in the fountain right below your balcony. He hated you too, even if he didn't know you, just because Marsus loved you."

Erastus looked away for a moment, as if he was afraid to show me even a glimpse of his heartbreak. It made no difference; I'd seen it clearly enough last time. When he lifted his gaze again, it was steely.

"Entellus," he said, as though committing the name to memory.

"Entellus," I repeated.

Erastus's throat bobbed. For a moment, I thought he was going to say something, but he just pressed his mouth into a tight line, nodded, and then closed the door in our faces.

I felt like a man who'd unloosed an arrow into the dark who couldn't see exactly where it would land.

But it was bound to hit something.

And after yesterday's failure, that kind of power felt good.

* * *

Word of Litus's death had spread, and I spent the afternoon holed up in my tablinum listening to Hursa turn visitors away from the door, and fiddling with the holly branches I'd grabbed off Calliope. She and the other indoor slaves were busy making wreaths for Saturnalia. When I was a child, I'd loved to join the slaves when it came to decorating. Today, I just fiddled with the branches, tested the skin of my thumb against the pointed leaves, and sat sunk in thought.

My star had been on the rise since Nero had made the whole city aware that he called me his friend, but there was an entire field of stars in the sky every night, and mine wasn't brighter than any other. I wasn't a nobody—someone with my pedigree was never a nobody—but I wasn't quite a somebody yet. I was part of the crowd of patricians hanging onto the wobbly ladder of the cursus honorum, just hoping not to lose our grips as we climbed to the next rung. The whole point was to try to get ahead of everyone else on the ladder, and to climb higher and stand taller. And in case nobody was aware of how that could go spectacularly wrong, Tarquinius Superbus had some gardening tips regarding tall poppies he could share. Although, if I was honest with myself—to be clear, I rarely was—it wasn't the political intrigue and risk to my personal safety that I hated most about climbing that wobbly ladder. It was the social obligations. I'd rather be locked in a dark room with a Parthian spy, a cup of poison, and a hungry lion than be forced to smile politely as I feigned interest in some senator's lengthy opinions about the latest grain prices and whatever trouble was brewing in the provinces. At least I stood a fighting chance with the spy, the poison, and the lion. And, if I failed, death would be quick.

Hursa, astonishingly enough, did his job well enough that I wasn't disturbed again until it was almost time for dinner.

"Sir." Hursa blinked at me as he hovered in the doorway like an uncertain bee. "I know you said that I shouldn't bother you, and you didn't want to see anyone, but…" He wrinkled his nose.

"Is Maro back?" I asked. "Or is it Atreus?"

Dealing with Hursa was a lot like dealing with blisters. Just fucking painful.

"No," he said decisively, and then smiled as though he'd been pleased to get a question right.

I fought the urge to throw my wax tablet at his head. "Then who is it, Hursa? Jupiter, it's one of the playwrights, isn't it?" I wasn't in the mood to deal with anyone today, the playwrights more than anyone else. "Shit. Is it Petronius?"

"It *is* Petronius," the man himself announced as he wandered past Hursa into the tablinum.

I shot Hursa a furious look that I was certain he failed to interpret and let out a breath. I suppose I should have apologised, but I didn't have the energy or the inclination. Mostly the inclination. I leaned back in my chair. "I'm afraid I'm not in the mood to play your games today, Petronius."

"Well, that makes two of us," Petronius said, and sat down across the desk from me. "You. Haystack. Go and fetch us some wine, hmm?"

Hursa blinked at him.

"Hursa," I said. "Wine. Go."

"The Juvenalia is going to be a disaster," Petronius said. "Poor Antigon is tearing out what remaining hair he has. Litus and Cilnius are dead, Entellus has probably already fled the city, and Marsus is dead too. That's half the writers gone, and the only actor worth a damned thing. What a mess."

I spun my stylus on my desk. "Don't give me that."

"What?"

"That puffed-up bullshit, like you're nothing more than *inconvenienced*," I said. "I'm not falling for it."

Petronius held my gaze for a long moment, and then let out a breath. He scrubbed a hand over his short-cropped hair. I'd never heard him speak before without a smile in his voice, whether it was delighted or barbed. I heard it now. "Why didn't I know? I thought it was funny, encouraging Hermes to make up his little poems. I thought Litus thought it was funny too."

I thought of the line of columns at the theatre, and the way taking a sideways step could make them suddenly appear. It was disorienting enough

223

when you took that step yourself—when someone pushed you, it had to be even more dizzying. Petronius's perspective had been forcibly shifted. He'd thought the jealousies and petty bickering of his friends was amusing, until it had turned deadly. And yesterday he'd seen it in person, when Litus had bled out on the stage of the elaborate scaenae frons. Petronius was a man who made a living out of skewering patrician society with his stylus. His methods of attack were sharp but bloodless. I wondered if he'd even seen a man killed before yesterday.

"Petronius," I began, and then paused when Hursa finally found his way back to us with the wine. I waited until he'd gone again, then reached over the desk to nudge a cup closer to Petronius's hand. "Petro."

That caught his attention, and he cocked a brow. I didn't know if the angle of his brow signalled that he was waiting for me to continue, or if he was silently admonishing me for daring to call him by a diminutive.

"The worst part of betrayal isn't that you couldn't trust your friends," I said. "It's that you couldn't trust your own judgement of them."

Petronius snorted and then took a sip of wine. "Very profound."

"You can steal it, if you want."

"I do *not* want," he said, his eyes regaining some of their customary mischievous glint. "It's lucky you do whatever it is that you do, Valerius, because you'd make a terrible poet."

I shrugged. "My poems would make you weep."

He cocked his brow again. "Agreed."

But the corner of his mouth twitched, as though he knew I'd cast my shield aside and stepped straight onto the point of his gladius intentionally. "Did you know that Nero asked me to decide whether or not you were worthy of being in his closest circle?"

"Of course I know," I said. "There was no other reason Rome's most famous and celebrated writer would suddenly invite me to dinner."

"And do you know what I told him?"

I drew a breath, bracing for another blow.

Petronius huffed out an amused breath at whatever expression I was making. "I told him I liked you. I told him I approved."

We both pondered that for a while, and then Petronius drank the rest of his wine and rose to his feet. He didn't look much happier than he had when he first arrived, but he looked as though he was coming to terms with his misery, which was an improvement. There was probably a Stoic philosophy wrapped up somewhere in there, but I couldn't be bothered trying to untangle it.

"You must come to the Juvenalia," he said. "It'll be a disaster, and the least you can do is suffer through it with the rest of us. And don't worry, you won't be the only one without a birthday present for the emperor. Otho and Poppaea are still scrambling to find something after Litus attacked their slave. Or was it Entellus? I can't keep the details straight."

And with that, Petronius left me alone with my swirling thoughts.

I flipped open my wax tablet and scratched a few lines on it; just something to keep my fingers busy while my thoughts wandered. I found myself scratching out a grid on the surface of the wax, like a latrunculi board, and thinking of how I'd watched Atreus frown down as he shifted pieces randomly yesterday morning. Except had it been truly random? He'd been on the edge of a revelation, shoving those pieces around the board, both paying attention to them and not, changing the patterns and hoping to see something new. He hadn't seen it in the board—he'd seen it at the theatre, where one column suddenly became a row of them—but maybe moving those latrunculi pieces around first had loosened his thoughts enough to make room for new ones.

I half listened to the sounds of the household outside my tablinum as I dragged the point of my stylus through the wax. I could hear the back-and-forth swish of a broom on tiles, somewhere nearby. From much farther away, there came a faint shriek of delight—either Mouse or Perella, or possibly both of them, playing in the peristyle. The stairs creaked as someone climbed them. From the kitchens, the faint clang of pots and pans sounded like the clash of cymbals, and my stomach growled, hangover forgotten, as I anticipated dinner. I filled in the grids with narrow lines.

When Atreus arrived, Hursa didn't announce him.

I glanced up from my tablet and saw him leaning in the doorway, as casually as I'd seen him lean against walls in alleyways in the Aventine. Like he belonged here just like he did there. Warmth spread through me.

Atreus straightened up and came into the tablinum. He looked down at my tablet. "Busy day?"

I hummed. "Just working on some ideas. Do you suppose there is a muse of murders? The sister that Erato and Euterpe and the others don't talk about?"

Atreus tilted his head. "A muse who inspires men to murder?"

"No, one who inspires those trying to *solve* murders." I set my stylus down and looked up at him. "I could use one, because what I don't understand, and what makes no sense, is why did Litus attack Iris? To muddy the waters?"

Atreus opened his mouth, and then closed it again. He was silent for a long moment, and then he shook his head. "He didn't."

"But it can't have been Entellus," I said. "We were watching him all night."

Atreus reached out and took my stylus, and then dropped it on the floor.

"What are you doing?" I asked, and he put his foot over it, just like little Nonus had with the coins in Antigon's office. And then, as suddenly as a man who took a sideways step and noticed a row of columns instead of just one, I *saw* it. I saw exactly how Iris had been attacked—the *only* way it could have happened—and exactly who was responsible. I stood up. "Jupiter. Have you been keeping this to yourself since Nonus?"

Atreus shook his head. "When I saw Nonus, something about it caught my attention, but I only just realised now what it was. It's the only way it works, isn't it?"

I didn't answer; I didn't need to. I stood up and left the tablinum and Atreus fell into step behind me. We headed for Juba's little room. He was seated on a stool outside, his head leaning back against the wall. He rose to his feet as we approached, and wordlessly opened the door to his room.

Iris was sitting cross-legged on Juba's mattress. Her one visible eye widened as Atreus and I entered the narrow room, Juba behind us.

"Hello," Atreus said. "Can you show me your hands, please?"

Iris looked to me, and then back to Atreus, and finally raised her shaking hands.

Atreus crouched down in front of her and took one of her hands in his. He inspected her palms carefully, and then released her and straightened up again. "I should have realised the moment I saw your hands that night, but I suppose there was so much blood to begin with that I didn't take proper notice."

Iris stared up at us, tucking her hands under her armpits as though if she hid them, they couldn't incriminate her any further. Her shoulders rose and fell with the shuddering breaths she pulled into her body.

"Nobody heard you scream because you *didn't*," I said. "And you have no wounds on your palms because you didn't defend yourself. There was no attacker."

Iris whimpered, and squeezed her visible eye shut.

"Was it your brother?" I asked, "Idaeus? Did he bring you the knife? Did he want to, or did you have to convince him?"

She hunched over and wept.

"Idaeus brought you the knife with your dinner," Atreus said. "You ate your dinner—you had to, because otherwise we would have known Idaeus had something to do with it. If you ate, and then you were attacked, that gave him an alibi. He was nowhere near your room by that time." He shook his head. "It must have been hard to swallow, knowing what you were going to do next."

She hugged herself hard.

Juba, standing beside me, was silent and watchful. I often joked that I couldn't read his expression, which usually meant I was making a point to remain oblivious to whatever disapproval and sarcasm he was radiating, but right now, I really couldn't tell what he was thinking.

Atreus said, "You slashed your own face, and then you put the knife under your mattress, knowing that everyone would be in such a panic when the old woman discovered you that nobody would look for it."

Iris's shoulders shook.

"But Idaeus knew he had to get rid of it," Atreus continued. "And he knelt down, his tunic long enough to reach the ground. It acted as a curtain while he retrieved the knife. And, of course, we were all busy with you."

"When we told him to go and get a doctor, he took a bundle of bloody cloths with him," I said. "I thought at the time he was just being a good slave, and that tidying up was some instinct trained into him—or beaten—even when he was panicking. But he had the knife, didn't he? He had to get it out of the room without anyone seeing it."

Iris made a broken sound.

"It was an impossible puzzle," Atreus said. "Confounding. But we were already confounded with whoever had killed Hermes and Marsus, which gave you and Idaeus the perfect opportunity to fake an attack and blame the killer." He gave a rueful smile. "And it almost worked too, except it was *too* impossible. It could only have been you and Idaeus."

"Sir," Iris said imploringly to Atreus, and then looked up at me. "Master, please. It was my idea, not my brother's. It was all mine! I made him do it!"

"I don't believe that for a moment," I said. "But I also don't blame you."

"Master?" she asked, her voice wavering.

"I don't know Nero well," I said, "but I know that he hates his mother, and that you look exactly like her. However decent a man he is, nothing good could ever come from that. I thought as much the first time I saw you. You must have been terrified."

Her chin trembled, and she nodded frantically.

"You don't know me, and you don't trust me," I said, "so listen to Juba instead."

I glanced at Juba and found him looking back at me. His expression was grave. Had he already known what Atreus and I had only just figured out? I thought he probably had. He was too smart to be the last one to know—that was my job. And I supposed I could have asked him, but I didn't really want to know what his answer would tell me. It would tell me that his loyalty wasn't as simple as I liked to believe. Juba had saved my life yesterday, and it wasn't the first time, and yet if he'd known about Iris and kept it to himself, it was because I was a master and he was a slave, and that was what the gods and fate had decided.

We were not friends.

"Explain to her that she's safe here," I told him. "Explain to her that—" I waved my hand. "Explain that whatever she thought was going to happen to her in Nero's palace is not going to happen here."

And then I swept out of his room because I no longer wanted to look either him or Iris in the eye.

I stormed out to the peristyle.

"Quintus?" Fulvia's voice floated out from the sitting room where she and Octavia spent a lot of their time, but I ignored her.

Mouse and Perella were no longer in the peristyle, and so I planted my arse on a stone bench, glowered at the winter-brown garden, and pretended I didn't realise how uncomfortable it was with the cold seeping into my backside.

Atreus had followed me, naturally, and now he sat down beside me. He knocked his shoulder against mine and, when that didn't get him whatever reaction he was chasing, he rubbed his hand down my back, and then up it again, finally curling his fingers around the back of my neck and squeezing gently.

I closed my eyes.

"You wanted her to be happy you know the truth, not scared," he said, his thumb rubbing against the sensitive skin at the nape of my neck. "But she doesn't know you."

"I don't care what she believes," I said, forcing my eyes open again.

It wasn't the truth, but it wasn't exactly a lie either. I didn't know Iris. But I'd thought I'd known Juba.

Atreus hummed, but there was a smile in the sound that made me bristle. Not for long, though, because the bastard squeezed my neck again, turning my spine to liquid. I wished we were at his place instead of mine. But I'd spent the last week running around the city like a headless chicken, I'd been in a fight for my life just yesterday morning, and I owed my womenfolk a quiet night at home after the worry I'd put them through.

"Petronius has invited me to the Juvenalia," I said. I let my eyes slip closed again. "I suppose I'll have to go, as well."

"That's what happens when you have friends in high places."

"The highest," I said. "Of course, you'll have to come with me."

He dropped his hand away from the back of my neck. "Why would I have to come?"

"Because Nero likes you," I said, "and he does put on a good party."

Atreus ran his palm down my spine, and I wondered if he was thinking of the party at the palace, in that maze of a garden crowded with half-naked nymphs. I wondered if he was thinking of how he'd kissed me. I was usually the stupid, reckless one, and it made me burn with a strange sort of satisfaction to know that, just once, at least, Atreus had been stupid and reckless because of me.

"You're staying for dinner, aren't you?" I asked.

He drew a breath, and I had no doubt he was going to use it to push some excuse out of his mouth.

"You're staying for dinner," I said, and it wasn't a question this time. "I'll send Juba to fetch Lucilla, and she can join us. Do you know what this investigation has lacked, Atreus?" I turned my head to look at him. "The thrill of victory."

He raised his eyebrows.

"Cilnius killed himself out of remorse or fear—or perhaps he was killed by Entellus, who was afraid he would give him away, who knows? Entellus has fucked off back to his father's house, where we can't reach him, and Litus was killed by Juba, not by you or me. So I would like a victory, please, and you're going to give me one by agreeing to stay for dinner without arguing about it."

Atreus stared at me for a moment, and then rolled his eyes. "I would love to stay for dinner, thank you."

I grinned. "That's the right answer."

A breeze sighed through the peristyle, making the rosemary shiver, and I leaned closer to the heat of the nearby brazier.

"Is there ever the thrill of victory?" I asked.

Atreus let out a breath. "Not entirely. At least, not in my experience. It's been messy. And—and *pointless*. Not the investigation, but the murders themselves. Hermes was killed because he wrote insulting poems, and Marsus was killed because he wouldn't sleep with Entellus. Neither of those things is worth killing for."

He sounded personally aggrieved.

There were Atreus's ideals again, popping up at inconvenient times. He was born and bred in the Aventine, for Jupiter's sake. He dealt with the lowest of the low for a living. He must have seen hundreds of crimes that had been committed for no reason other than the perpetrator felt like doing it, and yet, as always, Atreus wanted things to be different. He believed that if there were moral laws to the universe, then people ought to follow them. He wanted there to be order and sense instead of chaos and pettiness. But when it came down to it, either the universe was chaotic and petty, or people were, and the universe didn't have the power or the inclination to stop us, and so we just kept getting worse. If there wasn't already a school of Greek philosophy built on that idea, somebody needed to found one. Heraclitus said that everything was in a state of flux and that you couldn't step into the same river twice. So, something like that, except that the second time you stepped in the river, it turned out that it was a sewer, and you found yourself up to your eyebrows in shit.

I mean, it probably wouldn't be a popular school of philosophy, but that didn't mean it was wrong.

I leaned back into Atreus's touch. "Cleverer people than us haven't been able to figure out how the universe works, or the minds of men either. We solved the riddle, Lucan is no longer in any danger—well, he never was, but that's not the point—and we're not dead. You want the universe to make sense, and I want the thrill of victory. The Stoics would probably tell the both of us that we need to adjust our expectations."

"I think you've adjusted yours," he said.

I raised my eyebrows at him in a silent question.

"Dinner," he reminded me. "You're settling for dinner with me and Lucilla."

"It doesn't feel at all like settling, though," I said.

His thumb rubbed against the short hairs at the nape of my neck, and I heard the smile in his voice as he replied, "I know."

And that, I supposed, was a victory of a different sort, and one that I could very easily live with.

Chapter Twelve

S everal weeks after the murders, on the Twenty-First of December, Nero's Juvenalia was held at his theatre in the Gardens of Agrippina. Much to the shock of everyone who had any knowledge of the leadup to the celebration, it was a roaring success. Spirits were still high from Saturnalia, although they were slightly frayed in my home, where, despite my objections, which had been overruled by Fulvia and Octavia, Hursa had played master for the day and had naturally made a dog's breakfast out of the whole affair. Despite the short days and the long, cold nights, the mood in the city was warm and festive. The Juvenalia was not a public affair. The theatre and the surrounding gardens were full of invited guests of fame and renown, but that didn't mean the plebeians were neglected. Nero had men ride through the streets on chariots, tossing coins and gifts into the cheering crowds. Rome rang with the emperor's name.

Antigon, despite losing three writers and an actor, managed to put on a show for the Juvenalia that people would be talking about for years—and not just the dull old moralists who had conniptions at the idea of patricians performing on a stage, however private it was. With the sort of backdoor deals and promises that could only be leveraged by the imperial slave who'd once been in charge of the divine Claudius's travel schedule to Britannia *and* his triumph when he returned home, Antigon had somehow managed to convince what felt like half the patricians in the city to participate in the festivities, and the night's reduced theatrical performances were paced out with singing and dancing. Aelia Catella, who must have been eighty if she was a day, made a surprisingly limber nymph. She was smiling the whole way through as well, so fuck anyone who claimed it was shocking and undignified. And Nero, despite the fact that the Juvenalia was a celebration of his moving out of adolescence and into adulthood, was as delighted as a child at the celebrations. He sat front and centre in the cavea, his acolytes and admirers spread around him like bright, fallen petals.

Fulvia and Octavia came with me to the Juvenalia, as did Atreus. Mad Uncle Maro also attended and was so enthusiastic about the entire event that I wondered if he'd switch his crazy obsessions from home renovations to the theatre in the future. I hoped not. As much as I hated having to dodge tradesmen whenever I visited his house, I'd hate to run into Ammenius even more. Give me a phalanx of surly plasterers any day.

During the performances, Petronius detached himself from Nero's retinue and climbed the steps to where we were seated.

"You've done well, Valerius," he said, taking a seat beside me. On stage, a group of youths sang and danced. "We wouldn't be here tonight if it hadn't been for you."

It seemed in bad taste to point out that about half of them weren't here tonight, but I did it anyway, and it made him laugh.

"Your scene is going ahead then?" I asked him.

His laughter faded, but a faint shadow of a smile remained on his face. It was more pensive than joyous. "Yes. The new boy is no Marsus, but he will do. The gods know I'm not going to win the prize tonight anyway." He shook his head. "A play about a fucking *bee* has no business being that good."

Oh, yes. Cripplingly shy Hosidius had shocked everyone who ever knew him, and everyone who didn't, by having produced what was so far the best piece of the evening.

"I believe Terence wrote that nothing is said anymore which has not been said earlier," I said, "but it turns out he was wrong, and what we were missing this whole time was a new dramatisation of the story of Jupiter and the bee."

"We live in a universe of no rules," Petronius said, but there was a delighted gleam in his eye as he spoke. He was a devoted child of Chaos. "The only consolation is that Otho is still running around like a headless chicken squawking that he has no gift for Nero. It's cheered me right up."

I laughed at that.

Petronius snorted, and then cut me an appraising glance as he dived into a more serious subject matter. "Did you hear about Entellus?"

"What about him?" I asked, my stomach clenching in anticipation.

"His father thought to send him away to Athens," Petronius said. "For his education, of course, and despite ruining whatever career, and influential friendships, he was making here in Rome. It was quite the perplexing decision."

"I'm sure that it was."

"He was meant to leave yesterday," Petronius said, "to get ahead of any scandal, I suppose, though I've found that the right sort of scandal will always ride hard on your heels."

I hummed.

"Apparently, he ran into some trouble with some local roughnecks at Ostia. Nobody seems to know exactly what happened, but they slit his throat and hung him up by the ankles like a butchered pig."

"What a strange coincidence," I said, enjoying the malicious thrill that ran through me. Erastus had worked fast.

"I dislike coincidences; too many, and they cheapen the entire play." Petronius slapped me on the back. "But I am a fan of poetic justice, in whatever form and through whichever unlikely agent it takes."

I hummed again, and pointedly ignored Atreus's narrow look. Then, when Petronius left us to rejoin Nero, I pretended to be very interested in the spectacle on the stage. Whatever the dancers were doing, they were fluttering a lot of scarves while it happened.

"You went to see Erastus," Atreus said, his tone low.

"He needed to know. He *deserved* to know." I ignored Fulvia's concerned look.

Atreus's eyes blazed. "He's a dangerous man."

"Which is exactly the reason I told him," I said firmly. "If someone I loved was murdered, I would want to know the name of his killer. Wouldn't you?"

I was right, so he didn't have an answer for that. And later, I was sure, he would grumble and glare until I apologised for putting myself at risk, as though I was some pampered child who'd never held a gladius. It rankled. Maybe I couldn't hold my own in a street brawl with a dirty fighter like Erastus, but I'd seen the horizons at the edges of the empire. I'd crept into enemy territory with only a few scouts, our camp tens of miles behind us. I'd heard the Parthians howling like dogs at night to let us know they hunted us. I liked that Atreus had my back, but I hated that he thought I needed it every time I was out of his sight. We had edges that didn't quite meet, Atreus and I, but we were both still learning. And those gaps would always be there. They were there in every relationship—between fathers and sons, husbands and wives, brothers and sisters, and lovers. Plato may have been right about his idea of every soul having another half, but life and experience knocked those matching edges out of shape so that by the time your soul found its missing part, it took a little more battering to get it to fit again. Plato called it the wound of human nature, a hurt that we strived to heal from the moment we were born.

There was an echo of it on the stage right now. Two dancers, held apart by the rest of the troupe, reached for each other. Then, just as their hands touched, they were whirled away in different directions. It was meant to be heartbreaking and poetic, I guessed, but even though I'd never seen this dance before, I knew how it ended. Because on stage, things always ended neatly. This was rarely mirrored out in the rest of the world, which was so often cruel and unfair and unfeeling, and was the reason I would never regret giving fate the nudge it needed by going to tell Erastus about Entellus. And why I knew that Atreus, although he didn't approve of my methods, couldn't fault my motivation. In a day or two, tonight's mismatched edges would be hammered flat, and some other jagged parts of us would snag and clash instead. And I trusted it would be worth it.

Fulvia found my hand and squeezed it.

When the dancers finished and were ushered off the stage with warm applause, a man climbed the steps from Nero's seat and approached us. He looked vaguely familiar, but I recognised his boots before his face: Rufio, the Praetorian from the Milvian Bridge. He might have been fancied up in a toga tonight, and his clothing told me he was more than a common legionary—a tribune, perhaps? —but his boots were still a soldier's.

"Aemilius Valerius," he said, and dipped his chin. "The emperor would like to speak to you." His gaze took Atreus and my womenfolk in as well. "All of you."

Under the jealous stares of most of the rest of the theatregoers, we stood. I took Fulvia's arm to help her down the steps, and—before Atreus could do it—Rufio held his elbow out for Octavia. She slipped her arm into his, throwing him an appraising look. I decided not to notice how he smiled in response.

Nero rose from his seat to meet us, a gesture that would not go unnoticed or unremarked upon. Lucan was seated near him, but there was no sign of Seneca tonight. I didn't know if Seneca really had any strings left to pull behind the scenes of the imperial palace, but it probably wasn't an accident that he wasn't here. Nero was shedding his childhood, and whatever their relationship was like now, that included his childhood tutor.

"Valerius," Nero said with a smile. "We always do meet in the aftermath of such strange events." His smile slipped into an expression of gravity as he greeted my sister. "Octavia Junilla."

I was glad he'd remembered that Octavia's husband had died for Rome, and for him. I was glad for Octavia's sake. Only very few people knew the truth of Nasica's death, and of Octavia's sacrifice. It deserved remembrance.

Nero leaned close and said something into Octavia's ear that I couldn't hear. My sister nodded, and blinked rapidly, and then reached out and clasped the emperor's hand. Nero's courtiers murmured like waves at the shore at her boldness.

But what did Nero care about propriety? He was young and brash, the most powerful man in the world, and this was his birthday celebration. He leaned down and kissed her hand, the sort of deferential kiss a grateful client gave to his patron, or a soldier to his commander, and then he straightened up and smiled broadly again, while an entire theatre full of people wrote scandals and conspiracies in their heads and shared them immediately with their neighbours.

It might have bothered me once upon a time, but not now. Octavia could handle a little gossip. Knowing her stubborn streak, she might even enjoy it.

And as it turned out, Nero's kiss wasn't even the most shocking act of the night. After we'd spoken with Nero for a few moments, Rufio indicated that it was someone else's turn. Fulvia hooked her arm in mine, and we stepped aside for the emperor's newest visitors.

It was Otho and Poppaea Sabina, and they both looked perfectly primped and pampered. It was hard to say which one of them had spent more on cosmetics and clothes for the occasion. They glittered like a pair of dragonfly wings in the sunlight.

And, as Poppaea moved forward, her glimmering stola slipped and revealed a tunic underneath. The fabric was sheer, but just to be sure, there was also a long slash in the front of it, proudly revealing Poppaea's gold-dusted breasts.

Well, then.

It looked like Poppaea had figured out what to give Nero for his Juvenalia after all. And, by the shocked expression on his face, this was the first Otho knew about it.

I would have loved to be a fly on their bedroom wall later tonight, presuming Poppaea came home. And—I caught a glimpse of Nero's expression as I turned to look one last time before returning to our seats— that didn't seem very likely at all.

* * *

It was almost dawn when Juba and Atreus and I arrived in the Aventine. A pair of drunks staggered past us, their arms flung around each other's shoulders as they weaved their way along the street. I couldn't tell if they were holding one another upright or dragging each other down. They probably couldn't tell either. A beggar sat under the closed awning of the caupona on the corner, huddled into her threadbare cloak. Atreus veered away from us as we passed and said something in a low voice to the woman. I didn't hear her reply, but I saw the moment she reached up and took the coin he passed her. In the Aventine, a man in Atreus's profession was either loved or hated, depending on which way the wind blew, and sometimes by the same people at the same time.

We climbed the stairs of Atreus's insula. It was dark inside, but there was a warm glow coming from the crack underneath Atreus's door. When we reached it, he knocked, and said, "It's me."

I heard the soft shuffle of footsteps, and then Iris opened the door. The bulky bandage that had obscured half her face was gone, but she wore her hair hanging loose so that it hid the still-healing wound that bisected her cheek from the edge of her eye to her chin. It would leave an awful scar. She avoided my gaze as she stepped back to let us in.

"Is Lucilla asleep?" Atreus asked her.

"Yes, sir," she said.

He nodded and unfastened his cloak. She reached for it, and he held onto it, and then they both dropped it at the same time. Atreus bent down and scooped it up before Iris could.

"It's fine," he said. "Go to bed, if you want."

Iris nodded, and darted toward the bedroom.

Atreus gave me a look, and I gave him one right back.

And this was another reason that I wouldn't push him too hard to not only admit that he thought I couldn't look after myself, but also to apologise for it. When I'd told him that I had no use for Iris in my house, but that he did in his, he'd allowed it to happen. We'd both known that his childcare arrangements for Lucilla weren't adequate, but he'd finally allowed me to chip away at his pride enough to offer him the solution. Not only was Lucilla now looked after properly, but Atreus's apartment was neater than I'd ever seen it. Iris might always be timid and shy, but I hoped that in time she would realise that she didn't need to be afraid. Atreus would never mistreat her. In the meantime, he'd given up his bed for her and Lucilla, and was sleeping on the couch in the main room. My next goal would to be to get him into a better apartment, but I wouldn't spring that on him for a while. He needed to recover from this first.

I grabbed some bread and some oil and went and sat on the balcony. Atreus joined me after a moment, and we tore chunks off the bread and softened it with the oil before eating it. It was a cold night, but a pleasant one. Atreus's neighbours weren't even screaming at each other.

From inside, Juba hummed softly.

"What's the plan for tomorrow?" I asked, putting my feet up on the railing like I owned the place.

Atreus made a considering noise in the back of his throat. "I believe there was a murder in Ostia I might know something about."

"That's well out of your jurisdiction," I said, "and it was probably a tragic accident."

He huffed out a faint laugh. "A tragic accident?"

"Happens all the time," I said. "You slip, you fall, you somehow find yourself strung up upside-down with your wrists slashed. Could happen to anyone."

He stretched. "I heard there's a baker near the Temple of Diana who uses false weights."

"That sounds like something you really don't need the help of a magistrate's assistant to investigate," I said.

"There may be honey cakes."

"Well, I could probably take a look then. Since it's a matter of public interest."

The faint moonlight caught on the curve of Atreus's smile. "Your help would be invaluable, I'm sure."

I was already dreaming of honey cakes.

I knocked my shoulder against his and caught his hand in mine. And then we sat together on the balcony, our breath making mist on the cold air, as dawn very slowly crept over the city.

Acknowledgement

With special thanks to Sylvia and Jane, who read along in bits and pieces as this was taking shape, and who supported, encouraged, and/or harassed me as required.

About the Author

Jennifer lives in tropical North Queensland, Australia, with three cats, two dogs, and more geckos than she wants. She spends half her time as a government minion, and half her time writing. She studied History and English at university, though she likes playing with them more than she ever did studying them. Jennifer also writes mm romance under the pen name Lisa Henry.

AUTHOR WEBSITE:
jenniferburkebooks.com

SOCIAL MEDIA HANDLES:
x: @jenburkebooks

Also by Jennifer Burke

Sub Rosa (A Valerius Mystery #1)

As Lisa Henry
Full Throttle
Not Until Noah (Star Crossed #1)
Because of Ben (Star Crossed #2)
Only for Ollie (Star Crossed #3)
The Parable of the Mustard Seed
Anhaga
Two Man Station (Emergency Services #1)
Lights and Sirens (Emergency Services #2)
The California Dashwoods
Adulting 101
Sweetwater
He Is Worthy
The Island
Tribute
One Perfect Night
Fallout, with M. Caspian
Dark Space (Dark Space #1)
Darker Space (Dark Space #2)
Starlight (Dark Space #3)

With J.A. Rock
No Business Like Snow Business
Fran Cuthbert Ruins Christmas
When All the World Sleeps
Another Man's Treasure
Fall on Your Knees
The Preacher's Son

242

Mark Cooper versus America (Prescott College #1)
Brandon Mills versus the V-Card (Prescott College #2)
The Good Boy (The Boy #1)
The Boy Who Belonged (The Boy #2)

The Playing the Fool Series
The Two Gentlemen of Altona
The Merchant of Death
Tempest

The Lords of Bucknall Club Series
A Husband for Hartwell
A Case for Christmas
A Rival for Rivingdon
A Sanctuary for Soulden
An Affair for Aumont
A Scandal for Stratford

With Tia Fielding
Family Recipe
Recipe for Two
A Desperate Man

With Sarah Honey
Red Heir (Adventures in Aguillon #1)
Elf Defence (Adventures in Aguillon #2)
Socially Orcward (Adventures in Aguillon #3)

Cool Story, Bro

Awfully Ambrose (Bad Boyfriends, Inc. Book 1)